THE
PROSTITUTES'
BALL

...

STEPHEN J. CANNELL

■ ■ ■ ■ ■ ■ ■ ■

THE PROSTITUTES' BALL

■ ■ ■ ■ ■ ■ ■ ■

ST. MARTIN'S PRESS
NEW YORK

This is a work of fiction. All of the characters, organizations, and events portrayed in this novel are either products of the author's imagination or are used fictitiously.

www.stmartins.com

Book design by Kathryn Parise

ISBN 978-0-312-55730-0

First Edition: October 2010

10 9 8 7 6 5 4 3 2 1

OPENING
CREDITS

· · · · · · · ·

This book is for J. Rickley Dumm. Rick and I were roommates and Sigma Chi fraternity brothers at the University of Oregon. More important, had it not been for Rick, I would never have pursued my dream to become a writer. I had left that idea behind when Rick came to L.A. after college and convinced me that we should write TV scripts as a team. We sold our first projects together and joined the Writers Guild on the same evening in 1968. We learned many of the hard rules of writing behind closed doors, when only our wives knew we were "in the biz." Since this novel is about a police case destined to become a screenplay, I know my old writing partner will get a kick out of it. Rick and I have worked together many times since those days in the early sixties. We've been friends since the journey began, still are, ever will be.

I love you, Bro . . . In HOC.

Midway upon the journey of my life,
I found myself within a forest dark,
For the straightforward pathway had been lost.

Dante Alighieri
THE DIVINE COMEDY

PROLOGUE

■ ■ ■ ■ ■ ■ ■ ■ ■

• CHAPTER •

1

This is a story about a story.

It's also a story which, despite all my efforts to the contrary, seemed destined to become a major motion picture.

It began a few days before Christmas, but it's not a Christmas story. It's about lost generations and emotional desertion, and about a Los Angeles family with way too much money. So I guess at its heart, it's a story about greed, corruption, and loss.

With those themes, what better place to start than at an office Christmas party? But before we begin, just a few preliminary remarks.

I'm a homicide detective, and as such, I'm carefully schooled in the three concepts mentioned above. I work at an elite LAPD detective division known as Homicide Special. Our unit was reconstituted after the O.J. Simpson case, another L.A. story of greed, corruption, and loss.

After losing that high-profile media trial, it occurred to our command floor managers that maybe it wasn't such a good idea to have homicide detectives carrying blood evidence vials around a crime scene where they could later be accused of planting it.

As a result, Homicide Special was completely reorganized and staffed with our most seasoned detectives. I'm lucky to be assigned there. It's a great gig.

My name is Shane Scully, and for this story I will be your host narrator. It's going to be a fast ride through L.A. with a lot of reckless driving. Look out for abrupt lane changes, freeway shootings, and dangerous hairpin turns. As a police officer, I'm required to advise you to fasten your seat belts.

All set? Then let's go. . . . Cue the opening theme music. Fade slowly up from black, and we'll begin at:

THE
INCITING
STORY EVENT

. . . .

▪ CHAPTER ▪
2

The chief's Christmas celebration was being held at the Magic Castle, an old baroque mansion in the foothills just above Hollywood Boulevard. It was a private club that normally catered to L.A.'s large population of magicians, but was also available to rent out for special occasions such as this one.

Half a dozen professional sleight-of-hand performers were ripping up twenty-dollar bills or cutting apart ugly neckties then magically restoring them before a crowd of half-lit captains and deputy chiefs who'd seen their share of deception and were squinting through alcohol filters, trying to bust these tricksters.

The party was for the chief's command staff and their spouses. More than a few of the braided hats were getting seriously hammered at the open bar, sometimes exposing their dark, competitive natures or revealing dangerous political aspirations. The music was about peace on earth, goodwill toward men, but most of the people in this room had seen too much street crime to believe it.

Our chief, Tony Filosiani, mingled happily, wearing a blue double-breasted pinstripe over his lunchbox-shaped frame. On his shiny bald head was a Santa hat. He moved through the room, grinning and slapping backs, the ridiculous red hat bobbing along, identifying his position like a hazard warning.

It was hard not to wonder what would happen once this half-lit badge-heavy crowd hit the street and ran into the poor stiffs in our Traffic Division.

As usual, my beautiful wife, Alexa, was the center of attention, her looks both a blessing and a curse. Gleaming black hair, reefwater blue eyes, and high fashion-model cheekbones made Alexa attractive in a way that drew people to her but also made it impossible for a few of the old boy cops in this room to accept her as a division commander. Some of the wives stared enviously, while others wondered openly about her.

I was only here as Alexa's husband and was haunting the corners of the room, trying for invisibility. I look like a middleweight club fighter with a nose broken too many times and short black hair that never quite lies down, so people stay out of my way.

On that December night, Alexa was riding on a political wave of congratulatory remarks. The day before, it had been announced that she was being promoted to captain and would finally be able to drop the word "acting" from her title of Detective Division commander.

For two years she'd been running the Detective Division that supervised three hundred plainclothes cops. In L.A. only captains can head police divisions, but she took over the job as a lieutenant and the "acting" adverb had been haunting her authority like an asterisk. With her appointment to captain came full-fledged membership in the department's double bar club.

I watched as a few of the more aggressive career assassins mingled and schmoozed, wearing big, deceptive grins. They cruised the party like ocean predators, their dangerous personalities barely visible, only the hiss of their dorsals giving them away.

"You ready yet?" I asked Alexa, trying for the third time to get us out of there. I'm a line officer, a Detective III. I don't mix well at these things. Because I was uncomfortable, I wasn't drinking alcohol, so I wouldn't inadvertently insult somebody who could later decide to wreck my career.

"In a minute," Alexa said, turning toward a florid-faced commander named Medavoy, who ran the Special Operations Support Division. I knew he had actively opposed Alexa's appointment to captain, but you'd never know it as he congratulated her, gave her a big, expansive hug, and told her she was the absolute best. The putz.

I wandered off to find a backwater as the music changed and the annoying strains of the Chipmunks singing "We Wish You a Merry Christmas" began to claw relentlessly at my brain.

"Shane?"

I turned to find Sally Quinn, my partner from Homicide Special.

"Sally! What're you doing here?" I was surprised to see her because this was a command-floor-only party. Short, with a bob hairstyle and freckles, she looked as uncomfortable as I did.

"Cal invited me as kind of a going-away thing," she said, referring to both Jeb Calloway, our captain at Homicide Special, and the bombshell she'd laid on me without warning that afternoon.

"I was hoping to get some time with you before I left tomorrow," she said.

Sally and I had been partners for three years, although much of that had been interrupted, first by her maternity leave and then by medical complications she'd had following the birth of her daughter. I got benched right after she got back because I'd been wounded and needed time off to recover. As a result, we'd only been working the job together for a little over eighteen months.

Earlier this afternoon, she'd informed me she was taking another family leave. She and her husband had just received the difficult news that their little two-year-old daughter, Tara, had been diagnosed with autism. Sally had decided to stay home to work with her.

"Now that it's sunk in, I hope you're not too upset," she said. "You seemed a little quiet after I told you."

"Of course I'm not upset." I took her hand. "I'm gonna miss having you as my partner is all. I thought we were finally through the medical stuff and ready to kick ass."

"I'm sorry we had such a choppy go. After the baby, I had more stuff going wrong than a Russian airline." She squeezed my hand. "I just wanted you to know I think you're a great partner and I'll be back once Thomas and I have a good support program set up."

"I'll be waiting," I told her.

"You know yet who Cal is going to assign to our desk?" she asked.

"Nope."

"I hope it's not Hitch. You deserve better than that."

"I doubt he'll put Hitchens with me." But the truth was, I'd been worrying about that ever since Sally told me she was taking another home leave.

Sumner Hitchens had been bouncing between partners, hitting the guardrail, getting slapped to the center, and ringing all the tilt buzzers, before ending back in the return tray like the kinetically overshot pinball he was. We were currently the only two unattached detectives at Homicide Special.

A captain from Ad Vice jostled us as he made his way back to the bar. "These guys look sloshed," Sally commented. "It's dangerous to drink at these things."

"It's a Christmas party," I said noncommittally. "Hopefully, Yellow Cab's gonna make the difference."

Sally hugged me and we wished each other luck.

Twenty minutes later I had Alexa by the arm and we were mercifully out of there. We walked to the valet stand out front, followed by the faint strains of "Frosty the Snowman."

My black MDX pulled to the curb and we both got in. Alexa and I had ridden in together this morning because of the party. My wife never drinks at police events either, so thankfully, with what was just about to happen, we were both completely sober.

I turned out of the parking lot and headed down the hill, then took a left on Franklin, making my way toward the Hollywood Freeway.

According to the Communications Division, the radio call we answered a few minutes later hit dispatch at 10:13 P.M.

It was December 22nd, three days before Christmas.

▪ CHAPTER ▪
3

LAPD protocol demands you always keep your police scanner on even while off duty. Alexa reached into the glove box as we hit the 101 freeway and flipped the switch. A steady stream of low-value mistakes bubbled out at us, all of it delivered in a flat, rambling female monotone.

"One X-Ray Seven, meet L-Fifteen Code Six at the market, 3316 West Olympic," the RTO said. "Cross street is Western. Felony 211 suspect needs transport to MCJ for booking."

It went on like that. Nothing too big seemed to be going down at the moment.

Since it was relatively late, I was using the freeways, taking the long way home in miles, which at this hour should turn out to be the short way in minutes.

I was tooling along, glad to be out of that party, when Alexa said, "I saw you talking to Sally. What a shame about her little girl."

"Yeah, she thinks if they start working with specialists right now, they can minimize the effect of the autism. Tara's so young, it's hard to test her, so the doctors don't really know how severe it is yet."

Because Alexa ran the Detective Bureau I couldn't help but wonder if she'd seen Captain Jeb Calloway's new Homicide Special partners list, so I casually floated the question.

"I'd sure like to know who Jeb's gonna put with me. You heard anything?"

We were about five miles from the transition to the San Diego Freeway, which would take us to Venice Beach, where our little canal house was located on one of the waterways there. When Alexa didn't answer I glanced over.

I knew that expression. She was trying to make up her mind. It was always a problem for us when she knew something that affected me but that she wasn't supposed to confide.

"I'm hoping it's not going to be Sumner Hitchens," I gently prodded.

Then she said, "I think Detective Hitchens is going to be transfered to CAPS in the Valley. But please don't say anything because I don't think he's been told yet."

CAPS was Crimes Against Persons, and if that was true, it was a big demotion for him to go from the elite Homicide Special squad where he was currently assigned to some Valley purse-snatch detail.

Hitchens, or "Hitch" as he preferred to be called, had somehow gonzo'd his way into our unit, then had burned through three partners in less than a year. All of them eventually became so frustrated with him they demanded reassignment.

"You sure he's going to the Valley?" I asked.

"It's just something I think I heard," she responded vaguely.

"Okay, that's good. Actually, that's great. But it leaves us with an odd number up there. Means they'll have to transfer in someone new to partner with me. Bobby Shepherd has been trying for the unit. I worked great with him when we were in patrol. You think you could put in a good word? I'd love to get Shep as my new partner."

She poker-faced my dash.

"I hope making captain isn't going to fuck up that nice, easy management style you're so widely appreciated for," I said, trying to kid her along.

"Come on, Shane, you know who gets in Homicide Special is Jeb's call. I can't micromanage my commanders and then hold them responsible for their performance."

At that moment the radio call that put this story in motion burbled out of the scanner.

"All units and One Adam Twenty. A 415 with shots fired at 3151 Skyline Drive. Nearest cross street is Mulholland. One Adam Twenty, your call is Code Three."

"Isn't that about a mile or two up there?" Alexa said, pointing off at the hills to my left where some very pricey real estate was located. We'd both been patrol officers for five years and as a result had a pretty thorough knowledge of the city.

"Yeah," I said. "I think Skyline Drive is just off Mulholland near Laurel Canyon."

Alexa snatched up the mike and keyed it.

"This is Delta Fifteen. Scully and Scully. Off duty, but in the immediate vicinity. We will take the Skyline Drive 415 shots-fired call."

"Roger that," the RTO replied. "All units, all frequencies, Delta Fifteen is in the vicinity of 3151 Skyline and is responding Code Three. All other units, your call is now Code Two."

Code Three is red lights and siren. I hit the switch, and the strobes I'd had installed in the grille and back window of my Acura flashed on. Simultaneously Alexa reached out and flipped another toggle and as the siren began to bray I floored it.

A 415 radio call is a disturbance where the 911 caller is so hysterical or incoherent that dispatch doesn't know the exact reason or nature of the event. In the Patrol Division, 415s were dreaded calls because you could be rolling on anything from an old lady locked out of her house to something as deadly as the North Hollywood bank shootout.

One night, years ago, when I was still in an X-car, I got a "possible major 415 with knives and chains." It sounded like a riot. We squealed in with our adrenaline surging and our weapons out. It turned out to be two eighty-year-old men fighting over a garden hose. We were so keyed up, and the lighting in the backyard was so bad, we could have easily shot one of them by mistake.

You had to be extremely careful but ready for anything on 415s. The shots-fired tag definitely upped the ante.

We exited the freeway on Laurel Canyon and headed into the hills. Out of the corner of my eye I saw Alexa fishing in her purse for her 9 mm Spanish Astra. I caught her eye just as she tromboned the slide, kicking a fresh round into the chamber, then clicked on the safety.

"Merry Christmas, sweetheart," she deadpanned.

· CHAPTER ·

4

We powered up Laurel Canyon with the siren squealing and turned right onto Mulholland Drive, which runs for a way along the top of a mountain ridge that separates Hollywood from the Valley. The road was almost a thousand feet up and provided spectacular views of Studio City on the right and Hollywood to the left. The view was the reason so many multimillion-dollar estates dotted this hillside.

About a mile down Mulholland, we saw Skyline Drive. It cut in on the left heading farther into the mountainside. As I made the turn I almost hit a blue Maserati that flashed past, speeding onto Mulholland. Alexa snapped her head around to look through our back window but the car had already disappeared.

"Didn't get it," she said, referring to the license plate.

The engine on the Acura roared loudly beneath my siren as we continued up the grade, passing more cantilevered mansions that hung off the mountain like glass-walled palaces. We were in the 2800 block, which meant we still had a ways to go.

Then a red Ferrari Mondial sped past us. There were two people inside. The savvy driver flashed his high beams up into our eyes so we couldn't read his plate.

"Didn't get that one, either," Alexa said. She was looking out the back window again but missed the rear plate because of the dark, underlit street.

We passed two bumper-chasing Escalades. Both had their headlights off and were screaming down the hill. No front plates. Next, a half-million-dollar Mercedes McLaren whipped past, its high beams blinding us, followed by a Bentley Azure, then another Maserati. This one was yellow with a maroon racing stripe.

"Nope," Alexa said, turning again. It was way too dark to see much.

"Cockroaches running for the baseboards," I muttered as I grabbed a curb number. 3140. The house we wanted was going to be near the top of the hill.

The last car to pass us was a new black Mercedes 350. It was also running without lights, but this time as Alexa spun around she managed to catch the first four letters on the back plate.

"4 L M C!" she exclaimed. "Didn't get any other numbers."

We got to the address and I skidded the MDX to a stop, flipping off my emergency package as Alexa and I bailed.

I clawed my party gun, the backup Taurus Ultra-Lite .38, from my jacket-slimming ankle holster and we both surveyed the scene, our hearts pounding.

3151 was at the very end of Skyline. The driveway looked like an extension of the street leading up a hill onto a large property dominated by a looming overgrown mansion on the left. We were the first unit on the scene.

The huge house was a big, rundown Spanish structure that looked like it was built in the early 1900s, well before the rest of the sixties-style neighborhood had filled in around it. The front yard had gone to seed. An old wooden gate was hanging crooked but standing open across the driveway. I could hear Christmas music coming from the back—Bing Crosby singing "Silver Bells."

"Let's clear it," Alexa said.

I nodded and we passed through the open gate and started up the drive with our guns drawn, moving carefully, ready for anything.

The mansion was dark. As far as I could see, not one light was on inside. We walked up the steep drive, hugging the mansion's south wall, heading toward the sound of the music.

When we neared the top of the hill a huge eight-car garage came into view and we could see lights coming from a large backyard area. We crested the drive and saw that the house sat right on a promontory point. A magnificent half-acre pool area with a spectacular view overlooked the lights of the Valley on the left and parts of Hollywood on the right.

There were neighboring houses on either side but they were newer and sat a little farther back from the point, allowing them views in only one direction or the other. This property was obviously the first estate up here and, as a result, was in the prime location.

There was a pool house with Spanish arches that matched the old architecture of the estate, but newer plate-glass windows indicated it was a more recent addition. It looked empty but was ablaze with lights. The Christmas music seemed to originate from a sound system located inside.

We kept our backs to the wall and edged around the corner to get a better look at the layout.

It was then that I saw two female bodies floating facedown in the rectangular, Olympic-sized pool. Their tangled hair and colorful dresses were illuminated by the powerful underwater lights. Both appeared to be Caucasian, their inert bodies leaking large amounts of dark arterial blood into the turquoise water.

Alexa and I continued to stand with our backs to the wall of the house, surveying the terrain for any sign of movement. In addition to the two women floating in the pool, I could now see a third person. There was a man bent over the back of a pool chaise with his ass poking up in the air. His face was looking down at the green canvas chair pad as if it contained something of great interest to him.

"Police! Stay where you are! Put your hands in the air!" I shouted.

He didn't move—didn't twitch. In that instant, changing categories, going from potential adversary to victim number three.

"Go," Alexa directed.

While she covered me, I ducked through the gate into the backyard and sprinted across the deck to the side of the pool house, throwing my back to the wall. From where I now stood, I could see the rest of the backyard. It looked deserted.

"Backyard looks clear," I called as I raised my gun into a firing position to cover Alexa. "Go!" I shouted and she sprinted across the lawn, past my position and into the pool house. I followed behind her and covered her as she threw open changing room doors, checking both bathrooms.

"Clear," she called.

I left her and sprinted to the far side of the house to check the north side of the property and the path that led back to the street. It was also empty, the pathway lit by an old rusting Spanish-style carriage lamp.

"North side clear!" I shouted, then checked the back door of the house. It was fastened securely by a heavy commercial-sized Yale padlock. The bracket was bolted to the side of the house and attached to the door with two-inch bolts that went all the way through the solid oak.

I looked through the kitchen windows into a pantry. The house was dark and appeared deserted—more than deserted, it looked to be in terrible disrepair. For some reason only the backyard and pool house of this estate had been maintained.

Next Alexa and I checked the mammoth garage. All eight pull-up doors and the side entrances were securely padlocked.

Once we were finished we returned to the man who was still bent over the pool chaise, obviously very dead. He was a middle-aged Caucasian, and had three huge grapefruit-sized exit wounds in his back. All of them were oozing thick blood the consistency of ketchup but the deep purple-reddish color of eggplant. He'd been shot with some kind of large-bore weapon.

"I'll check on the others," Alexa said, moving toward the two women floating in the pool.

They looked young and fit, both in colorful strapless party dresses, which in death had floated up around shapely thighs. Their leaking wounds were now beginning to turn the Olympic-sized pool a weird greenish pink.

Alexa grabbed the nearest one by the arm, pulled her over, and checked for a pulse. Then she repeated the process with the second body.

"Both dead," she said, but made no attempt to pull them out of the water. We had to leave the scene pretty much as we found it for the homicide tech teams and photographers because our 415 with shots fired had just morphed into a triple 187.

As I studied the bloodstained man bent over the pool chaise, I noticed a wallet in his back pants pocket. I carefully fished it out using my thumb and index finger, then dropped it onto a nearby glass-top table and took a pen from my jacket.

I flipped the wallet open, revealing a driver's license encased in a plastic sleeve. The picture of a tanned, good-looking man smiled out from under the State of California seal. The date of birth on the license revealed that he was fifty-five. Then I read the name.

"You won't believe who we have here," I called over to Alexa, who was still by the pool. "This vic is Scott Berman."

Alexa stood, her face now drawn. "Then we're sitting on a full-blown disaster," she said.

Bing Crosby didn't seem to get it. "Have yourself a merry little Christmas," he sang happily.

This incident, I later learned, was something screenwriters call the inciting story event. But for me, it was the beginning of two weeks I'm going to call "Shane's Midlife Crisis."

ACT ONE

■ ■ ■ ■ ■ ■ ■ ■ ■

· CHAPTER ·

5

Scott Berman had produced some of the biggest movies in the history of Hollywood. Until tonight, he'd sat atop a massive production empire located at Paramount Studios, where I'd read he had just made an overall deal. His last three blockbuster hits had been produced there. Berman was an A-list Hollywood player, one of the few world-famous producers whose name was as important as those of the stars who worked for him.

I was already the primary responder on this 187, being first on the scene. Because I was also assigned to Homicide Special, which handled high-profile celebrity murder cases, I knew Jeb Calloway would probably assign this one to me.

We turned off the music and marked a predetermined access and egress path on the grass at the far side of the driveway for the patrol cops who would soon arrive. We didn't want them blundering in, disturbing any trace evidence that might exist. By the time the first black-and-white had pulled up, the crime scene was basically locked down. Seconds later two more X-cars chirped in.

"We're Code Four," Alexa called to the six armed cops who were running up the drive with their safeties off.

Alexa got on the phone to Jeb Calloway to notify him we had a department red ball, slang for a big media case. Next she dialed the district attorney's twenty-four-hour desk to start the process of getting a judge to write us a warrant that would allow CSI to do a search of the property at 3151 Skyline Drive.

I organized the patrol guys, got them stringing tape, and expanded the initial area that Alexa and I had secured. I had them block off Skyline Drive all the way down to Mulholland. I like to start with a big campus, because I've learned it's easy to shrink a crime scene but almost impossible to grow it.

I nabbed one of the patrolmen and told him to keep the crime scene attendance log, cataloging the names and times of arrival for everyone. Then I walked down and retrieved my crime scene notepad out of the car, returned to the pool area, and began sketching the positions of the three dead bodies in the large backyard. I walked around the main house checking every opening. Every door on the ground floor of the old mansion had been securely padlocked, every window locked.

We didn't find any IDs for the two dead women in the pool. One of the people escaping in those fancy cars must have stopped to gather up their purses so we couldn't identify them, making me wonder why they'd taken the time to do that but had left Scott Berman's wallet in his pocket where it was sure to be found.

Besides sketching the physical layout, noting first impressions, and making a list of vehicles we'd passed coming up the hill, along with that one partial plate on the black Mercedes, there wasn't much I could do until the warrant, ME, and CSIs arrived.

While I waited for forensics and the medical examiner, I decided to go next door to see if anybody had witnessed the shooting. My best bet was the house on the Hollywood side of the property because it sat slightly above, although a little back from the promontory point. There were a few dark windows on the north wall that looked like they had a decent view of this backyard.

As I headed away from the pool area I again studied the landscaping. Unlike the paint-starved, weed-choked mansion that fronted it, the backyard had been scrupulously cared for. Newly planted winter cyclamens showed bright red and white faces as they peeked over low hedges in freshly manicured flower beds. The pool house looked recently painted.

Again, I wondered why the mansion was such a wreck, while the backyard could have been a photo spread for *Better Homes and Gardens*.

Arleen and Cecil Prentiss lived next door and they supplied the answer.

"Nobody's lived over there since way before we moved in ten years ago," Cecil said.

He was a tall, gaunt, fifty-year-old character with a chin patch and frizzy hair that was growing in a Bozo the Clown half-moon shape. His wife, Arleen, was one of those thirty-five-year-old Hollywood health club exhibits—too thin, too buff, too tan, with bleached-blond hair and the required silicone enhancements.

"Did you hear the shots?" I asked them after we'd exchanged introductions.

"We were the ones who called it in," Cecil said. "We heard it, but didn't see it because it was getting pretty racy over there. We have a ten-year-old, so once they started groping each other, we pulled the blinds down on the back windows."

"Let's start with what you saw before you pulled the shades," I suggested. "Did you recognize anyone?"

"Nobody," Arleen said. "But whoever they were, they had money. The girls were beautiful, at least from a distance. Looked like actresses. The guys seemed older. Bunch of fancy cars parked on the street. There's a foundation that owns that place. They only rent out the backyard. Mostly it's for charity events and parties but we've heard the house is completely off-limits."

"Yeah, it's all padlocked," I told them.

"During the holiday season, there's something going on over at that pool house all the time," Arleen continued. "We complain, but the city-use ordinances in this sector are pretty loose, so we can't get them to stop. If it gets too noisy, then Cecil has the number to the pool house, which has its own line. He phones over and if we threaten to call the cops, that usually quiets things down."

"Who got killed?" Cecil asked, as he craned his skinny neck forward and began wringing bony hands, taking him out of his friendlier Bozo persona and into a less attractive praying mantis mode.

"Not sure, yet," I told him noncommittally. "You get any license plates for the cars parked out front?"

"No," Arleen said. "A year or two ago we might have, but it's sort of become like a normal thing, so we're just trying to deal with it now."

"What did the gunshots sound like?" I asked.

"Like some kind of machine gun. BLAPBLAPBLAPBLAPBLAP! Like that," Cecil said, mimicking the sound of the weapon.

"And you didn't look out?"

"Yeah. After we heard the shots. But by then, everybody was running like crazy. I couldn't pick out the person with the gun. They were gone in seconds. Car doors slamming, engines starting, tires squealing."

It turned out Cecil was a TV producer. Arleen had just started working with him and was, as the saying goes, learning the biz. They had offices at the old MGM studio, which is now Sony.

"Maybe this will finally end all of this," Cecil said, more concerned with the area's use and noise regs than the three dead strangers in the neighboring backyard. "We've been talking about getting the City Council to pass a number of night location rules, like they have over in Pasadena. Maybe this will finally get somebody's attention."

"You never know. Could happen," I said.

After we exchanged cards, I walked out their front gate and saw Captain Jeb Calloway pulling up in a brown Crown Vic Interceptor. His D-car was followed closely by a new, top down, midnight blue Porsche Carrera Cabriolet with a tan interior.

"Shit," I muttered as the Carrera pulled in and shut off its lights.

Sumner Hitchens unhooked his seat belt and exited the hundred-thousand-dollar sports car. He paused for a moment to straighten the creases on his expensive pleated trousers.

As usual, Hitch was dressed like a runway model. This evening it was a dark rust-colored suit, purple shirt, black silk tie with matching pocket square. His shoes were glittering Spanish leather. An oversized thirty-thousand-dollar special-edition Corum wristwatch flashed rose gold from under French cuffs with diamond links. His neatly trimmed mustache and handsome coffee-colored face were lit by his standard devilish grin.

Hollywood Hitch, mean and lean, had made the scene.

"Hang on, Skipper," he called to Jeb Calloway, hurrying after our captain, who was heading up the drive toward the crime scene.

I've been a cop for almost half my life and other than Sumner Hitchens, I've never heard anyone on the job call a police captain "Skipper." That only happened on TV, in the movies, and in Hitch World, which I had come to learn had a very large zip code.

The way the story went, Sumner Hitchens had sold one of his big homicide cases to the movies. That happened just a year before he was transferred to Homicide Special. Back then Hitch was a detective in the Metro Division downtown. He and his homicide table had busted a dangerous serial killer, a nutcase who thought the only way he could nourish himself and stay alive was to drink the blood of his victims.

Paramount produced the film and Jamie Foxx ended up playing the starring role of Detective Sumner Hitchens. The movie was entitled *Mosquito*, and the damn thing grossed over six hundred million dollars worldwide. Hitch had two back-end profit points—hence the hundred-thousand-dollar Carrera, the pricey watch and wardrobe, as well as his new multimillion-dollar house in the Hollywood Hills, all of which he never tired of bragging about. His Hollywood representatives were a gang of sharks at United Talent Agency.

In my opinion, Sumner Hitchens was the ultimate pretender so there was no way I was going to let that hairbag end up as my partner.

He spotted me standing on the neighbors' steps ten yards away.

I must have been frowning because he waved and shouted, "Hey, dawg, cheer up. It's you and me now, brother."

▪ CHAPTER ▪

6

Patrol had already taped off a media control area in a vacant lot half a block away. It was currently empty, but we all knew before long this would get phoned in by a neighbor and once the press got wind of the fact that Scott Berman was one of our vics, they would be covering this place like a red carpet awards show.

Crime techs were arriving down by the main gate, talking in low voices while they waited for an ADA to show up with a search warrant so they could start collecting evidence. Until then there wasn't much anybody could do.

Hitch tried to approach me once or twice, but I gave him the slip by saying, "Just a minute, Hitch. Be right with you." I didn't want to give our new partnership even six seconds of emotional currency.

As the primary along with Alexa, I was one of the few people who were permitted to stay on the scene before the warrants arrived. Another exception was my immediate supervisor. I was looking to pull Jeb aside and start with my list of complaints. I'd paid my dues and like Sally said, I deserved better. No way I was going to work with Hollywood Hitchens. Jeb was just going to have to see this my way. I was rehearsed and ready to make my case when I finally caught him alone. He was standing at the side of the house, out of the immediate area of interest, talking on his cell.

"Captain," I said as I approached, but he held up a hand to silence me.

"I don't care who's in the regular rotation," he said into his Black-Berry. "I want you to handle it personally, Meyer. We're gonna need a pile of cover on this."

Meyer was Bert Meyer, better known in police circles as Meyer the Liar, head of our Media Relations Department.

"We're gonna need a media war room with daily press briefings and handouts," Jeb continued into his cell. "This is gonna be everybody's lead story. Matt Lauer will probably be out from New York tomorrow, doing stand-ups in front of this place."

I looked down and saw an old paint-peeled Prime Properties Real Estate sign that had been ditched back here years ago. Underneath, hanging from a chain, was a dirt-smeared placard that read: A BEVERLY BARTINELLI LISTING. I wrote it down.

Jeb finally hung up and turned to me. "I don't wanta hear it, Shane," he said before I could even get started.

"But Captain . . ."

"You're gonna work with him. It's my call and it's already settled. That's all there is to it."

"Captain, can I at least make my case?"

Jeb Calloway was originally from Port-au-Prince, Haiti, and still spoke with a slight French accent. He was marble hard, black ebony with a torpedo-shaped head and Mighty Mouse build. We sometimes called him the Haitian Sensation because of his comic-book proportions. He was a good guy but when he got pissed he could really break your balls. The whole package, every ounce and fiber, now looked extremely menacing. He glanced down at his watch impatiently.

"Go! You've got forty seconds."

"I only need five. Hitchens is a total waste of space and a raging asshole. I won't work with him."

A uniformed patrolman started down the path by the side of the house, stringing perimeter tape.

"Can you give us a minute?" Jeb said, and the cop abruptly spun and left us there. Jeb turned back to me.

"Shane, I try to be fair to everyone. You know I've got a three-strike rule. He's down to his last swing and, like it or not, you're it."

"Three strikes? He's already had 'em, Captain. Dick Parsons dumped him over that evidence-tampering thing that went to IA, Chris Molina for being a total dickhead and crashing their unit twice. Barbara Palma last week for seducing her twin sister after the police academy picnic. That's three."

"The Barbara Palma thing was a foul tip. Some people misunderstand what Hitch calls personal charm. He and Babs were chemically incompatible. It was my idea to split 'em up, so that one doesn't count."

"Captain, please."

"Shane, work with the guy. He needs your guidance. You're my cleanup hitter. My *cheval de guerre*. Get Hitchens out of the ditch and back on the road."

"Do you really want this numbnuts working on Scott Berman's

high-profile homicide? Forgetting his agents at UTA and the fact that when the movie comes out, Howie Mandel is gonna be playing you in blackface, he's completely unreliable. He's gonna screw up."

"You're the one who's working the case. I'm looking to you. He's just driving the car and learning from a master." Then Jeb looked down at his watch. "You're done, Scully. Request denied and you got a whole two minutes instead of just forty seconds. See what a nice guy I am? Now go out there and hit it. Bring me back a collar and do it before this is next week's cover story in *People* magazine."

During the intervening hour, the rest of the CSI responders hit the scene along with the medical examiner and his staff. They continued to mill around at the foot of the drive, waiting for Carla Morris from the district attorney's office to show up. She finally arrived with the warrant signed by a superior court judge.

"How come this warrant is only for the backyard? What about the house?" Alexa asked as she stood by the sagging driveway gate with a swarm of evidence techs and glared at the paper.

"I thought you said the bodies were in the backyard. I don't think you said anything about a house," Carla said. "If you want me to go back and get a new warrant, it's gonna take another hour."

Alexa pondered this for almost a minute.

On a murder scene, time lost at the outset can allow a perp to get away. Prints or other evidence, if recovered soon enough, could allow us to effect a quick arrest. Since the house was locked and probably not part of this anyway, Alexa made her decision.

"Let's get started. If we need to, we can go back and get a paper for the house tomorrow."

With the warrant in hand, about twenty CSIs and coroner's assistants carrying their crime scene kits full of investigatory tools started up the path Alexa and I had marked in the grass by the side of the drive.

Except for pointing out areas of examination, the primary homicide detective is a third wheel during this stage of an investigation. The tech squad and coroner had full control of the scene.

The CSIs began by setting up an inward spiral search, walking the outside circle of the yard, moving slowly in toward the pool, where the bodies were. Ten investigators walked in a line, looking down, marking anything that looked like evidence with cards that were folded into a teepee shape with numbers that corresponded to a master sheet.

Slowly, they began finding 9 mm brass shell casings and meticulously gathering and cataloging potential evidence, photographing footprints and blood spatter.

I walked around the edge of the backyard, looking for my new partner. He was off talking to Tom Rosselli, the crime scene photographer.

I thought, *Well, okay. This is good. At least he's working, helping the guy set up his photo log.* But as I got closer, I realized they weren't talking about the case at all.

"You gotta pound the sucker with a hammer," Hitch was saying.

"You always wanta go to town with the hammer," Rosselli answered. "Is that like an African-American thing or something?"

What the hell is this? I thought and slipped behind the pool house so I could eavesdrop.

"Don't be starting in with me on how to prepare the meat," Hitch was saying. "You gotta hammer it first to make it tender."

"We're talking about a Sicilian meat roll, asshole. It's *supposed* to be a little chewy. I'm *Sicilian.* You're from fucking Sixty-sixth Street in South Central. Whatta you know about Sicilian cooking?"

"I'm the king of Sicilian cooking," Hitch shot back. "Check it out. You arrange your meat on your wax paper, you arrange the ham slices on top of the meat—"

"Ham goes on the outside, not on top, dipshit."

"This is so pathetic," Hitch said. "You make your living photographing dead people. What am I wasting my time on you for? It's like talking to a garbageman about the ballet."

Not as bad as I first thought but still pretty awful. Here we were at one of the hottest murder scenes of the year and Sumner Hitchens was distracting the videographer with an argument over Sicilian cooking when Rosselli should have been doing his initial walk-through to memorialize the scene before the swarm of techies moved anything. I stepped around the side of the building and faced him.

"Let's go," I said. "Let Rosselli do his job. You're with me."

I left abruptly and Hitch followed me across the pool deck.

"Try the recipe my way," Rosselli called after him.

"I gave up vomiting after meals when I found out Lindsay Lohan was doing it," Hitch called back.

I led him to a place near where Alexa was standing.

"After the bodies are processed I want you to go to the ME's office with Alexa. Witness the autopsies with her." Thinking it would at least get him out of my sight for a while.

"I'm not gonna be that easy to ditch," he said. "I already had this out with Jeb. I'm not the kind of partner you can bullshit. I know I'm junior man, but that's only in hours. When it comes to working this case, I'm your tight. It's you and me, cheek to cheek, brother."

He pulled out a red notebook. It was covered in expensive leather and had gold-embossed edges. Across the center, engraved in gold script, it said: MY JOURNAL. The thing must have cost him three hundred dollars.

"This isn't going to be a movie," I informed him. "So you can put away your little writer's journal."

"I know you're upset, but I'm gonna grow on you, man. I got this feeling."

He smiled at me. He was handsome. He was charming. He was hard not to like. But he was also a hopeless bullshitter and opportunist. At least, that was my take back then.

"I'm not going to the morgue. I can't," he added.

"Why not?"

"I don't get along with dead people. I don't like them; they don't like me." His smile widened. "Besides, I already secured some valuable info for us. The morgue is backfill on any investigation. With a red ball like this, time is everything. We need to be moving forward. Somebody else can watch the coroner fingerpaint."

I stood there, not sure how to play it.

"I called a friend of mine in real estate who sold me my Hollywood house last year." He grinned again. "LeAnne has a big case on the Hitchmeister. I'm otherwise involved right now so I haven't gotten around to her yet, but the girl's managed to secure a spot on my farm team. That means she's eager to help me so she ran the title on this house. It's owned by something called the Dorothy White Foundation. It's some kinda trust and the primary beneficiary is listed as . . ."

He flipped open his leather notebook. "Brooks David Dunbar, 236 Schuyler Road. Schuyler Road is a primo street in Beverly Hills, by the way. I've also got the zip if you want it, but I hate showing off."

After the coroner left with the bodies I handed Alexa the keys to the MDX. She was still on the dispatch sheet as one of the primary responding officers so she was going to accompany the ME to the morgue and cover the autopsy. Then she would officially sign off on the case.

Since CSI would have control of this crime scene until almost morning, I agreed to follow up on the Brooks Dunbar lead that Sumner had just supplied.

I told Jeb and Alexa where we were going, then Hitch and I walked down to Mulholland where our cars had been reparked by patrol.

We got into Hitch's Porsche Carrera. As I sat in the soft tan leather passenger seat, he turned on his scanner. Then we pulled out and sped toward Mulholland, top down, both straight pipes snarling like angry jungle cats.

▪ CHAPTER ▪
7

"What was that all about with Rosselli?" I asked as we raced across the mountain ridge on Mulholland to Coldwater, then made a left turn and headed down the winding canyon road into Beverly Hills.

"Rosselli thinks he can cook," Hitch answered, using the Porsche's mid-engine cornering dynamic to take the S-turns on Coldwater at nut-puckering speeds. "Fucking Italians. All those greaseballs ever came up with that was worth anything was pizza and that's just a cheese sandwich with anchovies."

"And you're some kind of expert?"

"I've trained at the Cordon Bleu. I fly to France and take cooking classes on my vacations."

"I didn't know bullshit could be prepared in the French style," I said.

"Bullshit is a French specialty." He grinned. "And don't knock my cooking 'til you've tried it. Wait 'til you taste my eggs Portugal."

"What I meant was, what kinda deal do you have going with Rosselli? You get him movie premiere tickets or actress phone numbers, he sends you your own personal copies of the crime scene photos so you can include them in your movie pitches at UTA?"

"Come on, Shane. Let's not do this, okay? Everybody in this town is in business. Even you. We just have different profit expectations. Don't tell me you never flashed your badge to get out of a speeding ticket." He smiled. "Besides, how many L.A. cops have sold cases to the movies before me? LAPD Sgt. Joe Wambaugh single-handedly turned that into a cottage industry. *Onion Field, Lines and Shadows, Echoes in the Darkness,* just to name a few.

"We got a front-row seat to the greatest show on earth. You want to just write this stuff up in some stupid case file and forget it? I'm asking you to take a minute here and clear your bowels, man."

"We're working a triple homicide, Sumner. I told Jeb I'd work with you, but if I lose patience and throw you back like all your other partners, then you'll be out of Homicide Special and down to chasing smash-and-grabs in the Valley. We do this my way or you're gonna get your next decent police posting about the same time we colonize Mars."

He took a moment, grimaced, then said, "You're being very short-sighted."

"This case is not going to end up in a theater near you. It's gonna end up in court."

After a minute where he raced through another S-turn, causing me to grab the door pull, he said, "You need to relax on this, Scully, because a case like *Mosquito* doesn't come along very often.

"Granted, when it does, the Hollywood *gantseh machers* will drop trou and grab for the K-Y 'cause most studio execs have business degrees from Princeton or Yale, but they got no story imagination. What they *do* know is, they've got a much better chance of getting a picture greenlit if it's been a big national news story first, making it what we in the biz call a 'presold title.' Right now this Skyline Drive case is just an interesting springboard with no ending." He turned and focused the Hollywood Hitch persona at me. "Lemme give you some Screenwriting 101 here."

"That's okay."

"No, you should hear me out 'cause I can tell you're needlessly freaked. On this Scott Berman thing we're only at the top of Act One. The central job of Act One is to define the problem. Admittedly this inciting event has a high-value player and two hot-looking dead chicks floating in a pool, but while all that is mildly interesting, it won't carry a picture. There's gotta be something much more menacing hiding under the surface that drives the action forward. Something nobody sees that will rise up and grab the audience by the throat in Act Two. So far we ain't got that. Not even close. Meaning we got a ninety percent chance this story dies right here at the top of Act One."

"I think when you get to Lindacrest you want to go left," I said.

"Got it." A moment later he turned on Lindacrest but the writing lesson continued. "Like, suppose it turns out Scott Berman was cheating on his old lady and she got fed up, hired some guy with a harelip to put Scott on the ark. Bing, bang, boom, end of story. Provocative start, no ending. See what I'm saying?

"For a movie to have legs, you need a great first act with a sharp attack on the story, then a complication in Act Two with some hellacious moves where the antagonist is rippin' up the landscape.

"Next comes your second act curtain where the hero ends up on the balls of his ass, completely destroyed, or, alternately, where something so big happens it puts the screenplay in a whole different place. In *Mosquito*, by the way, it was when I almost became victim number six. Then Act Three needs a firestorm ending where you blow the shit outta something big.

"On a true-crime story it's okay to embellish a few flat spots slightly to keep it interesting because as Albert Einstein once said, 'imagination is more important than knowledge.' But that's it. Believe me, we're a long way from having something we can sell for megabucks like *Mosquito*."

I was getting a headache.

A car full of girls in UCLA sweatshirts pulled up next to us and started honking and waving. Hitch honked and waved back.

We left them as they turned on Sunset Boulevard, heading to the UCLA campus while we continued on down Lindacrest Drive, navigating the narrow curving streets, finally arriving at 236 Schuyler Road five minutes later.

It was another huge house located behind closed gates. Another Christmas party was in progress. My third in one night and I don't like them much to begin with.

We pulled up in the Carrera with the top down and Hitch smiled at the gate guard, a black guy with shoulders like a bookcase and a CIA-style earpiece jammed in one ear.

"Sumner Hitchens," he said. "I'm sure I'm on the list. My office at Paramount phoned my acceptance in late this afternoon." All this before I could stop him.

"Just show him your fucking badge," I growled under my breath.

I pulled my creds out and held them across his chest for the guard to see. "Police. We're here to talk to Brooks Dunbar."

"Okay," he said. "But I have to announce you."

"Fine, just open up."

He pushed the gate button and Hitch squealed up the drive.

"You gotta chill, dude," he said as we approached the palatial house. "I know this place. It's a Hollywood landmark. Elton John used to own it. Then Spielberg before he got married. They call it Knoll House. When a mansion has a name it means it's like one of a kind. There's some major weight living on this six acres of manicured velvet. I know how to play this crowd. We won't get anything butting heads."

"If you so much as open your mouth I'm gonna fill it with shoe leather."

"Suit yourself, but you'll see."

We pulled up in front. More Christmas music was leaking out of the open front door. About twenty-five fancy cars were in the huge driveway, as well as one or two limos with their liveried drivers standing beside them.

"The guests at this Christmas party might be stoned, but hopefully they won't be dead like at the other one," Hitch said as he parked and we got out. Another security guard was in the doorway with a clipboard. This guy was Hispanic with a weight lifter's build. We approached him in the entry.

I showed my badge. "Detectives Scully and Hitchens from Homicide Special."

"Hey, nice to know you," he said. "I work at the Police Administration Building too. LAPD Sergeant Bob Cruz. I think I've seen you guys around."

"What are you doing here?" I asked.

"I moonlight for Ameritech Security after hours. This is one of my semi-regular accounts." Then he leaned closer. "Homicide Special, huh? What's up?"

"We're working a triple murder that took place tonight on a property Brooks Dunbar owns in the Hollywood Hills," I told him. "Before we talk to him it might help if you could give us some background."

"Welcome to the care and feeding of the asshole elite," off-duty Sergeant Cruz said. "Brooks Dunbar has his head so far up his ass he's looking at most stuff through his navel. This kid is twenty-four and says he's a movie producer, or sometimes it's an art dealer, but what he really does is snort dope and throw up in the backseats of cars. His buds call him Heir Abhorrent, which might give you an idea."

"Who owns this place?" Hitch asked. "Looks a little lush for a twenty-four-year-old drug addict."

"You're right. His dad, Thayer Dunbar, owns it. He's a big Texas billionaire who lives half the year in Houston, checking on his oil leases. He's divorced. The mother lives in Malibu. Brooks has inherited money, but since his parents know he's a total nimrod, they've locked it all up in trusts.

"Ameritech has the contract to protect the property. But for parties like this one, Brooks takes on extra people like me, 'cause he's got this thing about paparazzi getting shots of him that will piss off his dad. But when you work for Brooks you gotta get your money up front 'cause he's a very slow pay. Slow like in months."

"Can I help you?" a young man said.

He had appeared out of nowhere and was standing behind us. This guy was thirtysomething, dressed in an open-collared silk shirt and gabardine pants. He had a glass with some kind of foamy Christmas punch in his hand, eggnog maybe.

"We're police, here to see Brooks Dunbar."

"That's what they said when they called up from the gate," the young man said. "I'm his attorney. I'm afraid you'll have to start with me."

▪ CHAPTER ▪
8

The young attorney introduced himself as Stender Sheedy Jr. He was with the famous Century City law firm of Sheedy, Devine & Lipscomb, where his father was the letterhead Sheedy. Junior informed us he was in the entertainment law department and handled Brooks Dunbar's film and music business, which if Sergeant Cruz was correct probably consisted of phone camera gags and recorded farts.

As we stood in the massive marble-floored entry, I could see a swarm of young revelers partying in the huge living room beyond.

"Could I possibly use the men's room?" Hitch said.

"It's right through there on the left," Stender said, pointing.

After Hitch left, young Stender tried to tell me that I'd have to come back in the morning—that Mr. Dunbar was hosting his annual Christmas Do, and could not be pried away from his important guests, who, from what I could see, were just a bunch of stoned Hollywood leeches and midnight club crawlers.

"Let me put it to you another way," I said, politely. "Your client owns a property at 3151 Skyline Drive. A triple homicide was committed there tonight. My partner and I are working that crime, which means that Mr. Dunbar can talk to me here, right now, as a friendly, cooperative material witness, or he can talk to me at Men's Central Jail as a guest of the city."

"This is not a good time. We're just starting holiday follies," Stender protested. "The Truth or Dare is about to begin. It's a tradition."

"I'll make it as quick and painless as possible."

Sumner hadn't come back from the men's room so I did a quick scan of the party and to my dismay saw he hadn't gone in there at all, but was over by the floor-to-ceiling windows, already talking to a pretty girl in a green sequined miniskirt. As I watched he handed her his business card.

"Okay, Detective, if you'll make it quick, let me see what I can do," Stender said, as if it was his choice, not mine.

He escorted me into the massive hotel-sized living room. The center had been cleared of furniture with the big, snow white sofas pushed up against the far walls to make room for the festivities. There were at least forty people in here, all of them very hip and trendy. Nobody over the age of thirty-five.

"Okay, okay," somebody shouted shrilly above the noise as I entered. "But if I do it, Sandra, then you gotta do me." I turned and saw a slightly pudgy guy wearing baggy jeans and a T-shirt that had FUCK ME screen-printed across the front. He was shouting at a young, shapely girl with a rich tan set off by a strapless white mini.

"You ain't got the stones, mate," the girl yelled back with a New Zealand or Aussie accent. The crowd was hooting and shouting insults at the pudgy young guy.

The chub squealed. "That's the bet, right? If I do it, I get to put my schmandra in Sandra." He laughed. It was actually more of a high-pitched giggle.

"You gotta catch me first," the girl yelled. She was drunk or stoned, so that probably wasn't going to be much of an issue. She took a step forward and stumbled, almost going down.

Without warning, the pudgy brat grabbed a taser up off a nearby table and shouted, "Don't taze me, bro!" Then he slammed the gun up on his chest and fired.

The tazer zapped the T-shirt. Flesh and fabric burned. His body leaped backward, hit by fifty thousand volts of electricity. He bounced off a sofa by the wall, then rolled onto the white plush pile carpet and started vibrating violently under a table like a hype with the dries. "Ooow-Ooow-Ooow! That smarts!" he yelled while the room hooted and cheered.

"I'm hoping that's not him," I said to Stender.

"That's him," he replied.

"Who are these other people?"

"Agents, studio development people, celebutantes."

I didn't ask what a celebutante was but guessed it was a famous heiress who did nothing but party.

"Somebody cut me a line. I need medication!" Brooks shrieked, as everyone laughed.

A fresh line of cocaine was cut on a table as the Heir Abhorrent crawled over to it on his hands and knees. Somebody handed him a straw and, while his friends shouted encouragement, Brooks hoovered up the blow.

I'm not in Vice, and I didn't want to waste three valuable hours at the top of a murder investigation booking this jerk at Men's Central, but I have to admit I was tempted. I turned to Stender instead.

"We've got two ways of doing this. You can bring him to me in another room or I can badge this whole bunch of loadies and end this party right now with a trip to jail. Your call."

"There's a den back there," he said, pointing. "I'll show you, then bring him."

"Good choice."

I caught a glimpse of Sumner Hitchens, caucusing with four Hollywood film types whose hair was moussed and styled in interesting shapes. Hitch had his hand on one guy's shoulder, chatting him up relentlessly. I left him there because bottom line, I preferred to do this alone.

Stender led me to the den and left. As I waited I decided to have round two with Jeb over my new partner first thing in the morning.

The den had beautiful whitewashed ash walls. It was large and square, with a high carved-wood ceiling. Bookshelves dominated three walls and framed historic documents with some familiar signatures—John Hancock, Benjamin Franklin, Thomas Jefferson—hung in lighted alcoves. There were certificates of authentication mounted beneath each priceless artifact.

In one corner of the den, inside a magnificent glass box, was an antique six-shooter. The plaque read: COLT SINGLE-ACTION .44 PEACE-MAKER: JESSE JAMES 1881.

As I was admiring it, the door opened and a very stoned Brooks Dunbar stumbled in followed by Stender Sheedy, who closed the door immediately and moved up to take a guardian's position between us.

"You have a card?" Stender demanded.

I pulled out my creds and showed them to him as he wrote down my name and badge number.

"I don't want to talk to this fucker, Sten," said the pudgy little twenty-four-year-old monster in the pornographic tazer-burned T-shirt.

"Shut up!" I snapped at him, spittle flying.

He jumped back and looked at me with an expression of disbelief as if I'd just dropped down from the chandelier wearing a cape and spandex tights.

"You can't shout at me!" he said. "This is my house!"

It was actually his father's house, but I was beyond quibbling. Brooks seemed badly offended by my behavior. It seemed that nobody ever spoke harshly to him.

"Wait 'til my dad finds out about this," he said petulantly. "He'll get you fired."

"I'll risk it. You've got some questions to answer, Mr. Dunbar. They're not difficult, but they will require accurate, sober responses. I understand you own an estate at 3151 Skyline Drive in Hollywood. Is that correct?"

"Huh?"

I turned to Stender and shot him a frustrated look.

"Brooks, tell the detective what he wants to know," the young attorney directed. "Then I'm sure he'll leave."

Brooks Dunbar wiped some runny powder off the edge of his nostrils with the back of his hand. "Shit . . . I gotta . . ." More silence. "This fuckin' sucks. My party's totally going to shit out there," he complained before finally heaving a big, frustrated sigh. "That property, if you have to fucking know, is like an investment, which is in my dumb trust, which I can't fucking use. Why I gotta talk to this guy, Sten?"

"Three people died by the pool up on Skyline tonight," I told him.

"You mean like they overdosed or something?"

"Yeah . . . On 9 mm bullets."

He held my gaze, a shrewd crafty look finally coming into his bloodshot eyes. "Is that supposed to be like my fault or something?"

"Do you own a machine gun, Mr. Dunbar?"

"A machine gun? I got . . . I got . . . like a— I got . . . I really don't wanta do this now, Sten. This is so fucking unfair."

"Just please answer his question, Brooks," Stender Sheedy prodded gently.

"I can run a firearms check," I said. "I'm gonna find out so you might as well tell me. You own one or not?"

"I got like an old antique something or other. It's got a model number but I can't remember. It's a fucking— All I know is I had to register it when I bought the damn thing." He glowered, then mumbled, "You're not supposed to let shit like this happen, Sten. I'm not approving of this at all."

I waited for more, but that seemed to cover his thoughts on the machine gun.

"Is it here?"

"What?"

"The machine gun."

"In my room."

"Let's go."

He looked at his young lawyer. "The Truth or Dare is getting trashed while we mess with this shit."

"Let's just get it over with, Brooks," the wise, still sober, Century City mouthpiece advised. He set down his drink and led the way.

We walked down a hall and out into the beautiful six-acre backyard that featured a commanding view of the sparkling lights of Bel Air. We headed along a hedge-trimmed path to a carriage house, which was bigger than my place in Venice. Brooks opened the front door.

The main room was a mess. Beer cans, empty scotch bottles, and old fast-food boxes littered every surface. Girls' undergarments bloomed like lacy, pastel mushrooms on the furniture and floor. There was a dusting of white powder on most of the tabletops.

"'Scuse the mess," Dunbar mumbled as he led me upstairs to the large master suite.

The bedroom looked like a bomb had gone off in a men's store.

I followed him over to a table littered with a ton of debris. He swept it off onto the floor with his hand and there, serving as an elaborate base for a glass-topped coffee table, was a .50 caliber, water-cooled, antique Browning Model 1809 machine gun from World War I. It was sitting on a low tripod stand.

"Does it even work?" I asked.

It looked like an art piece, a decorative table base for gun freaks or Rambo fans. It was undoubtedly welded in place and missing the firing pin. I was starting to fantasize about smacking this little chump.

"I don't know," he whined. "How should I know? Can I go now?"

"Do you know Scott Berman?" I asked.

"The producer?"

"No, the butterfly collector."

I was losing it.

"I think my dad knows him. He's been here at parties and stuff. I don't pay much attention to shit like that. I got my own life."

"What *do* you pay attention to?"

"The color of Lindsay's or Paris's undies or the lack thereof." He giggled. Then he touched the burn marks on his T-shirt. "Man, that taze was brutal. My nipples are still stinging."

"Detective Scully, is it really necessary to do this tonight?" Stender Sheedy Jr. interjected.

"Yes it is." I turned to Dunbar. "When was the last time you went to your house on Skyline Drive?"

"I don't go up there. I told you, it's a fucking investment. It's in my trust."

"The Dorothy White Foundation?"

"Yes."

"Who is Dorothy White?"

"My mother. It's her maiden name. They named my dumbass trust after her for some fucked-up reason nobody can ever quite explain."

"And you never go up to 3151 Skyline?"

"It's an *investment*," he almost shrieked. "I don't fuck with that shit. I have people who do that for me." He was becoming very agitated.

Then, apropos of absolutely nothing, he said, "It's fucking Christmas, dude. You know, *Christmas?*"

"How much cocaine do you do?"

"I'm taking the fifth on that one, buddy," he sneered angrily.

Now Stender Sheedy, sensing my displeasure and his client's jeopardy, stepped forward. "Brooks wants to cooperate, Detective, it's just hard when he has fifty guests."

I turned to Brooks. "Where were you between ten and ten fifteen tonight?"

"He was here," Stender said.

"Yeah," Brooks agreed. "I was right here, asshole."

"The party started at nine thirty," Stender said. "He's got fifty witnesses. He doesn't know anything."

Which had to be the understatement of this entire holiday season.

"Okay. Here's the deal, Mr. Sheedy. You have your client in my office tomorrow morning at nine A.M. Have him cleaned up and sober. Otherwise, I'm going to issue a warrant for his arrest as a material witness."

I already knew that this stoned pudgeball wasn't involved in my triple murder, but I had some more questions that I needed to ask him on background. As it was, he was so loaded I'd have to do all of this again anyway, because a statement taken while a witness is under the influence of a powerful drug wouldn't hold up in court. I took out two business cards and handed one to Brooks, the other to Sheedy.

"Where do they make these up, Kinko's?" Brooks said, frowning at the department-issued card.

"I'll find my partner and get out of here," I told Sheedy. "Have him there on time tomorrow."

"He'll be there," Stender promised.

I walked back to the main house and was just heading into the living room when I saw the girl in the green sequined mini come out of the powder room.

"Excuse me, miss. Did my friend just give you his business card?"

"Huh?"

It was a sharp crowd.

"My friend, the handsome African-American in the rust-colored suit. I think he gave you the wrong card. We just got new ones."

She pawed into her purse, her expressive brow furrowed in concentration. She dug through bags of powder, pills, and beauty aids before finding the card and pulling it out.

I looked at it. An expensive gold-embossed number, definitely not from Kinko's. Nifty little picture of a golf flag in the top right corner. Underneath it said:

HOLE IN ONE PRODUCTIONS
SUMNER HITCHENS
PRODUCER & CEO

▪ CHAPTER ▪
9

I told Sumner what I'd learned from Brooks and Stender Sheedy in the carriage house as we headed across town to meet with Alexa. Once I was finished, I also gave him a good sanding down over his professional demeanor and investigative methods.

"You were down there passing out your little production company cards to a room full of coked-up agents and D-girls while you were supposed to be working this case with me. I'm trying to be patient, but this shit's gotta stop or I'm gonna make a serious move on you."

"I was on the job, Scully. There's more than one way to prepare Courgettes Provencale."

"Please stop with the cooking metaphors."

"I was in the zone, brother. While you're up in the carriage house with Lord Fauntleroy, I had those freaks in my crosshairs working ground zero, collecting facts."

"If you got something, let's hear it," I said, wondering if maybe I'd jumped too fast.

"I always get something, my man," he shot back.

"Make it great, *my man*."

"Brooks Dunbar is broke," Hitchens began. "What our moonlighting sergeant from Ameritech told us is true. His trust is all locked up. As a result he's a thief. He waits 'til his friends are stoned or passed out then steals credit cards out of their wallets and runs up huge tabs. I learned from one guy that some Russian oligarch's kid got hit for almost two hundred grand on his black AmEx a month ago.

"When his victims start hiring bent noses and talking about his kneecaps, young Brooks takes them to expensive Melrose stores like Louis Vuitton, Fred Segal, and especially this place called Cruel Hearts which is right down from the Ivy. It specializes in expensive S and M leather and jewelry. He got his mother to set him up accounts at these places. To keep his friends from killing him, he buys time by letting them charge expensive stuff on his mother's accounts there. His mother, by the way, is Dorothy White. They named Brooks's trust in her maiden name." I had that last part, but little else.

"Among other things, this kid also owns Eagle's Nest Productions," Hitch continued.

"You shitting me? Wasn't that a huge privately owned TV studio back in the eighties? They used to have half a dozen shows on the air. I haven't heard anything about them for almost twenty years. It explains, I guess, why Stender Sheedy is his lawyer."

"Under Brooks Dunbar's astute guidance, Eagle's Nest now only makes the occasional Paris Hilton *Look, Pa, No Bra* video. The last one didn't make back its production costs so Stender probably doesn't have to work too hard on that account.

"His art-dealing business consists mostly of stealing a few of his dad's paintings—out of the guesthouse so his old man won't notice—then fencing them in Melrose Boulevard antique shops." He looked over and smiled. "There's more if you're interested."

"Yeah, I'm interested." I had to admit, he'd done better than I had.

"So his art and movie businesses are both a joke, like Sergeant Cruz says. Nobody likes this kid. He's been cut off by both his mom and dad, which is why he's such a thief. Dorothy Dunbar still thinks little Brooks will pull out of his drug-induced tailspin, but nobody else believes it. They're using him. He's using them. All of this useful intel was obtained by Sumner Hitchens, Esquire, while you were in the carriage house examining a fucking table base."

I didn't respond. When you're right, you're right.

"An apology would be nice," he prompted.

"I'm not gonna apologize to you just because you did your job, Hitchens."

"Why not?"

"Because I don't want to."

"Courtesies of a small and trivial character strike deepest in the grateful heart," he said.

"Who said that? Sure doesn't sound much like Einstein."

"Henry Clay. You should start reading more than department wanted fliers." He snap-shifted the Porsche and we sped on.

Sumner pulled in at a pancake house restaurant located in a strip mall off Mission Road near the medical examiner's building. It was after one A.M. I'd called on my cell and knew Alexa would be waiting.

Hitch chirped the car lock and we walked past a space where my Acura was parked.

Inside, as we approached a back booth where Alexa was sitting, I could see a worried look on her face. Before we even sat down I knew she had more bad news for us.

· CHAPTER ·
10

"Both of the dead girls were high-dollar Internet prostitutes," Alexa said as soon as we slid into the booth with her. "The blonde was named Chrissy Sweet. Her working name was Slade Seven. The brunette was Paula Morgan, working name Steel Cavanaugh. These were five-thousand-dollar dates. They worked for Yolanda Dublin, the Mulholland Madame. This hooker angle is gonna be media catnip so the case just got more sensitive, if that's even possible."

"Doesn't Yolanda Dublin run an Internet site called the Double Click Club?" Hitch asked.

"Right," Alexa said. "And from their pictures on that site, the girls were both gorgeous."

The waitress came and Hitch and I ordered coffee, along with ham and eggs and orange juice because we were probably going to be up all night, working through breakfast.

After the waitress left, Alexa continued. "The way her Internet site works, a client gets thoroughly screened by Yolanda first. Then, if you pass muster, you're issued a password which allows you access to the exclusive services section of the site. There, you can scroll the girls' pictures and streaming videos. The rates are listed on each girl's page as a modeling or therapist's fee. If you're a preferred client, once you double-click on a girl, the date is made."

Hitch was writing this down in his journal.

"Detective," Alexa said, and Hitchens looked up. "Hopefully this won't be talked about to third parties operating outside the scope of the investigation."

"What exactly does that mean, Captain?"

"UTA," I said. "Jamie Foxx. Studio development execs."

He smiled at her and nodded. "Me and Shane already been through this," he said, collegially.

"Good." Alexa smiled.

"Anything from Ballistics?" I asked.

"There were nine bullets, three in each body. All of them were 9×18 mm Makarov slugs. The most common machine gun weapon that fires those is a Russian-made Bizon. Ballistics says a Bizon uses a standard sixty-four-shot helical mag and can burn through six hundred rounds a minute. According to the people who heard the gunshots, and from the number of brass shell casings we retrieved so far, I think he must have gone through most of that magazine."

"Is Ballistics trying to confirm the weapon?" I asked.

"We're going to test fire a Bizon to see if the ejection striations on the brass are similar," Alexa said. "Tomorrow you guys are going to have to get back out there on the crime scene with CSI and some metal detectors and find all the stray slugs and brass. We need to know exactly how many rounds he squeezed off."

Hitch looked up with a thoughtful expression on his handsome face. "We can't ignore the idea that this could have been a contract hit and if it was, then we probably have only one primary target. That would probably be Scott Berman, which would make the two other vics collateral damage."

He looked down at the notes he had made in his red leather journal, then clicked his pen and tapped it on the tabletop. "There could be a lot more going on here than we can see on the surface."

That last remark sounded to me like a man still scaring up interesting plot points for Act One.

"There's always that possibility," Alexa agreed. Then she picked up her purse. "I'm gonna take the Acura and go on home. Sumner, will you take Shane back to the office so he can check out a slick-back to drive?"

"No problem."

I left Hitch in the booth and walked my wife outside to the car.

"How's it going with him?" Alexa asked as she unlocked the MDX.

"I'll find my way. We're still circling each other, checking out punching styles."

"I will not look kindly on leaks," she cautioned.

I kissed her and said, "Stop being such a—"

"Such a what?" she interrupted, smiling.

"A newly minted, tight-ass captain."

"You wanta talk tight asses, you need to come home," she teased. Then she kissed me again and drove off.

After she was gone, Sumner Hitchens and I sat in the restaurant, finishing our early breakfast without talking.

"I'm thinking we need to go badge Yolanda Dublin," he said as we were paying.

"Yep, that's definitely the next move. Let's go get the Mulholland Madame out of bed. Try and catch her with a head full of cotton."

"I ran her while you were outside. She lives out on the Coast Highway in Santa Monica. 2300. That's up by the Malibu line. The even numbers are on the beach side of the road."

Pricey.

▪ CHAPTER ▪
11

The first good thing that happened since I got this damn case was parked in the driveway in front of Yolanda Dublin's multimillion-dollar beach pad. It was a new black Mercedes 350 with the partial plate number 4 L M C. The rest of the plate read 292.

"That ride was coming down Skyline Drive when Alexa and I got the call and were going up," I told Sumner.

He shined his Mini Maglite inside the Mercedes. The top was up and both bucket seats as well as the back bench were empty. We proceeded up the walkway to the house and rang the front doorbell. The lights were on inside so apparently we weren't going to be gaining an advantage from the element of surprise.

Yolanda Dublin was a well-known Hollywood fixture who had once been a five-thousand-dollar-a-night girl herself, a centerfold who had gone into high-end hooking and then management. The word was that she was occasionally still available to party with clients, but only if she liked them and that was extremely rare, if it happened at all these days.

The door was opened by a striking six-foot-tall woman in her late thirties who had shiny long blond hair, a very nice shape, and a freckled beach tan. She was barefoot, wearing tight white jeans and a tank top. Her outfit complemented a spectacular body.

"Yes?" she said.

"Yolanda Dublin?" I asked.

"Yes."

"Police."

She looked over her shoulder and called out, "Edith!"

A few seconds later Yolanda's exact physical opposite lumbered up a short flight of stairs from the sunken living room and stood a few feet behind her.

This woman was built like a refrigerator. Big enough to get picked for the NFL draft, she was even taller than Yolanda and weighed well over three hundred pounds.

She had a feathered masculine hairstyle that was carefully trimmed. Her mahogany brown suit jacket and long skirt were tailored to camouflage her boxy shape, but managed only to accentuate it. Piano legs with anvil-sized feet encased in flats held it all upright. Her jaw was set pugnaciously, projecting an overall impression of severe, relentless aggression. She looked vaguely familiar to me.

"This is a police matter," I said, and we showed them our credentials. "I'm Detective Scully from Homicide Special. This is Detective Hitchens."

Yolanda Dublin didn't seem surprised that we'd come calling, so there was little doubt she'd been expecting us.

"This is Edith Stillwell. She's my attorney," Ms. Dublin said, confirming my suspicions. She'd obviously called Stillwell for help and they'd been sitting here well past two A.M. waiting.

Now I remembered where I'd seen Edith Stillwell. It was in the hallways at the Criminal Courts building.

"Edith advised me that I don't have to discuss anything with you guys," Yolanda said in a sexy, contralto voice.

"So you know then, that two of your working girls were found dead in a swimming pool up on Skyline Drive along with an unidentified man."

I thought it was best not to throw Scott Berman's name out at first. I wanted to see if she volunteered it. We were still on the front steps. Nobody had asked us inside yet.

Hitch shot Yolanda Dublin a smile that showcased his whole sparkling porcelain tray and said, "I could really use a glass of water."

Yolanda looked over at Edith, who said nothing, but Hitch's request worked, because Yolanda stepped aside to allow us to enter.

There was a Chinese man wearing a white shirt and black pants standing in the kitchen doorway that adjoined the entryway.

"Yeo-Sing, could you bring us a tray of ice water, please?" Yolanda said and he left quickly to get it.

"By working girls, are you implying that they are prostitutes?" Yolanda Dublin said. "Because no matter what you think you've heard about me, I run a legitimate modeling, escort, and physical therapy service. It's not a prostitution ring."

I let that go and replied, "Since you didn't ask us who the dead girls were, I'm going to assume you're pretty caught up on what happened on Skyline tonight."

"I think it would be foolish for you to assume anything, Detective," Edith Stillwell said. She was big in a way that made her appear uncomfortable. However, above the linebacker shoulders her hard, dark, gunfighter eyes left no doubt that she was all business.

"We're investigating a triple homicide," I said. "This is not going to go away. Your best bet is to cooperate with us."

"Let's sit in the living room," Yolanda suggested.

She led us over to a grouping of sofas and chairs by a large floor-to-ceiling window overlooking the ocean. The outdoor spotlights were on, illuminating a low surf, which was pushing a line of bubbling foam up onto the damp sandy beach.

Yeo-Sing returned with a silver tray and passed out four iced glasses of water, each with a lemon slice perched festively on the rim.

After he left, we settled in and Edith Stillwell immediately took the offensive.

"Yolanda admits to nothing. At this point we're willing to listen—nothing more. She has rights and I'm here to make certain they are scrupulously observed."

"Here's the bad news, Ms. Dublin. I happened to be the one who got the initial shots-fired call. I saw that black Mercedes out front coming down the hill on Skyline Drive. I was in the MDX you almost hit."

"There are lots of black Mercedes 350s in L.A.," Yolanda countered.

"Not with a partial plate of 4 L M C. You're busted as a participant at that Christmas party. That makes you anything from a material witness to an accomplice in a triple murder. Don't be lying to us. If we decide to make you an accessory after the fact, you're as good for this as the doer."

"Hardly," Edith said. "But it's good rhetoric."

"Okay, then I'm going to make an arrest."

I stood and reached for my cuffs.

"Wait a minute. Put those away," Edith said. "I guess Yolanda can answer a few nonincriminating questions."

I kept my cuffs out as an unstated threat, but sat back down and said, "Let's start with the dead man. You know who he was?"

"Scott Berman," Yolanda said softly. "I guess you know he's a world-famous producer."

I nodded. "Why was he there?"

She glanced at Edith, who dropped her head imperceptibly in a subtle affirmative. "He was a client. He was also an amateur figure photographer who sometimes hired our models for stills. He was nice. He treated the girls well. Since they're both dead, I guess I can tell you Chrissy Sweet was there as Scott's date. What he and Chrissy did on a date was their own business. He was divorced many years ago. That's about all I want to say right now."

"Who else was up there? What other clients?"

"I'm not going to tell you."

"That's sorta not your choice," Hitch said.

"Sure it is," Edith shot back. "She has confidentiality agreements."

"You gotta be joking. A modeling or escort service doesn't get a psychiatric or marriage privilege," I said, jiggling the cuffs in my hand softly. "You have some jeopardy here, Ms. Dublin. You tell us what we need to know and maybe we can work something out. You get balky, I'm gonna roll you up."

"Yolanda is in a personal service industry," Edith said. "She has some nondisclosure issues. You can threaten all you want, but she's not an accessory after the fact and you know it. The best you could possibly manage here is an arrest and a seventy-two-hour hold as a material witness. If she has to do a few days in jail, we won't be happy, but she can deal with it."

I knew she was probably right.

Edith continued. "Yolanda is not going to give up the names of clients or the professionals who work for her. If she does that, she'll crash her entire, totally legitimate business."

"Read the Heidi Fleiss book if you don't believe us," Yolanda said softly, then added quickly, "Not that my business is anything like hers."

"Okay, but you need to give us something that moves this case forward so we won't get stuck on you. If you don't, I'm willing to take this to the district attorney. I'm betting he'll see things my way and will charge you with a felony."

I was trying to bump her slightly to get her talking.

It worked.

12

"Instead of threatening let's try and work this out," Edith suggested.

"Tell me a little more about Chrissy Sweet and Paula Morgan," I said to Yolanda. She looked over at her attorney, who again moved a muscle or two, but remained almost still.

Yolanda leaned forward. "Paula Morgan was the dark-haired girl. She was an ex-actress who did some modeling for us, some massage therapy, full body rubs and the like. She was from Texas—Dallas. Wonderful girl. Nice family. She came here to get into films. It didn't work. She was a dear friend. I'm going to miss her terribly. End of story."

"And the other girl?" Hitch asked. "Ms. Sweet?"

"Chrissy was born in Long Beach. She was fun and sort of goofy. One of those surfer girl, pixie personalities. But despite being sort of uncomplicated, she made a lot of bad choices in her personal life.

When she wasn't working, she hung with some extremely trashy people but, for some reason, didn't seem to know it. She was strikingly beautiful, but I think it's safe to say not too smart."

Yolanda glanced over at Edith, who gave her a tiny little head shake, so she stopped abruptly.

"You two are going to have to stop with this semaphore system of yours," I said. "I need answers to these questions. I know you were having a Christmas party of some kind tonight, so let's talk about that."

Yolanda lit a cigarette. So few people smoke these days that when it happens it often feels staged, like she was buying time to think.

"The party was my annual Christmas ball," she began. "We have it every year. The models, escorts, and massage therapists on our Web site get to pick their best client and invite him. It's all free to the client. They have a few drinks, they dance, they do what they want to do.

"The clients are very grateful and will often give the girl an expensive Christmas gift, a diamond ring or necklace. The client pays for nothing except any present he might choose to give. I've been doing it for three years now. It's been very successful and makes satisfied customers. As I said, Scott was one of Chrissy's regular accounts. I think he liked it that she was fun, but not too deep."

"Who did you rent the house up on Skyline from?" I asked.

"Brooks Dunbar."

"From his foundation," I clarified.

"No, from Brooks himself. Seven thousand dollars in cash. That was for the backyard only. We had use of the pool house but there were strict provisions that we couldn't use the main house. It was padlocked."

"Brooks says he doesn't know anything about it. That he never goes up there."

"He's lying. I met him up on Skyline two days ago and put the cash right in his pudgy little hand."

Hitch and I exchanged a look before I went on.

"Besides Scott Berman, how many clients were there?" I asked.

"About twenty."

"Did you see the shooter?"

"No."

"Did anybody?"

"I don't know. I doubt it. It was over in seconds. For reasons of client confidentiality, we didn't use a caterer to serve hors d'oeuvres or drinks. After they set up, they left. Yeo-Sing and I did the serving. I was in the pool house with him pouring champagne. We heard the shots. It sounded like a machine gun. A lot of bullets, people screaming. We both dove under the serving table so we didn't see anything."

"You have no idea who the gunman was?"

She hesitated for just a second before she said, "No."

Her pause was the tip-off. She was holding something back. I set the cuffs on the table in front of her.

"I thought you were going to cooperate," I challenged.

She again glanced at Edith, who I don't think moved a muscle this time, but she was coaching her client to be quiet, nonetheless.

"I can go on the Internet and start downloading pages," I said. "We'll run every one of your models through Vice. We'll get old arrest records, start pulling people in. We'll sweat names and build this party list. It's a lot of work but we can do it, and then once we're through, I'll come back here and bust you for obstructing justice and failing to cooperate with a homicide investigation."

I looked her right in the eye. "I'm not Vice, Ms. Dublin. I may have opinions about what you do, but I'm not the morality police. I've got three dead bodies. One of them is an international celebrity.

"This is going to be big news tomorrow. It's gonna mushroom out until the politicians in this town get itchy and decide to make an example of someone. You look like a good candidate. It's as much in your interest to put this down fast as it is ours."

"I can't give you the names of my guests. Some are married. I'll go to jail first."

"Then you better find something to give me that goes someplace," I said.

She sat silently for a minute, considering it. Then she stubbed out her cigarette, got to her feet, and said, "Come with me."

She led us into her media room, where she sorted through a stack of DVDs until she found the one she wanted. Then she put it in the player and fast-forwarded until she came to a picture of a man pulling up on a motorcycle in front of her house. Obviously this was a security video.

On the screen we watched while the man took off his helmet. He was a blond, scruffy-looking guy with a low forehead who gave off a bad vibe even on video. He looked angry and slammed his gloves into the helmet as he dismounted the bike.

"That's Carl Sweet," Yolanda said. "He was Chrissy's about-to-be-ex. She had just filed for divorce. He's originally from Czechoslovakia and if you ask me, he's nuts. She moved out on him two weeks ago and into an apartment I helped her find. After Chrissy moved out, he came here looking for her. My security cam got that shot. He was screaming at me over the intercom. He wanted to know where she was. I wouldn't tell him."

"And you think this guy is the shooter."

"Maybe. He's violent enough. He used to beat Chrissy. There were times when she was so messed up I couldn't send her out on modeling assignments or dates."

She shut off the camera, then turned to look at us. "Does that buy me some space with you, Detective?"

"We'll see. I'm going to need that DVD." She nodded and handed it to me. "Do you have the address where they used to live?"

"After Chrissy left, she told me the landlord threw Carl out, so the old apartment's been re-rented. Carl's always broke. When they were married and living together, Chrissy paid for everything. After she split and filed, he had no steady income. I have no idea where he lives now."

"How about the address of the new place you helped Chrissy find?"

"I'll copy it down for you."

She got it from her address book, wrote it on a slip of paper, and handed it to me. It was an apartment in Glendale, on Brand Boulevard.

Once we were outside and back in the Carerra, Hitch paused before starting the car. "I've heard of that Christmas party," he said. "It's called the Prostitutes' Ball."

"But unfortunately for you, it seems Act One just fizzled big-time," I said. "Carl Sweet kills his wife and Scott Berman, hits poor Paula by mistake. Like you said—bing-bang-boom. End of story. No movie."

"Yeah." He grinned. "But what a title, huh? *The Prostitutes' Ball* . . . Who wouldn't go see that one?"

· CHAPTER ·
13

Before we left Yolanda Dublin's driveway I picked up the mic for the police radio in Hitch's glove box and ran Carl Sweet for wants, warrants, and DMV.

The run came back empty. He wasn't in our system, not even at Motor Vehicles. Then I put in a request to run him with the state to see if he had a Russian Bizon machine gun registered to him. We probably wouldn't get that info back until tomorrow.

"If the guy was beating on Chrissy, it's hard to believe he didn't get at least one spousal abuse complaint," Hitch said after I hung up. "He should be in the system."

"Maybe Sweet's not his real name," I said as Hitch put the car in gear and pulled out.

"How's that possible, Shane? Alexa ran Chrissy. She checked out. It was Chrissy's married name, so it had to be his."

"You're right. Just thinking out loud."

We got on the Coast Highway, heading toward Brand Boulevard in Glendale. I didn't trust Hitch's motives, so it was hard to solicit his opinion. But I've been trained to always check with my partner after an interview to see if he or she picked up on something I'd missed.

"Gimme your take on what just happened back there," I said as Hitch drove.

"Some lies are more believable than truth," he replied.

"Who dropped that pearl of wisdom?"

"I did, just now." The dashing smile was gone, replaced by a seriousness that gave me hope.

"We walk in there and after a few rounds of 'No, I won't,' 'Yes, you will,' out comes the little DVD with Carl Sweet," he said. "I know it's almost Christmas, but do we really think there's a Santa Claus?"

"Good point. But sometimes it happens that way."

"*That's* not a take. That's wishful thinking."

"You're still looking for first-act moves," I told him, my disappointment showing. "If Carl Sweet, a jealous husband, shoots his ex and her boyfriend, you got nothing to give the movie department at UTA."

"I'm just saying, before we ring up SWAT to go out and throw a net on this guy—if we can even find him—I think we need to check out Scott Berman, work on some victimology. My gut tells me we're going to find some juicy stuff there."

"We'll get to the victimology tomorrow," I snapped. "Tonight we're following leads and this lead points to a dead girl's apartment in Glendale."

It wasn't going well between us. We didn't speak again until we got to the address on Brand Boulevard. It was a small, seventies-style building, boxy but neat. Each unit had its own garage in back. Chrissy Sweet was renting B-6 on the second floor. We found her five-year-old silver BMW still in her parking spot.

"So Scott Berman must've picked her up here, driven her to the party up on Skyline," Hitch said.

"Which begs the question of who drove Berman's car off Skyline Drive after he was dead and where is it now," I replied.

We woke up the manager. It was three thirty in the morning and he wasn't happy about it.

"Jesus Christ," he griped.

"Nope," Hitch said. "But people tell me there's an amazing resemblance."

The manager didn't find that funny. Neither did I. He was a grumpy bald guy who didn't know anything about Chrissy Sweet. He also didn't seem to be very shocked that she was dead.

"I try not to get involved with my renters. L.A. is transient and superficial. People move on, they transfix, they die."

"Gee, good one," Hitch said. "We should get that off to Deepak Chopra immediately."

The manager led us to Chrissy's apartment, opened up, told us to drop the key in the slot when we were done. Then he returned to his apartment and went back to bed.

There wasn't much here. The small one-bedroom had the look of a hideout. Very few clothes, a makeup case that was well stocked. No drugs, no pictures. A few teddy bears, but no real personal effects. We searched it for almost half an hour, came up with nothing.

"The unlucky, lonely life of a tragic beauty," Hitch whispered softly, sounding like that guy in all the movie trailers.

We locked up, dropped the key in the slot, and left.

"I'll have Impound pick up her car and tow it to the forensic garage," I said. "Probably nothing in there, but we gotta look."

"Maybe we'll get a latent print hit for Carl. If we do and Sweet is an alias, maybe it gets us another name," Hitch suggested.

"Maybe."

When we got back to the Porsche, we took five minutes just sitting at the curb in front of Chrissy's apartment, thinking out loud. It was almost four thirty A.M. The sun would be coming up soon.

"Where do you want to go from here?" Hitch asked. "It's too late to go to bed. Or make that too early."

"I got that little puffball, Brooks Dunbar, coming in at nine A.M.," I said. "Yolanda Dublin says he rented her the house for the party and that she met him up on Skyline two days ago and put the cash in his hand. He says he never goes up there. I'm gonna bust his grapes with that. There's opportunity in deception."

"We also need to go to Paramount and check on what was going on with Scott Berman before he died."

"Right," I said. "Paramount would be a good place for you to pass out some Hole in One business cards."

"Knock it off, Scully. You know we should cover that. We gotta see if Berman was on anybody's shit list, if his life was being threatened. There might be another suspect other than Carl Sweet."

"You mean one that doesn't wrap the movie up too quickly."

"You're reading my mail, homes," he said irritably.

He put the Carrera in gear and chirped rubber pulling away from the curb. We stopped for some coffee and rolls on the way to the office, said very little in the next hour, and then hit the PAB parking garage at a little before six.

Hitch and I looked at the phone sheets and checked my computer. CSI had e-mailed over the initial case notes.

They had collected twenty brass cartridges and fourteen bullets, photographed and plastered eight male shoe prints and six female, all of different sizes. They were now starting the slow process of trying to identify the shoe manufacturers by the sole shapes and tread patterns.

The blood spatter was high-energy droplets, which was consistent with the machine gun fire description that the Prentisses and Yolanda had mentioned.

CSI's notes also indicated they were beginning the painstaking step of dusting every brass casing they'd found, looking for fingerprints the doer might have left when he was loading the clip. From what Hitch and I read, it looked like the forensics part of the case was moving along.

Stender Sheedy showed up at our office at nine o'clock sharp carrying a very expensive wafer briefcase, which looked like it was real alligator. His suit was Savile Row, his watch a Rolex. One of his cuff links could have paid my monthly mortgage. He was only in his thirties, but already owned an extensive collection of fancy accessories.

"Glad you could make it," I said.

By ten thirty, it was pretty obvious that Brooks had missed his bus. Stender was on the phone making calls. His client either wouldn't answer his home or his cell phone, or he was vibrating under a table somewhere with his nipples stinging, checking out some celebutante's undies.

"I'm filing the warrant," I told Stender.

"Detective Scully, I know how this looks," he pleaded. "I know I promised I'd have him here and I'm sure you don't care about mitigating circumstances, but Brooks has had very little love or parental supervision in his life. As a result he doesn't react well to overt instructions. But I promise on my life, I will have him here by noon. I throw myself at the mercy of the Los Angeles Police Department."

He rendered this argument with such passion and remorse that

I took pity on him. Despite his prominent father, at least Stender Sheedy Jr. had managed to make it through Harvard Law or wherever it is these kinds of guys matriculate.

"Okay," I told him. "But that's your last chance. After that, I'm going to jail your client."

"He'll be here," Stender promised.

When he left, I watched Hitch put some fresh business cards in his wallet and we headed out to Paramount Studios on Melrose.

I thought we were probably still somewhere in Act One, but I didn't want to ask. Frankly, operating with no sleep, I was getting a little confused.

14

We didn't have studio passes to get onto the Paramount lot, but we had badges, which worked just as well. We were allowed to park in the big lot just beyond the main gate. Hitch and I got out of the Carrera and followed the map the guard gave us to A-Building, where Scott Berman's offices were located on the second floor.

Hitch pointed out the Groucho Building to me on the way. As we passed the commissary, Hitch said the food in the executive dining room was interesting fare and the chef made a great lamb osso bucco, which was simmered in red wine until it fell off the bone, but he only served it on Fridays.

The other side of the restaurant Hitch called the "little people" side. The food there was standard cholesterol-clogging cafeteria chow. Hot dogs and lasagna. Better to stay away, he warned.

"That's Lucy Park," he said as we passed an open patch of grass, pointing out landmarks like a driver on the Hollywood tour. "I understand that Lucy and Desi used to eat their lunches out on that lawn, sitting on those very metal benches."

A-Building was a two-story stucco structure that Hitch said was the first building on the lot.

"Howard Hughes had his office here when this was still RKO."

We took the carpeted stairway up to the second floor and turned left into a hallway whose walls were covered in rich brown fabric and decorated with movie posters in simple brass frames.

"Berman's undoubtedly got Howard Hughes's old office. It's a celebrity suite. Has a big Hollywood history. After Hughes, Lucy had it for years. Stephen J. Cannell was there for a while in the eighties, Sherry Lansing after him, then Tom Cruise before he got the boot by Sumner Redstone for jumping on Oprah's couch and tanking the opening of *Mission Impossible III*. That office has seen a lot of shit go down."

"Hitch," I said, and he turned to look at me. "Stop it."

"I just thought."

"Just stop it, okay?"

"Jesus Christ," he muttered.

"No, but people tell me there's an amazing resemblance." Now he was sulking, but I'd had it.

"And while we're on it, why do you say shit like that?" I asked. "It makes you come off like a total dipshit. We're supposed to be cops. Three people died last night. It's up to you and me to speak for them, to get them some justice. I don't care right now who had that office after Howard Hughes or where Lucy and Desi ate their lunch."

"Fine, then I'm not talking to you anymore," he replied petulantly.

We entered the outer office that serviced Berman's production company and found a pretty assistant. Her mascara had run. She'd been crying.

"We're homicide detectives," I said. "We'd like to talk to somebody about Scott Berman."

"You should talk to Shay. Let me see if I can get her," she said, then buzzed an extension. "Miss Shaminar, two police officers are here about Scott." She listened for a minute. "Okay."

She hung up. "Miss Shaminar says you should wait in Mr. Berman's office. She'll be with you as soon as she's off the phone. As you can imagine, it's been pretty stressed around here this morning."

She stood and led us into Scott Berman's office. It was huge. Six beautiful leaded-glass windows lit a lush, paneled room. Two of the windows looked out over Lucy Park, the others were in a dining conference room, which we could see through a large opening in the south wall of the office.

The executive desk was big enough to play table tennis on. There was a big marble-faced fireplace fronting two wine-red sofas with a glass-top table set in between. All of the walls were dark wood. The modern art that hung inside each of the paneled insets looked stupid enough to be expensive. It wasn't hard to imagine Howard Hughes running his empire from this suite.

A few minutes later, a very slim, very directed black-haired woman with olive skin and a classic profile swept into the room. Her hair was pulled back in a bun. She was the executive assistant version of the beautiful librarian cliché. Severe suit, abrupt manner, glasses perched on her nose and secured on a no-nonsense chain around her neck. But you knew when she took those specs off and let down her hair, the results would be dazzling.

"I'm Shay Shaminar, Mr. Berman's executive assistant," she said. Her voice was crisp and strong, but underneath her command visage, you could see she was very upset.

It was the little things that gave her away. The rigid posture, the ring she turned manically on her right middle finger. But she was strong and kept a tight grip on her emotions.

We introduced ourselves and she motioned for us to sit on the wine-colored sofas near the fireplace. She sat opposite us, her shapely knees pressed together, her skirt just long enough to cover them.

"We're all a little shook up," she said. "Adding to Scott's horrible death, we were deep into preproduction on his next film, but now the studio is putting our picture on hold, which is a nice way of saying it's canceled."

"We'll only need a little time," I said. She looked very tense. I felt bad for her.

"This was Howard Hughes's office, wasn't it?" Hitch jumped in, asking her a question that was completely off the point.

"Yes. Back when he ran RKO in the forties, this was the studio headquarters. The RKO property was bought by Desilu, then became part of the Paramount lot in the late forties. Now administration is in the new building on the north side of the lot."

"Bet a lot of amazing stuff happened in here," Hitch replied.

It was a good play, so I went with it. People who are too locked up in grief miss details and don't give good interviews. It was a worthwhile technique to start by getting her mind on something else.

"Famous offices all have histories," she said, glad to talk about this and not the death of a boss she clearly worshipped. She seemed to relax slightly. Her expression softened.

"For instance, I ran into an old waiter from the commissary when I first came to work here," she continued. "The man was about eighty. He told me when Howard had this office, he used to order a tuna salad sandwich with chips on a plate every day. He wanted it placed right outside the door, which was always locked when he brought it. He was supposed to put the sandwich plate, covered in wax paper, on the floor at eight A.M. exactly. Then he had to come back at six and get the plate.

"But the sandwich and chips were always untouched. After a few days of this, he decided not to bring it anymore. At eight fifteen the next morning he got a call from Mr. Hughes. 'Where's my sandwich?' he shouted. The waiter said, 'But Mr. Hughes, you never eat it, so I didn't think you wanted it.' You know what Howard Hughes said?"

"No," Hitch replied, leaning forward, totally captivated.

"He said, 'I need to know it's there.'" She paused then smiled wanly. "Tells you a lot about the man, doesn't it?"

Hitch nodded. "Obsessive-compulsive."

That story had slowly brought her out, so I gently switched to the more painful topic of Scott Berman's death.

"I know this is hard, but can we start by talking a little about Mr. Berman's personal life," I said. "I understand he was divorced."

"Yes, from Althea," she told us. "His ex-wife was awful. A total bitch."

"Do you think she could have been involved somehow?" Hitch asked.

"I doubt it. She got a pile of money in the divorce. That seemed to be all she cared about. The settlement was almost five years ago. Since then, Mr. Berman's been all about his movies. He was married to his films. I know it sounds awful and shallow, but he was a celluloid artist. He didn't have time to invest in personal relationships. That's why he dated the girls from the Double Click Club."

"He didn't hide it?" Hitch asked.

"He didn't," she said, without rancor. "He even brought the escorts to studio functions. They were educated and beautiful."

"What about Chrissy Sweet?" Hitch asked. "We understand she wasn't exactly on the waiting list for Mensa."

"There's an expression in show business about beautiful, dumb actresses. 'God gives with one hand, but takes away with the other.'

That was Chrissy. She was gorgeous, but if you're a guy, don't get caught in a locked room with her when you're planning to keep your clothes on. You could die of boredom."

"And Mr. Berman liked that?" I asked.

"I think so. She was easy for him to be with. She made no intellectual demands."

"Can you tell me about the Christmas party last night?"

"He went to last year's party, so this was his second time. I bought a diamond tennis bracelet at Tiffany's for him to give to Chrissy as a Christmas gift. Fifteen grand. That's me, the working girl's friend," she quipped. Hitch and I both smiled at her attempt at humor.

"Did Scott have any enemies?" Hitch asked, getting to the meat of it. "Was there anybody you can think of who might have wanted to kill him?"

"You mean, besides the entire movie department at CAA and Endeavor?" she said, smiling. We nodded.

"As a matter of fact, he almost didn't go to that party because of Chrissy Sweet's husband, who she was divorcing. His name is Carl. He called here twice yesterday. He told Mr. Berman to stay away from his wife or there would be big trouble.

"Even though she was in the midst of divorcing him, Carl wasn't about to let go. He was extremely possessive. Scott wasn't going to go to the party because of that threat. Then unfortunately he changed his mind and went at the last minute. If I were you, I'd definitely go find Carl Sweet," she added. "If he doesn't have a hell of a good alibi, I'd bust him."

"Any idea where he lives?" Hitch asked.

"No. I don't think Scott even knew Chrissy's real address. It was one of Miss Dublin's strict rules. All dates had to be arranged through her Internet site. The girls were prohibited from giving out their addresses. At first, the only name we had for her was Slade Seven.

Eventually, she told Scott her real name. The Double Click Club kept it all very arm's length, because that's the way Yolanda wanted it."

We talked to her for another ten minutes, but that was all Shay could really tell us. As we stood to go, Hitch took her hand then bowed elegantly like Count Hollywood.

"Shay is a very beautiful name," he said in his most bullshit courtly manner.

"Thank you," she demurred. "My father was from the South Pacific. In some obscure Indonesian dialect, Shay means princess."

We left and walked back across the lot.

"Nice lady," Hitch noted.

But I had tuned him out. My mind was parsing another idea. By the time we were back to the car, I had it.

"If Shay means princess in Indonesian, I wonder how you say Sweet in Czechoslovakian."

"Wow," Hitch said. "Good get, homes."

Once we were inside the car, I picked up the radio mic and I called the research desk at LAPD. It took five minutes to find out that the Czechoslovakian translation for Sweet was "Sladky."

We ran "Carl Sladky," spelling the whole name out.

"Roger, D-28," the RTO came back. "But the first name is Karel, spelled with a K and an E. Sladky is as you spelled it. He has three outstanding domestic violence warrants, all for aggravated assault. The warrant delivery team says they have tried three times to serve those warrants, but have no current address. According to their notes, since his wife moved out on him, he lost his apartment in Hollywood. She was paying for it. They think he's living in his van."

"Already did."

After he left, we were pulled into Jeb's office. We'd been working the whole night and for us, it seemed like forever since we'd gotten the case. Jeb, on the other hand, had gone home to bed, and since Scott Berman's death was blasting out of every radio and TV speaker when he awoke, he was complaining about how quickly the press had gotten it.

We brought him up to date on Karel Sladky, who was a definite person of interest. The fact that we had a name to chase after seemed to please our captain.

"This is good progress," he said. "Good stuff. You've made me happy."

"We live for those moments, Skipper," Hitch said. I couldn't tell if he was kidding or just in the midst of a monumental ass kiss.

"You guys now have a prosecutor assigned to work with you," Jeb continued.

"Already?" Hitch moaned. "Aren't we supposed to arrest somebody before they assign a prosecutor?"

"District Attorney Chase Beal wants to make sure none of the evidence is compromised. He put one of his best gunslingers on this."

"Uh-oh," I said. "Who'd we get?"

"The Black Dahlia."

"Dahlia Wilkes?" we both said, simultaneously groaning.

"She wants to meet with you before the end of the day to be briefed. In the meantime, she gave instructions that she wants you to personally get back out to Skyline Drive with an evidence collection team and some metal detectors to locate every single slug that was fired from that Bizon.

"So far CSI got no prints off the cartridges they found," Jeb continued, "but they only picked up twenty casings and fourteen slugs. The Bizon's got a sixty-four-shot clip, so there's a lot still out there. It's a big job. Sorry."

· CHAPTER ·
15

We flagged the outstanding warrants so if the warrant delivery team finally pulled up an existing address on the guy, we would be on their contact list. Then I called in a new firearms check, giving them the correct name and spelling.

When we got back to the office, guess what? No Brooks Dunbar. Stender Sheedy was there with his little jar of Vaseline, trying to get another six hours. I jammed the warrant into his hand.

"That's a copy. If your client even makes an illegal turn, he's gonna end up in jail. You want my opinion, we should let it happen. He's got too many people protecting him. Next time he falls, you oughta let his ass hit the dirt instead of always shoving a feather pillow under him. Maybe some jail time will straighten him out."

"Don't do this," Stender pleaded.

"Hello, hello," I said, standing under the camera and sighting in the general direction it was pointed.

"I love it when we catch the killing on tape," Hitch said. "It really fucks with the defense attorney's head."

We followed the hidden ground cable to where it led into the mansion through a small hole drilled in the stucco at the base of the exterior wall.

"Video deck's inside the main house," I said. "Call Jeb and see if he can get us a warrant, or better still, to save all that trouble, maybe somebody from the Dorothy White Foundation will come out here and just open this up for us. Give us verbal permission to go inside."

While Hitch made the call, I walked around the side of the mansion and looked through every available window.

I hadn't done it the night before because I was positive that the house was deserted. I should have, because by the light of day, even though the windows were dirty, I could now see that the mansion still had some furniture inside, unusual for a deserted house.

Making this discovery even more intriguing was the fact that through one window I could just barely see a fully decorated Christmas tree standing on the far side of the solarium in the living room. The tree looked to be about seven feet tall and there were a lot of unopened Christmas gifts underneath.

Hitch came back after making his call and found me peering through the big round solarium window. "Jeb already called the lawyer at the foundation last night. They're gonna open this up for us without a warrant. What ya got?" he asked.

I pointed and he looked through the dirty glass at the sparsely furnished room and the fully decked-out tree and presents barely visible in the living room beyond.

"Thought nobody lived here," he said.

"Somebody's sure as hell all ready for Christmas," I said.

"Act One was on life support but it's sure got a nice heartbeat now," Hitch replied.

"We've gotta go through this house," I said. "If somebody's in there then they could be a witness to the shooting."

"Right."

"Why would everybody lie about this?"

Jeb Calloway arrived in about an hour, followed a few minutes later by Stender Sheedy Sr.

The legendary letterhead partner of Sheedy, Devine & Lipscomb turned out to be a seventy-year-old gray eminence in a charcoal suit with hair the color of roadside snow and such a pale complexion that it looked like he never got into the sun.

His manner indicated he was accustomed to being treated with deference. The only cops he'd ever dealt with had probably been holding traffic citations.

"I don't have much time," he announced abruptly. "I came personally because I conversed with Thayer Dunbar in Houston this morning and he's getting extremely annoyed. He doesn't want the house involved with all this."

What that had to do with a triple murder escaped me.

Stender Senior had a large ring of keys in his hand and walked past the pool where Chrissy and Paula had died without even bothering to glance at the blood-tinged water. Then he pulled up the ball of keys and, like a school janitor about to open a delinquent's locker, started trying keys in the heavy Yale padlock.

"We were told that nobody lived here," I said.

"Nobody does," he replied curtly.

"There's a Christmas tree in the living room with unopened presents under it."

He didn't bother answering as he continued to search for the right key.

"It's almost Christmas," I persisted. "That tells me somebody is living here."

He finally found one that worked, slipped it in, and twisted the padlock open. Then, once it was off, he turned and grimaced at me, exposing teeth almost the size and color of yellowing piano keys.

"*Nobody lives in this house,*" he said, enunciating each word slowly and carefully, as if speaking to a three-year-old child or an idiot. "That tree has been there since we purchased this property in eighty-two."

"Really?" I said. "If it had been up almost thirty years wouldn't it be nothing but twigs by now?"

"It's synthetic. It was up and the presents were all there when the house was sold to us. The Dorothy White Foundation bought the property as a real estate investment for the Dunbar family. Then, when Brooks was born, I was asked to do some estate planning and the foundation was transferred into his portfolio along with this mansion. Since we were holding the property for long-term capital gain, we never bothered to clean out the house. Does that answer all your questions?" Without waiting for a reply, he turned the knob on the back door and pushed it open.

We entered into a kitchen pantry. There was easily an eighth of an inch of dust on the linoleum floor. Several sets of footsteps were tracked in the dust.

"Somebody's been inside recently," I said, pointing at the tracks.

"The security company comes in to service the video surveillance. I'm sure the tracks will only lead to the laundry room downstairs where the equipment is."

He led the way down to the laundry room. As it turned out, he was right. The tracks led to the basement, where we found a new surveillance DVR and monitor mounted on a bracket near a laundry table.

Jeb walked over and shut it off, then said. "How long is this set to record?"

"Almost a month. I think the company said it works on motion detection." Stender Sheedy Sr. frowned at his watch.

"I'd like to take a look around in here," I said.

"I'm trying to cooperate," he said. "I realize three people died out by the pool. It's painfully apparent to me and to Thayer that young Brooks must have been secretly renting out this backyard to obtain extra money for his extravagant social habits. But even so, he was only making the backyard available and with that fact in view, I would suggest you confine your murder investigation to the pool area and keep the house out of it. I represent Thayer Dunbar, who intends to hold this property until Brooks is thirty-five. Then it will eventually be rehabbed and sold. He does not want the house included as part of your crime scene."

"Three people died here last night," I said.

"No. They died in the backyard." Then he heaved a theatrical sigh and began humoring us. "I'm sure it's not lost on you that many buyers are superstitious about houses, especially ones that have been involved in horrible murders. Once a house is rumored to be haunted the price drops precipitously. The backyard is one thing, but if the house becomes part of the investigation it could cost the Dorothy White Foundation a good deal of money."

"All of which means what?" I asked.

"I'm asking you not to create a problem where one need not exist."

"You mean, we'll have to get a warrant if we want to look around in here."

"I didn't say that. What I said was, please don't needlessly compromise this real estate investment."

We all stood locked in a stalemate. Then Jeb made a decision.

"Shane, let's start by looking at the surveillance video. If the shooter is on there, maybe this can just get wrapped up fast, like we all want."

"If that's your call, Captain," I said. Hitch shifted his weight and when I looked over at him I could see that, like me, he was uncomfortable with this.

"That's my call," Calloway replied stiffly.

I could tell by his voice that Jeb didn't like it either, but Thayer Dunbar and Stender Sheedy were part of L.A.'s power elite. They could pick up the phone and call people the three of us only read about in the paper.

We took the DVR into evidence and left without searching the house, although on the way upstairs from the basement I arranged to get myself lost for a minute so I could check out the Christmas tree. It was synthetic, just as Stender Sheedy Sr. had said. Everything, including the unopened presents, was covered in dust.

"You coming?" Jeb called out to me.

"Yeah, sorry, I thought this was the way out," I fibbed.

Stender locked the door and returned to his Century City law firm.

We returned to Jeb's office downtown and set up to watch the video. You wouldn't believe what was on there.

• CHAPTER •
17

Dahlia Wilkes came directly from the courthouse, where she was prosecuting a murder. When she arrived she was breathless from hurrying, trailing dangerous wisps of her hunter-killer personality like noxious fumes from a city bus. She was a thirty-six-year-old, drop-dead gorgeous African-American woman who didn't give anyone time to appreciate her beauty because she was always in your face before you even got a chance to smile. We all knew one another from past cases. The Black Dahlia got convictions but gave heartburn.

"I hope you two detectives have finally catalogued all of my missing Makarov nines," she said, before hellos were even exchanged.

"We've found fourteen more, so far," I said. "Plus the twenty CSI got last night and the nine that got parked in the three vics. That's forty-three total."

"I can do math, Detective."

"I didn't say you couldn't."

"How 'bout the brass?" she asked.

"Forty-five cartridges," I said.

"So you're still missing nineteen." We nodded. "If this guy, Carl Sladky, is our doer, I want to lock him up fast." She was looking at the monitor while Jeb fiddled with the DVR.

"Karel," I corrected.

"I'm sorry, were you saying something?"

She turned around and fixed coal black eyes on me. She was a real pistol, this one. I looked to Hitch. Since she was African-American, I figured maybe he might have some ethnic traction.

He picked up on my look and turned to her. "Ms. Wilkes, what my partner was saying is the man's name is not Carl, it's Kar-el, with a K and an E. Czechoslovakian."

"Then why didn't you say that?" she demanded.

"We just did," he replied.

"Stop babbling and play back the video. I'm on a short trial recess and my judge is a flaming asshole."

Jeb finally accessed the correct file and brought up the video. The initial image showed the gardeners working around the empty pool area early in the day. There was a time and date code running across the bottom of the screen. We fast-forwarded and then slowed the playback.

Yolanda Dublin and Yeo-Sing were the first to appear at a little past three P.M. We watched as they unloaded, put up a few decorations, and left.

Then a caterer arrived at six, set up buffet tables and a bar beside the pool and carried warming trays and food containers into the pool house before driving off.

Around eight P.M. Yolanda and Yeo-Sing returned, unpacked the food containers, and set out the hors d'oeuvres.

At nine, the gowned, beautiful girls of the Double Click Club began to arrive with their client dates. There was lots of arm's-length air-kissing at first, but before long things began heating up.

As the party got going, Scott Berman and Chrissy Sweet reclined on a pool chaise. It wasn't long before he had the top on her dress loosened, and they were nuzzling and drinking champagne.

Occasionally, Scott got up to make them fresh drinks. We watched as couples started dancing. There was a decent amount of crotch friction. I could see why the Prentisses pulled down their blinds to shield their child.

Then the same scruffy blond guy who was on Yolanda Dublin's security video walked casually into the backyard carrying something draped with a towel. He walked to a spot at the end of the pool and dropped the towel. We could clearly see a machine pistol in his right hand. He pointed the gun at Chrissy and shouted something. That was when the guests became aware of his presence.

Scott Berman and Chrissy Sweet scrambled up from the chaise and turned to run as Sladky let loose with a stream of bullets, first hitting his wife in the back.

The force of the bullets lifted her off her feet and she flew face-first into the pool.

Scott scrambled for cover as three rounds ripped open his chest.

He staggered back, spun, and flopped over the back of the pool chaise where we'd found him.

As the rest of the partygoers scattered in every direction imaginable, Karel Sladky started to spray bullets, turning and firing in a wide arc. People were running and screaming in terror, but the shots now weren't directed at anyone. Some crashed into the hillside, some into the stucco walls of the main house, some went into the night sky, where they undoubtedly landed half a mile away.

The last burst of gunfire inadvertently hit Paula Morgan, who had stupidly run out of the pool house, accidentally stumbling into the line of fire as Karel spun wildly around. When the bullets struck her she splashed awkwardly into the pool.

Karel Sladky turned and walked without hurry away from the pool area and was gone. A moment later Yolanda Dublin and Yeo-Sing ran out of the pool house. Yolanda checked the three dead bodies without touching them. She said something to Yeo-Sing, who fished into Scott's pocket and came up with his car keys. While he was doing this Yolanda gathered up the girls' purses and they quickly left. Once they were gone only Scott Berman, Chrissy Sweet, and the hapless Paula Morgan remained in the shot.

Jeb turned off the video.

"Fuck," Dahlia Wilkes said softly. It was the first time I'd ever seen her shaken.

"Think you can win the case with that?" I said.

She ignored me and began issuing instructions. "I want our CSI video guys to try and count the shots. Have them go frame to frame. I want every single slug that you can find, catalogued and cross-matched.

"I need the names of every person on that tape and all those people who were up there that we didn't see. Names, numbers, addresses. This is a good case, but it's a media red ball so it needs to be squeaky clean. No flaws, failures, or fuck-ups.

"You need to crank up the existing BOLO on this Sladky guy and red flag it. Have every squad room pass his picture out at roll call. I want him in custody."

She turned to go.

"Excuse me, Ms. Wilkes," Hitch said.

"What?!"

"Unless we can get an independent verification of who was up there, we may have trouble getting Miss Dublin to cooperate and supply any names."

"It's a triple murder, is she kidding?"

"I don't think so. She says we need to read the Heidi Fleiss book. I haven't had a chance to buy one yet but when I do, if you want, I'll pick you up a copy."

He was messing with her now and she scowled angrily. Dahlia was beautiful, strong, and smart, but all of those attributes were undermined by her intimidating personal interactions and her total lack of any humor. She drilled us with those deadly black irises. "Let me see what I can do to change that," she said.

"Good luck. Her attorney is Edith Stillwell," Hitch said.

"Shit."

She handed Hitch her notepad. "Write Yolanda's contact info there and get back out to Skyline and finish policing the crime scene. I want the rest of those bullets and casings, and I want them now."

"You saw the tape," Hitchens said. "He was shooting a lot of those rounds up in the air. I think it's reasonable to assume we won't find them all."

"Then focus on finding the rest of the brass. I need prints to lock this up tight. That stuff is out there somewhere. Go get it, Detective. And I don't want to hear a bunch of bullshit excuses either."

"Oh, lordy, lordy. Dontcha be payin' that no nevermind, missy." Hitch was bobbing his head up and down like Stepin Fetchit. "We field niggas ain't gonna be goin' and givin' no 'scuses, no siree."

"Go fuck yourself, Hitchens," she said.

18

The gun registration check on Karel Sladky came back empty. According-ing to the State of California, he was not the registered owner of a Bizon machine pistol, so it was probably a street weapon. But that actually didn't matter anymore because we had surveillance video showing him shooting up the murder scene and killing three people with a Bizon.

If it had been Sally who was working this with me, we would have been high-fiving each other right about now and talking about which bar we were going to hit for our celebration. The red-ball case was buttoned and we were down to mop up. Even better, we'd have done it in less than seventy-two hours. The tape left little doubt as to what happened and who the killer was. All that remained was to find Karel Sladky and get patrol or SWAT to hook him up for three murders.

But since it wasn't Sally, but Hitch, there was no high-fiving or celebrating. Instead we went back out to the crime scene with the evidence team to look for more bullets, per the Black Dahlia's instructions. We traveled in separate cars, a subtle but not unnoticed indicator of how badly we were getting along.

At the crime scene the press swarmed Hitch.

"I wouldn't let them take your picture," I told him. "You've been in that suit for two days. It's not good for your media profile to look like you sleep in your car."

"Go fuck yourself, Scully."

We pushed past the press to join a ten-person tech team waiting for us in the backyard in their blue jumpsuits. We put a DVD copy of the surveillance video into my new Apple MacBook, then ran the video for the CSIs, as on the screen, Karel Sladky began to fire.

"Some slugs could still be in that hillside," I said to the ten techies, pointing in one direction. "We got everything out of the pool house walls and off the house, but we need to check over by the pool heater. Looks like he squeezed off a burst in that direction. As far as the brass, since you did an outside spiral search last night, let's try a grid-and-graph search now."

Using the surveillance video, we went back at it.

While the CSIs and metal detector team organized their search, I wandered over and looked through the solarium window again. I really wanted to get into this house.

A lot of things had started to bother me. For instance, who buys and holds a multimillion-dollar mansion they're not going to live in for over twenty-five years? That story about holding it in Brooks's estate until he was thirty-five seemed like complete BS. And despite Sheedy's stated fear of starting a haunted house rumor and killing the market price, why was Thayer Dunbar so determined that nobody go inside?

I began calculating the potential hazard to my career that breaking into this house without a warrant might produce.

As I pondered this my pager went off. Across the pool, Hitch's went off at exactly the same time. I'd been a cop long enough to know that when this happens, something big is going down. Both of us clawed at our cell phones and hit programmed numbers. I connected with Jeb just a little ahead of him.

"What's going on?" I asked.

"The BOLO yielded results. They found Sladky. One of the Hollywood Division cops knew Chrissy. She used to strip at a club on Sunset called The Manhole. That's where she met Karel. We called over there and the bartender says Sladky's at the bar right now. He's kind of a fixture at that place. He does some bouncing for them from time to time—even sleeps in the manager's office. Because of that Bizon I've got SWAT rolling."

He gave me the address. I hung up and headed toward Hitch, who was yapping on his cell phone getting the same information.

"2556 Sunset," I told him.

"Just got it."

We sprinted down the long drive, but slowed to a walk as we passed the reporters so we wouldn't alert them to the fact that something was happening. We didn't want to show up at that strip club pulling a train of TV news vans and network anchors.

Hitch led the way because the Porsche was faster. He got permission to go Code Three and put on his custom window flashers. I tucked in behind him and drafted.

Twenty minutes later we were in a parking lot across the street from the club. SWAT was already there and was waiting for a lieutenant watch commander from the Hollywood station before going inside.

"One of us should case it," I told the SWAT commander.

"I should do that," Hitch volunteered.

"Except I'm senior man," I told him. "I'll keep my phone on and call you with any intel."

He nodded and I relocated my recently purchased Springfield XD(M) automatic pistol from its hip holster to the small of my back where it was easy to grab. The gun fired 9 mm parabellums with nineteen in the magazine, one in the chamber. I was glad I'd changed weapons.

I dialed Hitch's cell, left the line open so he could hear, then ambled across the street and walked lazily into The Manhole strip club to see if I could get a visual on our triple murder suspect.

• CHAPTER •
19

The early evening set at a strip club was usually a case of the new, the old, and the ugly. It tended to be a tryout session for dancers on the way up and sympathy work for those on the way out. Even so, it's hard to put on an enthusiastic show when nobody is paying attention.

Two semi-bored strippers were working poles, hanging like meat in an outdoor market. They spun around lazily, occasionally arching their backs to the four-four beat of the country western music playing through the bad sound system.

The clientele was a bunch of white guys in John Deere hats. Most had sun-reddened complexions, tattoo-laden loading-dock arms, and padded waistlines. Two waitresses wearing black vests, bikini bottoms, and heels wandered around the almost empty club carrying trays.

All ten or twelve people in here would have to be removed before

SWAT did the takedown. I'd have to find a way to get the half-drunk guys out without starting a head-butt festival. I didn't see Karel Sladky anywhere and hoped he hadn't been tipped by the bartender and skipped.

The guy behind the stick was an angry-looking asshole with a shaved head and water buffalo shoulders. He was watching a football game on a small TV with the sound muted under the bar top. I was sure he had some sawed-off crowd-control equipment hidden down there—a bat or a 12-gauge.

I snagged a menu off one of the tables, removed my police ID from its case, and slipped it inside. Then I took a position on the far end of the bar away from the other customers. When the bartender came over to take my order I handed him the menu.

"Surprise inside," I told him.

He opened it, looked at my creds, then closed the menu and handed it back.

"I'm looking for Karel Sladky."

"Yeah. I got a call from one of your sergeants about him an hour ago."

"Since he's not in here, I'm hoping nobody alerted him. He's a suspect in a triple murder."

"He's back there." The bartender pointed to a curtain.

"Manager's office?"

"There's a cot," he said. "Ever since Karel's old lady threw him out, Brad's been letting him use it. I think Karel and Brad got some kind of drug business going out on the corner. They bag the chronic back there, but you didn't hear it from me."

"Okay. We're gonna need to empty this place without making a big deal out of it."

"Unplug the music and close off the liquor," he said. "They don't come for the atmosphere. The waitresses and the dancers, I'll take care of."

"Want to do that for me?"

"No, but I guess I don't have no choice."

He walked over and shut off the music. The girls who were on the poles swung around to look at him, holding on like tree monkeys as they waited for the music to start up again.

"That the end of my set, Lou?" one of them finally called.

"Yep," he said. "Bar's closed." Then he turned to the guys at the tables. "You guys finish up and get out."

A few of the John Deeres knocked back their shots, got up and left. One by one the rest drifted out. I found a place at the back of the bar and, after the dancers and waitresses were gone, I spoke to Hitch.

"Okay, everybody's out. The bartender's locking the register and coming out with me. He says Sladky's in the manager's office."

"SWAT is ready," Hitch said. "The lieutenant watch commander from the Hollywood station just got here, so we're good to go. They want you out. Because of all the side exits, they asked if we could help by covering the parking lot in back."

"Works for me."

I walked out with the bartender.

A SWAT entry team crossed the street heading toward the bar. As they deployed out front Hitch and I went around to the back. We were all carrying walkie-talkies set on tactical frequency six.

Two guys from SWAT covered the windows in the front. The rest of the team, all wearing ballistic body armor and helmets and carrying 9mm H&K MP-5 submachine guns, headed across the street toward the entrance.

The MP-5s could be set on semi- or full-auto fire. They were great weapons, which only SWAT used to have, but in 1997 we persuaded the city to authorize them for regular cops because of how badly we got our asses kicked in the North Hollywood Bank shoot-out.

Hitch and I had found good cover positions in the back and on the side of the bar. There was a metal door in the center of the club's back wall. Hitch wanted to cover that so I took the west side of the building, which ran along an alley that separated the strip club from Lili St. Cyr's Exotic Lingerie.

This was the way I liked to serve warrants on machine-gun-wielding psychopaths. Let SWAT do the rough stuff. I'll cover the back every time.

Then it went down. The SWAT team had intended to kick the office door, swarm in, and take Karel by surprise, but something went wrong because we suddenly heard shouting, then shooting inside. The MP-5s made a unique short burping sound produced by their three-shot bursts. This was followed by the longer, louder retort of the Bizon machine pistol.

From my position in the alley I couldn't see Hitch, who was somewhere in the parking lot behind the back door. I was beginning to worry about him.

Obviously SWAT hadn't been able to take Sladky by surprise, and the odds were now pretty good that he would try and escape the club through the back door, leaving Hitch alone with only a pistol against a fully automatic machine gun capable of putting out 800 rounds per minute.

I could hear the Bizon chattering. Sladky was putting up a deadly fight.

I left my position and moved to the rear corner of the building where I could see the back exit and the parking lot, but I couldn't see Hitch.

Where the hell was he?

"Hitch, cover your position!" I whispered into my walkie. "I got the left side."

Two squelches came back as he acknowledged my transmission, but I still couldn't see him.

I moved into the lot with my pistol up, aimed at the back door. The Springfield XD(M) automatic had a four-and-a-half-inch barrel and was not very accurate at a distance. If Sladky came out that back door I needed to get a lot closer to be effective.

I sensed movement behind me and spun around. While I'd been creeping into the parking lot with my back to the alley windows, Karel Sladky had silently slipped out of one and had moved up directly behind me.

He had the drop on me with that monster Russian ventilator.

I dove facedown on the pavement just as he let loose with a stream of bullets. The 9 mm slugs dug into the black tar asphalt surface in front of me.

I had just barely survived the first burst, but was in a terrible predicament. I was facedown, ten feet from the shooter, seconds from death.

Then I heard three shots ring out. They sounded like balloons popping in contrast to the roar of the Bizon.

I looked up just in time to see Sladky fly backward. Three red spots blossomed on the front of his white shirt. He landed on his back and the Bizon fell harmlessly from his hands.

I turned and saw Hitch. He'd taken cover inside the trash Dumpster. When Sladky fired at me, Hitch had jumped up, exposing himself. Then he'd taken the Czechoslovakian down with three well-placed shots.

Hitch climbed out of the Dumpster. Coffee grounds and orange rinds stained the cuffs of his beautiful rust-colored suit. I wanted to kiss the guy.

"Good shooting," I said, my voice a croak.

The back door burst open and two gun-wielding SWAT officers

came running out. Two more rounded the corner at the side of the bar. All with their guns up and safeties off.

"We're Code Four!" I shouted. "Shooter's down."

The SWAT commander checked the body. Sladky was alive, but just barely. The Hollywood station LT called for the ambulance SWAT had standing by and seconds later it rolled into the parking lot. Sladky miraculously continued to breathe as he was loaded aboard a stretcher, leaking blood from three chest wounds. A few seconds later he was being rushed away, with sirens blaring.

The watch commander wanted Hitch and me to be transported directly back to Hollywood Division to complete a Daily Field Activity Report, which takes place immediately after every shooting where a police officer discharges his or her weapon.

A DFAR is usually done by a "shoot unit" headed by a sergeant from Internal Affairs. Afterward Hitch would undergo a full shooting review, also standard practice after an officer-involved gunfight.

When I finished with the lieutenant, he went in search of Hitch, who was supposed to be isolated in the back of a patrol car.

The watch commander couldn't find him and was starting to freak out. Hitch wasn't supposed to have contact with anyone until after his DFAR. The idea was to keep participants from getting together and organizing their versions of what happened.

"I'll find him, LT," I said, trying to calm the guy. "He's around here somewhere. Give me a minute."

I found Hitch behind the strip club in the very alley where Karel Sladky had gotten the drop on me and then been gunned down.

When I spotted him I thought he was cleaning the garbage out of the cuffs of his rust-colored suit. But he wasn't doing that at all.

He was bent over, throwing up on his Spanish leather shoes.

• CHAPTER •

20

The DFAR took place in the lieutenant's office at the Hollywood station. Sergeant Lena Fine, a thirty-year-old nondescript woman with mouse brown hair and a careful demeanor, from the Bureau of Professional Standards conducted the interview.

The interview was on a continuous tape and was witnessed by the lieutenant watch commander. The DFAR is conducted under oath and is basically the officer's retelling of the event for the official record. Hitch, as the primary shooter, went first.

I gave the supporting eyewitness statement and told my end of it, recounting how Sladky came out the window behind me after I had gone into the back parking lot and how he was dropped by my partner before he could get off a second deadly burst that would certainly have killed me.

I was told by Sergeant Fine that a separate shooting review would be conducted a day or so later at the Bradbury Building, and that I might be called to testify. She said because it was nearly Christmas Eve and even the headhunters from IA needed time at home with their families it probably wouldn't happen until after the holiday.

Hitch and I finished around eight. Despite the fact that I'd only had ninety minutes of sleep in two days, I was not the least bit tired, an adrenaline rush performing that miracle for me.

Hitch came out of the men's room where he'd been washing up and stood facing me.

"You wanta go home or do you want to let me buy you a thanks-for-saving-my-life-merry-Christmas drink?" I asked.

"Drink sounds good," he replied.

We went to a bar right across the street called Mulroney's Roost. It was a cop bar that catered to the Hollywood station. However, at eight P.M. this close to Christmas, the bar was pretty dead. Hitch and I took a booth in the back. We both ordered a Corona with lime.

"You okay?" I asked, looking at his tired expression and the rust-colored suit, which had endured a lot of abuse in the last two days.

"Yeah, I guess," he said, but he didn't sound too sure.

"You never put a guy down before, did you?" I said, remembering the image of him bent over in the alley, puking.

"No."

He sipped some of his beer; his handsome face was furrowed in thought. "Funny," he said. "Growing up in South Central I saw my share of bangers get taken off the count. Saw my first payback hit when I was in fourth grade. But . . ." He stopped and looked down at his beer.

"But it feels different when you're the shooter," I finished for him.

"Yeah, it does."

"Listen, Hitch. What you did for me this afternoon, that's something I can never repay. You know that, right?"

"Come on . . . guy was greasing off rounds at both of us."

"You stood up. You exposed yourself to fire and you saved my life. I'm not saying I exactly understand what you're all about yet, but that's something I'm not going to forget."

After a moment he nodded. I could see he'd taken in what I'd just said.

"You're gonna have some bad moments about it," I continued. "It's hard being responsible for ending somebody's life."

"He's not dead yet," Hitch said. "I called the hospital an hour ago. He's still in ICU."

"Come on. You put three in the ten ring. He might still have a heartbeat, but that guy's on the ark."

Hitch nodded.

"I've done this a few times. It's never easy. You gotta watch out for yourself these next few days. There's a guy in the psychiatric support unit who I've talked to a couple of times when this happened to me. It's standard procedure to send you to a shrink, so I'm sure Jeb will set you up to do that soon. But some of the head docs in psychiatric support are just clocking time. I want you to have this guy. His name's Dr. Eric Lusk. I'm gonna call him."

"Okay," he said softly. "Eric Lusk." We finished our beers and were getting ready to leave when he looked at me with an earnest expression I'd never seen before.

"I guess we did pretty good. I mean, we got lucky with that video, but we put the case down and we did it in less than two days. Big, media-intense red ball and we gonked it. Home run for big blue."

"Yes it is," I agreed.

"Okay, so what's our story, you and me? Where do we go from here?"

"You move over to my cubicle and take Sally's desk."

"Good." He smiled.

I nodded. "But do me a favor."

"Sure."

"Don't put those damn GQ photos up."

"Okay," he said. "Deal."

We shook hands and walked out into the parking lot and stood next to our cars, a little reluctant to let the moment go. We'd bonded behind the strip club and our partnership had found a heartbeat a few minutes ago. We could both feel it.

"Guess there's no movie," I said, grinning at him.

"Yeah." He shook his head in amazement. "But we had a pretty good one going for a while there. Great inciting event. Great characters—two dead hookers, Yolanda Dublin, a dead movie producer. Great title. But then I fucked it all up and shot the antagonist before we got out of Act One." He smiled. "And all I got in the bargain was you."

"Not much of a trade, but I'm grateful," I said.

We slapped palms, then he slid into the Porsche. "Merry Christmas. See you in a couple of days, dawg."

"See you then," I agreed. "Merry Christmas."

I drove home, kissed Alexa, called Dr. Lusk at the Psychiatric Support Unit and left a message about Hitch on his voicemail. Then I slept for twelve hours.

The next afternoon I turned on the news and found out that miraculously, Karel Sladky was still alive in ICU, although he was not expected to make it.

The news anchors all said that the huge Scott Berman murder case had been solved in record time and that the DA would file against Sladky for triple murder, that is if he didn't die of his wounds first.

On Christmas morning, after a crazy week, it just felt good to relax. We had the house to ourselves this year. Our son, Chooch, was on the road with the Trojans preparing for a national bowl game the following day.

We ate a late breakfast and opened our presents. Our cat, Franco, sat on the floor under the tree batting at Christmas ornaments. I saved Chooch's gift for last. It was a painting he'd had commissioned using the picture from the USC football media guide. It showed him dropping back, helmetless, the big number 9 on his jersey, about to rifle a pass. It would go in my den and I would treasure it.

On that quiet Christmas Day, I thought the case was over.

But it wasn't.

We were just beginning:

ACT TWO

■ ■ ■ ■ ■ ■ ■ ■

■ CHAPTER ■

21

We were having coffee and pancakes on the patio the Monday after Christmas weekend. Torn wrapping paper and Styrofoam packing peeked out of the trash cans and the empty boxes stacked around them. Franco was curled up under my chair sleeping.

"So then it's settled. You and Hollywood Hitchens are the new hot team at Homicide Special," Alexa said, smiling at me.

"Know any good agents?" I joked.

"Give it a chance. Maybe it's gonna work."

I finished eating and helped her clear the table and rinse the plates. We were both getting a late start. Alexa had slept in trying to stockpile some shut-eye because today would start the department's annual end-of-the-year budget review. Until it was complete she would be more or less sleeping in her office.

I was getting out late because Hitch had called earlier to tell me that Jeb had already set up an appointment for him at Psych Support. He was meeting with Dr. Lusk at eight A.M. I decided to time it so we would both get in about nine thirty.

On my way into work, one little troubling detail kept pestering me. It was keeping this cool red ball from being nothing but net.

The thing I couldn't stop thinking about was that damn 7.65 mm slug that we'd found by the trash area. It was the one piece of evidence in the Sladky case that didn't fit. Where had that bullet come from? Was it part of all this, or had it been fired years ago, and meant nothing? It was floating around in our case without a home.

I pulled into the garage at the PAB, parked in my slot, and went upstairs, where I found Hitchens already in our cubicle putting his belongings into Sally's old desk.

He was back to being a fashion elitist. Gray herringbone jacket, pleated gray designer slacks, maroon shirt and loafers, and a great-looking gray silk tie with matching pocket square. Sitting across from him I was going to look like a homeless guy.

"Morning, partner," he greeted me as I walked in and dumped my stuff on the desk opposite him. "How was your Christmas?"

"Great. How was the shrink?"

"Doc Lusk is tits. Thanks for the recommendation. He's gonna call Jeb this morning and approve me for duty. According to department shooting policy I gotta go to three follow-up sessions, but it's cool, 'cause we're doing them over golf on consecutive Saturdays at his club."

"How'd you sleep? Any bad dreams?"

"Had Czech psychos with Bizon machine guns chasing me around all night. 'Zat count?" The joke let me know he'd be all right.

One or two guys in the unit came up and congratulated him on putting an active shooter down and saving my life. I could tell from his expression that he hadn't been expecting this and that recognition of this kind was a new experience. He seemed almost shy as he accepted the praise.

Once we were alone again, he said, "Skipper says the Black Dahlia wants to talk to us. She's on her way over."

"Listen, Hitch, little tip since we're now gonna be full-time partners. Nobody, and I mean absolutely *nobody*, calls their captain Skipper. You're coming off like a bad episode of *Starsky and Hutch*."

"Here's the thing on that, Shane. A man has to have two things in life: his look and his style. We both know I got my look dialed in, but a man's style is infinitely more important than his fashion sense because it's all-encompassing. When you boil it down and remove wardrobe considerations, style is pretty much code and content, and a big part of content is syntax. Syntax creates perception. Perception often determines result. For that reason I—"

"Okay, okay. I give."

Just then I saw Dahlia Wilkes step out of the elevator. As usual, she was very pulled together in a no-nonsense black pinstripe suit and heels, carrying a big-ass briefcase from some expensive designer like Prada or Coach.

Hitch was sitting with his back to the elevator but stood up and said, "I just felt the temperature drop, so our ADA must be here. Let's go see the Skipper."

We walked into Jeb's office. Dahlia Wilkes was already by his desk setting down her big briefcase, removing binders and folders, all business. She didn't bother to mention Hitch's life-saving heroics.

"I just talked to the hospital," she started off. "Sladky is hanging in like he's union. His ICU doc now says he's probably going to make it. That means we gotta keep prepping the murder case."

"That's why we're here, Dahlia," Jeb said amicably. "We're always at the service of our talented team of county prosecutors."

"Right," I chimed in politely and looked at Hitch, who nodded and smiled warmly. I thought we were doing much better with her this morning.

"I'm looking for dedication, energy, and motion," she said. "Nothing more, nothing less. But I won't tolerate any goofing off on this just because we've now got the surveillance video showing Sladky doing the killing. We continue to work it as if we've got absolutely nothing."

"You won't ever find Detectives Scully and Hitchens goofing off," Hitch said sarcastically. "We're all about the motion. We don't even stand still on escalators."

From his tone I could tell he was back to messing with her, which was a really bad idea. She looked at him without expression, hands on hips. I thought she was about to fire back, but then, unexpectedly, she let it pass.

"Turns out, Karel Sladky has two prior felony convictions," she continued. "He won't plea bargain a third strike. That means our red ball is going all the way to trial. You two are going to be very busy. In the next week, I'm gonna want you to wrap up every loose end on my case."

Neither of us answered that. "I do not want to get surprised in court," she went on. "I want this policed perfectly."

"That's a two-way street, Dahlia," Hitch replied, giving her a sleepy little smile. "We're certainly gonna be policing the hell out of it, wrapping up all those messy little loose ends like you want, but we're also going to expect you to put our slam-dunk case on correctly and not fuck it up in court or lose it like you did on *State of California versus Menander* and *State v. Rosenard.*"

You could see her body stiffen. She looked at him for a long moment, forming her thoughts carefully before speaking, just like the well-trained attorney she was.

"Let's get something straight right now, boys," she began coldly. "I'm in charge of this case. Screw with me at your own peril, 'cause I'm not above turning both your lives into a shit soufflé. I can have you on your knees at my crime scene digging for brass 'til next April. I'm not looking for you to carry my books, Hitchens. But you better damn well show some respect or I'm gonna light you up and flick you to the curb."

He sat back and smiled vaguely at her. They obviously hated each other. My ethnic traction idea had failed spectacularly.

"One other thing," she said. "I want that 7.65 slug you found out of the case."

"It's evidence," I said. "We found it on the crime scene."

"It's confusing. It's suggestive. The defense will be all over it."

"You have the video showing Sladky doing the murder," I persisted. I figured this might be coming, but I kept paddling nonetheless.

"I'm sure you can endure a few meaningless questions about another caliber bullet. I really don't like removing evidence from a case file."

"Me either," Hitch said crisply.

"It suggests a second shooter," Dahlia argued. "We know there wasn't one, but the defense will say he could have been off camera, directing the show. They'll try and create doubt through confusion."

"One of the vics was Sladky's wife, who was in the midst of divorcing him," I shot back. "He was violent and jealous, and she was a high-roller hooker selling herself to guys like Scott Berman. How's the defense gonna get around that? It's pretty obvious what the motive was and why he shot them."

"I don't want that bullet in the case," she repeated.

"Except, we're not taking it out," Hitch said adamantly. "As the investigating officers, that's our call."

"I'm ordering you to."

"Can't do that," Hitch said, holding firm. "In fact, that would probably constitute prosecutorial misconduct. That bullet may be exculpatory evidence. You actually have an obligation to supply it to the defense on discovery."

Jeb was sitting at his desk with his head swiveling back and forth like a spectator at a tennis match. He hated this kind of stuff. But I knew in the end he'd come down on our side because we were right.

"The rule with juries is KISS, Keep It Simple Stupid," Dahlia countered. "I don't want any loose ends that I can't explain. My position is the 7.65 bullet was fired years ago and, as such, isn't part of my case in brief, and therefore, doesn't need to be supplied to the defense on discovery."

"We don't know it was fired in the past," Hitch persisted. "That's just your supposition."

"So you're not going to take it out," she said.

"Not unless the skipper directs us to," Hitch replied.

Everybody turned to Jeb.

"We cannot remove valid evidence in a homicide investigation just because it doesn't fit our theory of the crime," he told Dahlia. "You'll just have to deal with it."

"Okay, fine. Have it your way," the Black Dahlia snapped.

She closed up her books and folder, stuffing them angrily into her bulging briefcase. As she turned to go, she fixed a murder-one stare on all of us.

"I notice from the case notes you e-mailed over that you've still only recovered fifty-three of the sixty-four Makarov slugs that were fired, and that we're still missing four casings."

"That's right," I said.

"Then get back out there and start digging."

"The video techs couldn't determine how many rounds were actually fired. He might not have dumped the whole clip," I protested. "Besides that, as I've already told you, some of those bullets were shot up into the air and could be miles away. We're never going to recover all of them."

"Doesn't mean you shouldn't try," she replied. "That's why you're up here, right? Homicide Special—the best of the best. I know you hotshots are gonna come through for me."

We finally had her smiling, but believe me, there was no humor there.

"Excuse me, Dahlia," Jeb said. "But I don't want my detectives doing busywork. This is an active division. As far as I'm concerned this case is basically made and I need to put Scully and Hitch back in rotation. They'll continue to do normal wrap-up for you; take statements, build timelines and the like, but they're gonna get a new case to work. If you want more done at that crime scene, *you* should request a CSI evidence-gathering team out there."

"I'm sure you don't want me to bring Chase Beal into this."

She was referring to our county DA, who was already starting his campaign for L.A. mayor and was a dedicated politician. Whenever the media was involved he got squirrely.

"Let's just do it my way for a day or two," she said. "Then, if necessary, we can revisit it."

One of the other detectives in the unit tapped on the glass partition of Jeb's office and made a telephone sign, holding his thumb and little finger up to the side of his face, then pointed at his cubicle.

"Okay. You got 'em, but only for a day or two," Jeb said, getting up to take the call, glad to be out of there.

As soon as he was gone, Hitch switched tactics. He didn't want to kneel on a towel in his gray Italian designer slacks, digging in the dirt like a six-year-old, looking for bullets that were a mile away on some hillside or brass that wasn't there because it was probably never fired.

"Excuse me again, Ms. Wilkes," he said, standing up and putting on a full charm offensive. "Laying all of this aside for a minute, I'd like to say that I, for one, am glad to be at your disposal on this. I have nothing but the utmost respect for your work and hope you didn't misconstrue my comment of a moment ago."

She said nothing. She studied him like a spider in her closet, trying to parse this sudden change of course.

"Is that suit Dolce and Gabbana?" he asked, smiling.

Nothing from our beautiful, cold-eyed prosecutor.

"Because it looks stunning on you."

She just stood there looking at him, a frown now beginning to pull her eyebrows together like warring caterpillars, wrinkling her gorgeous face.

"Simply killer look on you," Hitch added. "That Italian cut is really happening this winter and I, for one, am glad to see it's back."

Still nothing. Not a flicker of interest. But I gotta hand it to him, in the face of this ice storm, he soldiered on.

"I know this might be presumptive, and please don't take it the wrong way, but as it turns out, I've been invited to Jamie Foxx's New Year's Day barbecue. It's going to be a pretty cool deal. Football and ribs. Lots of A-list Hollywood people. I was thinking perhaps, if you're not doing anything, we—"

"Which one is Jamie Foxx?" Dahlia interrupted coolly. "Is she the actress with the bad nose job?"

"Jamie Foxx is a guy. A major movie star. He played me in *Mosquito*."

"Really? How nice for him. So I guess if you want to be at that party on January one and not still digging in the backyard at my crime scene, you better get moving." She smiled coldy. "And it's DKNY, not Dolce and Gabbana." Then she swept out of the room.

Hitch turned to me. "I want it noted I was down for our team."

"Done. But on a more practical note, the way this is going, from now on we probably should start wearing blue jeans to work," I told him.

▪ CHAPTER ▪
22

We left Jeb's office and returned to our cubicle.

"I'm gonna take my own car out there," Hitch said. "I've got a thing I'm doing after work and it's out of my way if I have to come back here."

"Okay, see you out on Skyline."

I waited as he gathered up his stuff and left. I was glad to have a minute alone because I wanted to run something down. I opened my crime scene book to the page where I'd noted the Realtor's name I'd seen on the sign at the side of the Skyline Drive house. I found it on the second page. I'd written:

Prime Properties Real Estate
Beverly Bartinelli
Listing Agent

I called Information for the phone number and dialed Prime Properties. When the switchboard answered, I asked for Beverly Bartinelli.

"She doesn't work here anymore," the receptionist said. "Hasn't for a while."

"I'd like her number and current address if you still have it."

"I do have it, but I don't want to give it out to just anybody without her permission."

"My name is Shane Scully. I'm a homicide detective with the LAPD," I told her. "I'm working a case that she may have information on. You can call me back to make sure I'm telling you the truth. I'm at Homicide Special, extension 5675."

A minute later my phone rang and the receptionist came back on the line.

"Guess you're legit," she said.

"What about the phone number and address?"

"It's her residence. 1616 Maplewood Drive. I just checked the phone number I have but it's no longer current and I don't believe it's listed."

I thanked her and hung up. Rather than going to the trouble of running that number down through the department's reverse directory, I decided I'd just drop by. Maplewood ran parallel to Ventura Boulevard and was only about three miles away from Skyline, so it was on the way.

When I got to the parking garage I saw that Hitch's Carrera was gone. I climbed into my car and headed out to the Valley.

I was telling myself the reason I hadn't mentioned this errand to Hitch was because I was just indulging a stupid hunch that would undoubtedly go nowhere and it wasn't worth wasting his time on it. But the real truth was some part of me still didn't trust him. Hitch could be very efficient one minute, and the next, go totally off the reservation, like that smart-ass remark to Dahlia about those two old cases she'd lost.

Most prosecutors will only take slam dunks to trial and will plead out everything else so they all have at least a ninety-five percent trial win rate. Hitch had obviously gone to a lot of trouble to find the few losers in her package so he could jam them in her face. But for what purpose? It just pissed her off and now we were going to spend one and maybe two more days with CSI digging for lead and brass that probably wasn't even there. And that, I told myself, was why I was not confiding my hunch to him.

Despite all my rationalization, it really didn't matter, because when I pulled up in front of 1616 Maplewood Drive, Hitch's Porsche Carrera was parked at the curb. He was already inside talking to Beverly Bartinelli.

The guy had obviously spotted the same old real estate sign by the side of the house that I had. Worse still, he'd beaten me here.

The duplex was a neatly cared for two-story building with light yellow siding and white trim. I walked up the path to the front porch.

Before I could ring the bell, the door was opened by the Hitch-meister himself. He had a mug of Beverly's steaming black coffee in his hand.

"Saw you coming up the steps, dawg." He was grinning. "Guess you probably want to come inside."

CHAPTER
23

Before I could bitch Hitchens out for doing exactly what I was going to do, I saw Beverly Bartinelli standing a short distance behind him in the entry, so I put it on hold.

She was a pleasant-looking woman in her fifties with one of those faces that lacked guile and radiated warmth. Everything else about her was medium. Medium height, medium build, medium-blond hair.

After I stepped inside Hitch made the introductions. "Beverly Bartinelli, meet my partner, Shane Scully."

We shook hands and Beverly said, "Detective Hitchens was just asking me about 3151 Skyline Drive."

Hitch just shrugged at me. It was obvious to both of us that we were going to have to deal with this trust issue or our partnership was doomed.

"Can I get you some coffee?" Beverly asked and I shook my head. "Then why don't we sit in the living room? I'm sorry, but Christmas is still all over the place. I was at my daughter's house all day yesterday and Todd and I haven't had a chance to straighten up yet."

We sat on a sofa grouping, moving some new quilts and a few pillows in boxes to make room.

"It's strange seeing that Skyline Drive house after all these years," she said once we were settled. "It's been all over the news."

"Beverly was just telling me she had that listing in 1982," Hitch said.

She nodded. "I haven't been in real estate for a few years. I'm in computer sales now. That was one of my first listings when I went to work for Prime Properties over twenty-five years ago."

Hitch and I exchanged a look. One of us had to take the lead on this interview. Since I was senior man and still out of sorts about getting here second, I leaned forward and began.

"We're looking for some background on the property. Anything that you might know that could affect the triple murder that happened there."

"I'm certain nothing I know could have anything to do with that dead movie producer and those two prostitutes," she began. "I mean, it was December of eighty-two when I finally closed escrow."

"You're probably right, but nonetheless, we have some questions about the history of the place," Hitch jumped in. "Rather than us leading you, why don't you just tell us what you know and then if we have questions, we'll ask them later."

I shot him a look. He just leaned back and showed me nothing.

"Start with when you first listed the house," I said.

"Actually, it sort of starts a few months before I listed the house. I sold it for the estate of the late Thomas Vulcuna and his family. You may remember that name if you were around L.A. in eighty-one."

She looked at us to see if we responded. The name sounded vaguely familiar, but I couldn't quite place it.

"He was the head of a very successful television studio called Eagle's Nest Productions," she said.

Now Hitch and I traded startled looks.

"What happened to him and his family is one of those horrible L.A. stories," she continued. "If either of you were in town back then you must remember it."

"I was ten, living in South Central," Hitch told her. "The Crips moved onto my block in eighty-one so I spent most of that year hiding under my uncle's car."

"Why don't you tell us?" I said. "Start at the beginning."

"In 1981 Thomas Vulcuna had piled up a lot of debts at Eagle's Nest, a studio which he owned privately. I know a little about all this because his house on Skyline was actually put up as collateral on the Eagle's Nest bank loan. We had to untangle that mess before we could sell the property.

"Back then, Eagle's Nest had six TV series on the air, but the problem was they were spending more for each episode than the network gave them in licensing fees. Tom Vulcuna was losing hundreds of thousands of dollars per episode, and with the production company making over a hundred episodes a year, despite his success in getting his shows programmed, he was quickly outrunning his bank loan and going broke."

I was vaguely beginning to remember this now. It had been a big TV and newspaper story. A murder-suicide if I recalled correctly.

"Tom Vulcuna had all these production company debts and his bank was about to foreclose on the loans," she went on. "Then on Christmas Eve 1981, he came home from a Christmas party at the studio. He was distraught, he'd had too much to drink, and the police thought he got into an argument with his eighteen-year-old daughter,

THE PROSTITUTES' BALL ■ 133

Victoria. When his wife, Ellen, tried to break it up, apparently he just snapped. He picked up a ball-peen hammer that was lying around to hang Christmas wreaths and, in a frenzy, he beat both of them to death right there in the living room."

"I remember this now," I said. "He brought a handgun home from the studio or something. The police speculated he had already decided to commit suicide."

"That's right," Beverly said. "It was an old World War One Luger that he checked out of the studio prop department. Eagle's Nest was making a six-hour miniseries about Hitler's rise after World War One, and they had a bunch of those old Lugers for the SS officers to carry in the movie. They were props, but apparently the ones that weren't going to be fired didn't get altered by the prop master and still worked. He brought one of those home in his briefcase. After he killed his wife and daughter he went upstairs to the master bedroom, lay down on the bed, opened a copy of Dante's *The Divine Comedy* to a passage about death that he'd underlined, then he fired a shot into his head. When the maid arrived the next morning, she found them all dead."

"I remember," I said as my vague memory of it kicked in. "Big, big media case."

She nodded. "Because of the horrible, gory nature of the murders, the house was almost impossible for me to sell. Prime Properties assigned me the listing, but as soon as I took a client up there and they realized it was the Vulcuna house, any interest I had going evaporated."

"It's owned by the Dorothy White Foundation now," I said.

"I was the one who sold it to them," she said. "The foundation bought it at the Vulcuna estate sale less than a year later, in eighty-two. When we closed escrow, the Christmas tree with all their unopened presents was still in the living room. Last I heard, it was all still there."

"It is," I confirmed.

She gave us a weak, apologetic smile. "Anyway, it was quite a project selling that place. The production company owned the house. The bank had the production company in receivership. After the sale of all the studio's assets the bank only got twenty-five cents on the dollar and the sale eventually ended up in tax court.

"I finally got an offer from the Dorothy White Foundation. The easiest way for me to consummate the escrow was for the foundation to just buy the whole mess to pay back taxes. When escrow closed, they got the house and the defunct production studio along with some minimal tax loss carryforward."

"How much did they pay for it?"

"The house was a steal because of the murders. I think the end number was something like two point six million, but that's in eighty-two dollars. It would be worth a lot more today."

Hitch leaned forward. I could tell he had a question so I nodded for him to go ahead as if I actually had any control over him.

"Mrs. Bartinelli," he began, "it seems strange to us that a house worth that much money would stay vacant for over twenty-five years."

"Yes, it is, and it soon became apparent that the foundation had no intention of selling it either. Long after the stigma of the murders had passed, they were still turning down offers. We didn't represent the property any longer, but from time to time, people would be driving around up on Skyline and see it. We got our share of random inquiries.

"That mansion has the prime location right on the promontory point. People would want to buy it and fix it up to live in. I once submitted an offer for over seven million dollars to the Century City law firm that represents the foundation."

"Sheedy, Devine, and Lipscomb," Hitch said.

She nodded. "I dealt with one of the senior partners, Stender

Sheedy. It didn't matter how good the deal was, he always said no. The place just wasn't for sale.

"After a while, none of the Realtors around here bothered to even submit offers to them. It's just been rotting up there empty and run-down with that old dust-covered tinsel tree and all those unopened presents sitting in the living room, waiting for the Vulcunas' ghosts to float down and open them." Then she added, "Somebody ought to make that into a movie, don't you think?"

Hitch just nodded and smiled.

· CHAPTER ·
24

We stood out by our cars in front of the duplex apartment. Hitch was writing frantically in his red leather journal. It was just before noon.

"Put that away for a minute and let's talk about this," I said.

"You were right. There *was* a second shooter. The only problem was our time frame was off by over a quarter century. This story doesn't start with the Prostitutes' Ball and the Sladky triple. We gotta back it all up and start it on Christmas Eve 1981, the night Thomas Vulcuna bludgeoned his wife and daughter to death with a hammer then killed himself. Which, not for nothing, is a monster inciting event and the opening scene of our movie!"

"Listen, Hitch, put the movie on hold for a minute. Let's think this out."

"Right."

"I think World War One Lugers fire 7.65 ammo."

Hitch was grinning. "It's all one case, dude. Beginning in 1981 with the bloody Vulcuna double murder with the ball-peen hammer, then the suicide. The investigation and the closed case ends Act One. Then we move into Act Two with the Prostitutes' Ball triple-murder case that just went down on the same crime scene. The exciting cast of characters grows and now we got Thayer Dunbar and his cadaverous attorney who bought the house from Vulcuna's estate in eighty-two and then for some still-unknown, Act Three reason won't let anybody get inside for almost thirty years. We got little coked-up Brooks and the Scott Berman/Yolanda Dublin thing with the two gorgeous dead hookers. I mean, can you stand this? Topping it off, we're simply lousy with subplots. We got a once-powerful production company run by Vulcuna in eighty-one, which is today a shell of itself with Brooks making cheesy Paris Hilton videos. And tying the whole thing together is the German Luger and the 7.65 ammo that turns up in both triple kills, and we're just getting started. I'm telling you, dawg, this is one big, magnificent, kick-ass, go-to-the-bank movie."

He had again started to jot something down in his journal, so I took the leather book out of his hand.

"Stop writing and listen to me," I insisted.

He tapped his foot impatiently. "I'm listening, but can I have my book back?"

I gave it to him, then posed a question.

"If Vulcuna checked the gun out of the prop room and brought it home on Christmas Eve, and if the L.A. homicide cops found him dead with a 7.65 bullet shot through his head upstairs, then how come we found the 7.65 slug in the backyard by the trash shed? It should be in a wall upstairs in the master bedroom."

"I don't know. Maybe he test-fired the gun in the backyard first," Hitch said. "I can tell you this much, it isn't simple. Which means

Dahlia's gonna freak with all her KISS bullshit. We say anything about this, she's gonna try and get our bosses to transfer us to a traffic detail."

"I know. Too much collateral info for her Sladky jury."

"So we can't tell her, right?" Hitch continued. "We do what she wants, go up to Skyline right now, get the evidence techs working on a grid and graph, let them wave the little metal detector 'til there's no more joy in Mudville. While they do that, we work on this."

"Except what are we working on?" I said. "Is this somehow still part of the Sladky triple or are we now just working on Thomas Vulcuna's double murder / suicide, which was closed by our own department over twenty-five years ago and doesn't even have a case number?"

"I don't know," he said. "But you gotta admit, this is as intriguing as hell." He was excited; his foot was tapping maniacally. "By the way, this is exactly what happened on *Mosquito*. Things kept turning up, making the story better and better."

"You're saying we got two separate crimes here, but they're somehow connected? They happened twenty-eight years apart, both are triple killings, both occurred within days of Christmas, at the exact same location. In both instances, the guy who owns the house where the murders took place also owns the same Hollywood production studio, except because of the time span they're completely different guys and one wasn't even born when the first crime happened? I'm gagging here, Hitch."

"I don't know the answer, but it's certainly provocative."

"We need to get inside that house," I said, running the problem in my mind. "Except nobody's gonna write us a warrant. Vulcuna was solved years ago. That case is down. No need for further investigation. With the video we found of Sladky shooting up the party, that case is also down. Since both cases are solved, we got no PC to investigate that mansion. Sheedy will fight a search warrant saying the crime didn't occur inside the house and our spineless political hack DA will fold like a deck chair. So if we want to go in there we'll have to do it without a warrant."

"Right. Good one. Kiss your ass good-bye."

"I think we need to take a vow of silence," I said. "We pledge to keep this between us. Nobody knows. Not Jeb. Nobody. At least not until we figure out how we want to play it."

"That also include your wife?" he asked.

I didn't like keeping things from Alexa but Hitchens was standing there, his body language going more and more rigid by the moment, so I finally nodded.

Then his cell phone rang. He pulled it out of his holster and answered. "Yeah, sure . . . you bet." He hung up and put it away.

"Sadly, I won't be able to join you for the fabulous Dahlia dig up on Skyline Drive, which we've scheduled for this afternoon. That was the skipper. IA wants me over at the Bradbury Building ASAP for my shooting review board. I'm counting on you to handle my end of this search, bro. I want you to find every last piece of missing evidence for our exalted prosecutor. I wish I could be there 'cause I live for this shit, but sadly I'm needed elsewhere."

He shot me a peace sign, got in the Porsche and powered off, leaving me standing in the street.

• CHAPTER •
25

The week after Christmas is when all LAPD department heads have to prepare the year's budget review. They have to work up an annual cost-of-operation estimate for the coming twelve months and tender it to the chief, who then assembles the overall department budget and submits it to the mayor's office the first week of January.

Alexa is always completely buried by this fiscal process so I knew she would most likely be working until well past midnight.

I was thinking about what I would do for dinner as I faced six angry CSIs up on Skyline Drive, trying not to communicate my own displeasure about being forced to be here.

It didn't seem to be working because after I told them what Dahlia Wilkes wanted, they were glaring at me like I'd just delivered the wrong pizza.

"Is she kidding? We went through this place very carefully," Lyn Wei, the lead CSI, said. She was a twenty-nine-year-old Asian woman with a round face that wasn't helped by her severe helmet-shaped hairstyle.

"I don't think she was kidding," I told them. "Look, it never hurts to be thorough. I know you guys started with an inward spiral search pattern when you first got up here, then yesterday did a grid and graph, so why don't we try a parallel search today?"

Lyn Wei wrinkled her nose. "Did you and Hitchens do something to piss her off?"

"Miss Wilkes is a fine prosecutor," I said. "She tends to be a little obsessive on evidentiary and procedural stuff but let's bear in mind the terrific results she gets."

While they went to work, I sat on a pool chaise and looked at the big, empty house.

I thought about a distraught Thomas Vulcuna coming home all those years ago with that old prop Luger in his briefcase. Maybe coming out here half drunk to test-fire it, his hands shaking as he held a pillow on the barrel so he wouldn't alert his family inside. Then getting into an argument with his daughter, Vicki, killing her and his wife with a ball-peen hammer. Ugh.

A lot about that didn't track.

If he had the Luger, why use a hammer? I guess if it wasn't in the same room with him when he snapped and started swinging, you could find a way to get there. But still, I was suspicious of it.

Then after committing those ghastly murders he goes upstairs to the master bedroom where he opens *The Divine Comedy* to an underlined passage about death before he shoots himself.

I didn't like the *Divine Comedy* suicide note at all. I've been working homicide and suicide cases for a long time. Never seen that one before. People who write suicide notes are usually communicating important last thoughts to someone. It's something you do in your own words, not with a passage out of a book.

I also wondered if Thomas Vulcuna had removed his shoes before shooting himself. I'd noticed that on a large majority of suicides I'd worked, the victim had removed his or her shoes before doing the deed. It happened something like seventy percent of the time.

I'd asked a psychologist about it once and was told that the act of removing one's shoes prior to death was a ritual. This doc told me when we remove our shoes and socks before bed at night it symbolizes an ending. A suicide victim is involved with a final gesture—the end of life. By performing this task, the vic was subconsciously acknowledging the end of one state and the beginning of the next. At least that's what the shrink said.

I don't know how much of that I believed, but I certainly believed the overwhelming statistic I'd observed. It made me want to examine the autopsy and crime-scene photos of the Vulcuna murder to see if his shoes were on or off.

Of course, the fact that the '81 murder-suicide was closed almost thirty years ago was going to be a problem. But I'd find a way to deal with it.

I dialed Alexa to check on her schedule. She told me what I'd already suspected.

"I'm not going to make it home 'til very late," she said. "I'm collecting budget estimates from my division commanders right now and I'd like to get a preliminary worksheet done by the end of the night."

"Okay. I'm gonna pick something up," I said. "See you when you get home."

"If I get home," she sighed.

I stayed true to my promise to Hitch and didn't tell her about what we'd found out from Beverly Bartinelli, but I felt guilty as hell about it.

After I hung up with Alexa I called the Records Division and talked to an old sergeant named Leroy Porter.

"I'm looking for an eighties case file," I told him. "It was a murder-suicide that occurred in December of eighty-one."

"Vulcuna?" he said without hesitation.

"How'd you know?"

"Guy came in here and checked it out an hour ago. Two boxes. They were in the old evidence warehouse. That case was before we went on computers and it was stored in the hard copy room."

"Was Detective Hitchens the one who took it?"

"He'd be the one," Sergeant Porter said.

Damn, I thought as I hung up. Hitch had swung by on his way to IA. *He beat me again.*

My partner had a reason to be AWOL from our crime scene. He had his shooting review board. I, on the other hand, was stuck here. I didn't trust Dahlia Wilkes not to unexpectedly drop by to make sure we were following her instructions to the letter. She was gunning for us and certainly wasn't above that. I asked Lyn Wei when her team was scheduled to go into overtime.

"Six P.M.," she said.

It was four in the afternoon, so that meant I had to cool out up here for two more hours while Hitch was doing god knows what with the Vulcuna evidence boxes.

At quarter to six, I let the team of CSIs off fifteen minutes early. The crime scene had now been shrunk to just the property. The press had moved on to sit on another fence waiting to tear the flesh off L.A.'s next juicy disaster.

We all walked down the drive and got into cars parked by the sagging wood gate. I drove down Skyline and took a left on Mulholland on my way to Sumner Hitchens's house.

According to the detective roster at Homicide Special, Sumner Hitchens lived in the hills above Nichols Canyon in an expensive L.A. development called Mount Olympus, which was only a few miles from Skyline Drive.

I found I couldn't get there from Mulholland, which was the quickest route, because the feeder road, Woodrow Wilson Drive, was torn up and blocked by sewer repair. I had to go all the way down into Hollywood and approach Mount Olympus using Laurel Canyon.

Ten minutes later, I pulled through the kitschy, ornate, Olympian-style monument that marked the main entrance.

Sumner Hitchens, Apollo of Bullshit, appropriately enough lived on Apollo Drive.

I pulled up across from a very large two-story Georgian. The front lawn was almost an eighth of an acre of beautifully manicured rolling grass. I could see the Carrera parked under the porte cochere that overhung a sweeping circular drive.

From the look of it, this place had to be worth a lot more than three million, which was the rumored number around the water-cooler at the LAPD.

I fought back a wave of jealousy, got out of the MDX and walked up the steps to the large front door. Some kind of progressive jazz was playing from a sound system inside the house.

Before I could bang the brass lion's-head knocker or ring the bell, the large oak door was opened by a barefoot African-American beauty in her midthirties, wearing cut-off jean shorts, a tie-dyed T-shirt, and a commercial-looking chef's apron.

"So you're the infamous Shane," she said, smiling.

"I must be putting off a strong vibe," I answered. "I usually have to introduce myself first."

"Hitch saw you coming. We've got video." She flicked a thumb to-ward the porch surveillance cameras. "He couldn't come out 'cause he's in the kitchen, crisping the chickens, and that's the most critical part. We're making *galletto alla piastra*. He said I should bring you back. I'm Crystal Blake."

We shook hands. She had an athlete's grace and a dancer's legs, which I couldn't help but admire as she led me into the expensively decorated entry, across a carved plush pile rug, and through a beau-tiful living room where the walls were rose and the trim white.

The furniture was eclectic and tasteful, the artwork expensive but not overdone. Hitch had obviously spent a fortune decorating.

Off to the right, through plate glass, I could see the lights of the city winking and blinking like a carpet of jewels. A big wood deck overlooked the view. I could see patio umbrellas and expensive deck chairs out there along with a king-sized Jacuzzi that was bubbling like a witch's brew.

Damn, I thought. *Maybe I should take this movie stuff a bit more seriously.*

The kitchen was big and professional. There was a center island with a huge leaded skylight overhead, burnished stainless-steel appliances, and spacious, oiled wood counters.

Hitch was in Bermuda shorts, flip-flops, and a tank top that showed he was staying in shape. He was pressing an aluminum-wrapped brick down on some filleted chickens.

"Hey, be right with you, hoss. Crys, hand me the black pepper and that dish of chopped rosemary and sage leaves."

She grabbed a huge pepper mill and a glass dish with the chopped herbs.

"This is the tricky part." He grinned. "Can't take my mitts off these little gallettos 'til they're seared."

"How'd the shooting review board go?" I asked as he cooked.

"Only took an hour. It's closed. Not even going to call you to appear. Came down as an in-policy shooting because my three shots were determined to be IDOLs." He was talking about rounds fired in immediate defense of life—mine. "Your support statement clinched it," he added, sprinkling chopped herbs on the chicken.

"This is some place," I said, trying to keep the awe out of my voice. It's one thing to hear he bought an expensive house in the Hollywood Hills, it's another to actually see it.

"Check it out, homes." He pointed at the range he was working over. "Wolfgang Puck doesn't even have one of these. Ten burners. This is the NASA Space Orbiter of commercial grills." He grabbed another brick wrapped in aluminum foil and placed it carefully on top of the other two chickens, glancing at his thirty-thousand-dollar Corum watch.

"Three minutes, we flip 'em. Hardest part is to resist the temptation to peek."

"You want them to be golden brown," Crystal said. "If you lift them and peek it ruins the color. The bricks hold them close to the grill so they'll sear, but if you go too long they burn. Whole process, both sides, takes about seven minutes."

"Crystal knows her stuff. She's the pastry chef at Lucques. You should taste her desserts. Killer."

She put an arm around him and leaned a hip into his side. They were an affectionate, attractive couple.

"I thought you were a dancer," I said. "You move like one."

"Used to be," she said, but added nothing more to that.

Seven minutes later Hitch was pulling the four spring chickens off the grill and wrapping them in a cloth, which he explained was to soak up excess marinade.

"We're also having pasta ripiena, but it's lagging a bit. Crystal, can you keep an eye on this while I fix Shane a drink?" She nodded and he turned to me. "Let's go into the other room. I'm assuming you'll stay for dinner."

"Yeah, I guess," I said. "It smells great."

He led me out of the kitchen into the large den area, where a movie poster for *Mosquito* and half a dozen framed shots showing Hitch on the set with Jamie Foxx were hung behind the wet bar.

"I called Records," I said. "I understand you took the hard-copy evidence boxes for the Vulcuna case."

"Yeah, I did. But before we go through them, you and I need to get a few things worked out."

"That was gonna be my next suggestion," I said.

"Good. What are you drinking?"

"Beer's good."

"All I got is imported lager. I got a great Paulaner from Germany, okay?"

I nodded. He uncapped two beers and handed me one. We

went out on the deck that overlooked the city. The view was price-less.

"Okay, homes," he said, "time to get a few things out in the open."

"You're right, 'cause this still isn't quite working."

"We need to make some important partnership decisions."

"Exactly. Like how we go about doing this case without losing our badges or killing each other."

"Well, that wasn't exactly what I was talking about," he said. "We got more important issues to discuss."

"What's more important than that?"

"The back end on the movie. What we will accept as our definition of net profit. How many profit points we each get, stuff like that. If we do this now, before it gets too pregnant, we'll be cool. If we wait 'til some studio dumps a bunch of cash on the table, it inevitably turns into a brawl. You should have seen the mess my homicide table at Metro got into over the profit split on *Mosquito*."

"I don't want to sell this to the movies."

"Too late. This afternoon I sketched it out to my guys at UTA, who called me back an hour ago. They already have serious interest from Spielberg, Bruckheimer, and Joel Silver. This has just become the greatest of all the Hollywood nirvanas, the Weekend Auction. That's where you have three or more prime players fighting to control a hot project before start of business on Monday.

"Each of those guys will be desperately trying to keep it from the others, driving our sales price through the roof. A high-dollar auction like this only comes along once or twice a year in Hollywood. I predict *Prostitutes' Ball* is gonna be even bigger than *Mosquito*."

He reached out and clicked my beer bottle with his.

"You're gonna be rich, dawg."

· CHAPTER ·
27

"Hitch, I really don't want to be in the movie business," I said.

"Doesn't matter. I'm selling this story whether you like it or not. I got two back-end points on *Mosquito*. My agents at UTA say, because that was such a monster hit, I should be able to negotiate seven on this. Because you're my tight and because I always take care of my posse, I'm gonna carve out two of my seven points for you. That way you'll get the same on this as I got on *my* first movie."

"I don't want movie money for doing my job."

"You can set the money on fire or give it to charity. I don't care. But that's our split, seventy-thirty."

"And I got nothing to say about whether we sell it or not? Isn't this story half mine?"

"I don't need you to sell *my* side of the story. You can't stop me, because I own the rights to my own life. You can also sell yours if you want, but you'll get bupkis because nobody in the biz has a clue who you are. With no Hollywood representation you have no path to the market."

"I don't believe this."

"Believe it. I'm gonna try and convince you not to be stupid here. Your best play is to go in with me so I can help you maximize your profit."

This was coming at me so fast I was a little stunned.

"My guys at UTA think we can get five hundred grand for the story rights, then another half mil as a production bonus when it starts shooting." He went on, "I intend to get Jamie to do this as a sequel to *Mosquito*, and if that happens we could end up making millions more on the back end. He plays me, we get Brad Pitt or some other handsome asshole to be you. If I set this up right, Brinks will back a truck up to your front door and start unloading cash."

I sat in his lush house with his midnight blue Carrera parked out front, looking at his spectacular view and getting more confused by the minute. In that second, I realized it's very hard to say no to potential millions. You like to think your knees won't buckle over money and that, on principle, you'll be true to your code, but I have to admit, I was struggling.

"The reason I'm getting five points and you're only getting two is because, in essence, you can take a ride on my past success. Because of *Mosquito*, I'll get a big piece this time and I already have killer agents to hammer the deal points. That's the only reason we don't split fifty-fifty." He was selling this hard to me. "Seventy-thirty is eminently fair."

Crystal came out of the kitchen holding a big pasta fork. "The ripiena is cooling," she said. "You guys get your business sorted out?"

"Shane is having second thoughts about selling his part of *Prostitutes' Ball*," Hitch said.

"You should do it," Crystal advised me earnestly. "There's nothing wrong with it. Hitch knows the ins and outs of Hollywood and, as he's certainly proven, selling a movie concept doesn't stop you from staying on the job and being a highly respected cop."

"Not for nothing, but Hitch is not a highly respected cop. Even though he's obviously smart as hell he's also turned himself into a joke. The sole reason for that is all this movie BS."

Hitch frowned. "That may be a little harsh, Shane. I think it's probably worth noting that jealousy can often manifest itself as sarcasm and ridicule."

"I thought we were still in Act One," I said to change the subject, trying to keep myself from taking a dive. "I thought you told me we didn't have anything until we found that big, dark, scary complication that was hiding under the surface that suddenly reared up and changed everything in Act Two."

"It's already reared, dude. Act One is the whole Vulcuna mess in eighty-one. That's why we gotta get busy and figure that out. Then our complication comes in Act Two with the whole Karel Sladky thing culminating with three new murders. Then Act Three is going to be the breathtaking resolution that brings these two murder cases together in a spectacular conclusion that nobody in the audience sees coming."

"Act Three? You mean there's more? What the hell is going to be in Act Three?"

"We ain't quite got that yet, but once we do, then all that's left is we throw in a bunch of gun-wielding assholes in a helicopter, some shoulder-mounted Stingers to give us that Michael Bay factor, and, voilà, you got yourself a hundred-million-dollar domestic gross."

I started rubbing my eyes. I wanted to say no, but damn it, a million dollars is hard to walk away from. I put that thought on hold, hoping that events would submarine this whole thing and make the decision for me.

I thought my price for selling out would have been much higher than a few measly million, or better still, perhaps even be nonexistent. Apparently I lacked that kind of principle or moral fiber. It was a moment of sad realization.

"I'm not doing this," I whimpered, but quite frankly, as I sat there listening to the bubbling Jacuzzi and the distant strains of Dave Brubeck on his jazz piano, it sounded like a feeble protest even to me.

Hitch was up here on Apollo Drive living like a god on Mount Olympus, while I was in the flatlands on Anchor Way, living like an aging cop in a developer's scaled-down version of Venice, Italy.

The twinkling lights of L.A. graced Hitch's spectacular view.

A few plastic mossy-bottom gondolas greeted mine.

Was that fair? Shouldn't I be getting more perks in life?

"I think we should stop talking about it and let it settle in your mind," Hitch said. "I'm gonna assume you'll eventually come to your senses. In the meantime, we need to flesh out Act One and get working on Vulcuna."

He got up and walked into the house, leaving me with the lovely Crystal Blake. She was still holding the long-handled pasta fork. She looked beautiful in the gentle outdoor lights spilling out from under the eaves of the overhanging roof, throwing a rose glow across the deck and her life with Hitch.

"Thanks for being his friend," she said.

"Huh?" I replied, sounding like a stoned guest at one of Brooks Dunbar's parties.

"It's hard for Sumner. He has big dreams. But underneath it all he's always striving to live up to a higher version of himself. Nobody ever gave him anything and look what he's accomplished. But despite the money and fame, he's still that little boy hiding under his uncle's car trying not to join a gang."

"So that wasn't bullshit. He really did that?"

"His big brother was killed in the gangs. It's why he decided to become a cop. He could have quit the department after *Mosquito.* Jamie Foxx wanted him to run his production company, offered him a fortune, but Sumner said no."

"I didn't know that."

She smiled and nodded. "He has the same calling in life that you do. He loves being a cop, getting justice for victims. It's just with Sumner, so much is happening on the surface, it's sometimes hard to see what's going on deep inside. If you're not paying attention, you can miss it."

Then Hitch came out carrying two large cardboard boxes. He set them down on the table next to the Jacuzzi.

"Here's the Vulcuna case. The homicide team that worked this in eighty-one was out of Hollywood Division. Norris and McKnight."

"Jack McKnight?"

"Yeah, you know him?"

"Met him once. An old patrol car gunfighter who was working Hollywood Homicide about the same time I first came on the job. They called him 'Midnight Jack McKnight' because the guy was always working a bunch of moonlighting jobs. If I remember correctly, he lives at the marina now. Retired."

Hitch pulled out the leather journal and read from it. "Marina del Ray, slip B-243."

"We should go talk to him."

"I already set up an appointment to go out there at nine thirty, after dinner," Hitch said. "Tonight's his bowling night, but he said he'd be back by then."

"You were gonna go without me?"

"Yeah," he said unabashedly. "Until you showed up, that was my plan."

He reached into the box and pulled out McKnight and Norris's old murder book. It contained all their thoughts and drawings on the case. Usually it also had duplicate crime-scene photos and autopsy shots.

I flipped through, reading notes, studying their crime-scene pencil graphs, looking for photos of the double murder/suicide. There wasn't much here.

Hitch said, "Their notes say the Luger jammed after the first shot. Vulcuna fired one to his head. It went all the way through his skull and ended up in the headboard."

"There had to be two shots because we found the other slug in the backyard," I said. I continued to flip through the book and realized there were no crime-scene or autopsy photos in here at all.

Hitch reached into the box and pulled out the Luger. It was in a plastic evidence bag. The magazine was in a separate pouch. He took an inventory sheet from the box.

"Eight-round magazine. According to this, only one was fired. We'll get ballistics to match the slug we found to this gun."

I looked in the second box, which was loaded with physical evidence—labeled Baggies with hair and fiber, bloody clothes. Then I saw an old book with an ornate spine and pulled it out.

"*The Divine Comedy*," I said, reading the cover.

"That's right," Hitch said. "By Dante Aligheri. The guy was a great Florentine poet who died in the early thirteen hundreds. *The Divine Comedy* isn't a comedy like the kind Jim Carrey makes. In Italian literature, a comedy is defined as a story that begins in sorrow and ends in joy." Hitch was proving to be well read with wide-ranging interests, yet I didn't think he ever went to college.

I was looking for the marked passage. A paper clip pinned the page. I found the underlined paragraph and read it aloud.

"'Midway upon the journey of my life, I found myself within a forest dark, for the straightforward pathway had been lost.'"

"Kapow," Hitch said. I looked up and saw that he had made a gun out of his thumb and forefinger and had pointed it at his head.

"It feels like bullshit," I said.

"Ya think?" He grinned. "I'm telling you, Shane, there is a lot more here than a double murder/suicide. When we get it all together, Act One is gonna rock. The movie producer in me feels this fact resonating in my bones."

As I was closing the book, I happened to see something written on the inside of the front cover up by the top. In light pencil script, somebody had written *San Diego*.

"San Diego?" I said.

"Vulcuna or his wife probably bought that in a used book shop. These old books go hand to hand. Very few belong to the original owners. This one was published in 1912, probably sold at a bunch of book sales over the years. One was probably down in San Diego. God knows how many people could have owned that before Vulcuna finally got it."

"I wonder where the crime-scene and autopsy pictures are?" I asked.

"Old case like this, they could be anywhere. Lost even."

I put *The Divine Comedy* back in the evidence box.

"Let's eat," he said.

The *galletto alla piastra* was delicious. The pasta ripiena was also knockout. The wine was a Louis Jadot pinot noir. For dessert, Crystal brought out two plates of tiramisu.

She set one down in front of Hitch, the other before her own place. She went back into the kitchen and returned a minute later with a small platter of brown gunk with a parsley sprig stuck on the top.

She set it carefully in front of me.

I sniffed it. Smelled like peanut butter.

"What the hell is this?" I said, peering suspiciously down at it.

"Bullshit, prepared in the French style," Hitch said, grinning.

▪ CHAPTER ▪
28

I followed Hitch's Carrera into the parking area for the B-Basin 200 Dock at Marina del Rey and parked in front of the boat ramp. As we got out of our cars, Hitch was on his phone. He walked across the pavement toward me as he yakked, then flipped the cell shut and helped me lift the two evidence boxes from my trunk.

"That was McKnight. He's on his way up to let us in."

We walked to the locked gate, which was about nine feet tall. The dock was further protected by chain-link fencing on either side of the gate.

I saw a hunched-over figure of a man moving through the pools of light that illuminated the 200 Dock. He was lumbering along, limping slightly as he made his way slowly up the ramp to where we were standing.

"Hi," he said, a little out of breath. "I'm McKnight. Which one a you guys is Hitchens?"

"That's me," Hitch said. "This is my partner, Detective Scully."

"Hang on a minute while I get this open." He fiddled with the latch and pulled the gate wide.

We shook hands, which was a little tough because Hitch and I were each carrying an evidence box.

"What's in there?" McKnight asked.

"Vulcuna," Hitch told him.

"No shit. There's an old one," he said. "Come on out to the boat, I'm fucking freezing. You get old, you're always cold."

We followed him down the ramp onto the dock. He was much thinner and frailer than I remembered. Age was slowly pulling McKnight down as if it were a gnarled hand reaching up from the grave. Back when I was in patrol he'd been one of those robust street gorillas. Brass balls, big shoulders, and plenty of attitude. McKnight was never afraid to go through a door first. He'd morphed from that kick-ass cop into a craggy, wizened old guy whose face seemed arranged in a permanent scowl.

"Watch your step," he warned as we approached his slip. "This asshole neighbor of mine never flemishes his mooring lines."

He pointed at the ropes on the neighboring dock, which secured a thirty-foot Sea Ray and looked like a plate of spaghetti. By contrast McKnight had made neat, tight spirals of his. He mounted the gangplank leading to the beautiful forty-foot Bertram Sport Fisher. The mat on the dock by the boarding steps read: COME BACK WITH A WARRANT.

"Take off your shoes," he requested as he stepped out of his. "Saves the teak from getting scuffed."

Hitch and I shucked our loafers off, left them on the dock and stepped aboard. His boat was white with blue trim and was immaculately cared for.

It was set up for deep-water game fishing with large twenty-foot outrigger poles hinged up into the air on each side of the deck house, and a deluxe fish-fighting chair with two chrome pole holders located in the center of the teak back deck. There was a big circulating salt-water bait tank aft. Painted on the stern was CODE 4—the police radio designation for an event that was over.

McKnight led us into the spacious main salon, which had deep blue carpet and rich wood cabinets. There was a fancy entertainment center with a built-in flat-screen TV and stereo across from a large sofa and two club chairs. A step-down galley was forward, adjacent to the living area. In keeping with the fishing theme, McKnight had an expensive-looking glass-topped coffee table with two Wyland-like sculptures of jumping dolphins as its base. Their arched backs held up the inch-thick glass.

We set the evidence boxes on the counter separating the salon from the galley.

"So what're you two geniuses doing with Vulcuna?" McKnight asked. "You said you wanted to talk about an old case but that fucker has a long, gray beard."

"Yeah, we know," Hitch said. "Nonetheless, we wanted to ask you about it."

"I get it now. You guys must be the dicks who caught the Skyline Drive thing. The Czech shooter who took off the two Internet whores and that movie producer."

"That's us," I said.

"According to the news that case is already with the DA."

"Right, but we have a few little details to run down," Hitch said. "Some might involve the Thomas Vulcuna case you and Norris investigated at that same house. By the way, I couldn't find an address on Ed Norris."

"Ed currently resides in a pine box underground at 1656 Forest Lawn Drive. We all get there sooner or later. He took a shortcut called too much JD on the rocks. You guys want some coffee?"

"Good," I said, and Hitch nodded in agreement.

Jack McKnight poured from a pot sitting on the warmer. As he handed us our cups he asked, "So, how can I help?"

We told him about finding the 7.65 slug in the backyard of the house and how his report stated the Luger Vulcuna used to commit the suicide also fired 7.65 ammo but had jammed after one shot, leaving the one bullet in the master bedroom but only one round missing from the gun.

"So you're wondering how that second slug ended up in the backyard when there was only one missing from the clip," McKnight said.

"That's the question." Hitch nodded.

"Maybe he test-fired it in the backyard to make sure the gun worked and then reloaded before he pulled the trigger in the bedroom," McKnight suggested.

"Maybe, but it fights Occam's razor," Hitch said.

McKnight scowled. "And just what the hell is Occam's razor?"

I was wondering the same thing when Hitch explained. "It's a basic rule of logic that states in any complex situation where nothing makes sense, if you shave the problem down to its core issues the simplest solution tends to be the correct one."

"How does that apply to this?" McKnight asked, frowning.

"I don't think a guy who's planning to off himself test-fires his gun in the backyard and then reloads it because he likes a nice, neat suicide gun with only one round missing when they find him. Makes no sense. The simpler explanation is he was shot in the backyard by an assailant and the killer reloaded the gun because the missing bullet fucks up the suicide idea."

Not bad, I thought.

McKnight frowned. He was troubled. "So you're saying he was shot in the backyard and then moved?"

Something about the way he said this told me it wasn't a new thought for him. Then he added, "You think he got moved upstairs to the master bedroom by his assailant and then the gun was reloaded and fired again, so the suicide bullet could be found in the head-board. Sounds like an episode of *Columbo.*" His expression had gone flat and was now hard for me to read.

"There were no crime-scene or autopsy photos in your murder book," I said. "How come?"

"I don't know what happened to the photos. When the case got filed, they were already missing."

"That seem strange to you?" I asked.

"Yep. I think somebody went into our desks and took the pictures. Never figured out who." He hadn't poured himself any coffee and now he stood, walked to the refrigerator, and pulled out a beer. He levered off the cap and took a swallow.

While he had his back to us, I asked, "You remember whether Thomas Vulcuna had his shoes off or on when he died?"

"They were on," he replied, as he turned. "That matter?"

"Might," I said. "Most suicides take 'em off."

"Okay," he said as he returned to the salon and faced us. "I'm gonna give you guys some very friendly advice. Your Sladky red ball is down. You did it quick so you'll get good write-ups. Do yourselves a big ca-reer solid and take a deep bow, accept your praise, but let this old Vulcuna case go. There was big energy coming down from on high to have it listed the way it was. My guess is, there are some dangerous people still around who won't appreciate your meddling. You guys could get hit by lightning."

"'Zat what you and Norris did?" Hitch asked. "You two just cut and run?"

McKnight sat down again in the empty club chair. An angry frown creased his forehead.

Then he took a swallow of his beer and told us what had really happened twenty-eight years ago.

▪ CHAPTER ▪
29

"Me and Eddie also thought the murder-suicide angle was bogus," McKnight began. "There were a lot of little things that were pointing in the other direction. Like Vulcuna killing his daughter with a fucking hammer. I don't see the guy beating her bloody like that. Everything we found out said he doted on that kid. He was devoted to her. His wife too.

"And the bullshit suicide note—the *Divine Comedy* thing. Who leaves that kind of suicide note? In my opinion, that passage was picked by somebody to make it look like he killed himself."

We were all thinking the same way.

"Then there was the bedroom where he died. Vulcuna bled all over the bed but other than that it was a very clean crime scene. Me and Norris also suspected he mighta got shot elsewhere then was moved upstairs, where he bled out. If not that, then somebody came in and cleaned up the bedroom 'cause there was no blood spatter on the headboard or wall near where he died."

"So why did you write it up as a murder-suicide?" I asked.

"We didn't. We were working it as a triple 187, and we told our supervisor, Lieutenant White in Hollywood station, that's how we saw it. Nine hours into the investigation, while we were still doing our initial evidence pull, we get called back in to see the Loo and he takes us to Parker Center. We go into the Chief of Detectives' office where we're told that the case was over and that the coroner has just ruled it a murder-suicide. We're also told that the super chief himself has taken an interest in the case and also wanted it booked as self-inflicted."

This memory troubled him. He took another pull off the bottle of beer before going on.

"There was some guy in an expensive suit standing there—a big, lean, black-haired duck with a pale complexion—looked to us like some kinda power player. He was never introduced, but me and Ed thought he was maybe from Eagle's Nest Studios or maybe even the mayor's office."

"Stender Sheedy?"

"Don't know his name. Never found out. Never saw him again. But it was real clear to us that a lot of people high up didn't want this case worked and the mayor and super chief were definitely among them. It was closed that same night and we got reassigned. There was nothing me and Ed could do about it. We weren't happy, but we moved on."

He reached into the open box containing the bloody clothing and pulled out a frilly, bloodstained blouse in a cellophane bag.

"Look at this. His daughter was wearing it. Beat the poor girl's face flat. No dad did that, 'specially one who loved his daughter like

Vulcuna did. Whoever did this didn't know that little girl. The killer was a cold-ass impersonal monster."

"So if you and Norris were right, and Vulcuna didn't kill his wife and daughter and then shoot himself, that makes this a triple murder with the killer still at large," Hitch said.

McKnight dropped the bloody blouse back into the box and then picked up the bag holding the Luger. "You're right. And you're also right about that razor thing. Guy who's about to kill himself doesn't reload after a test shot. That's fucking ridiculous."

We all sat in silence thinking about it.

"But you got almost no chance of proving what really happened," McKnight finally continued. "It was more than twenty-five years ago. Lieutenant White has gone to the angels, the old mayor and police chief are retired. Nobody will talk to you about Vulcuna. Case has frostbite."

"There's still a few things we can do now, that you and Norris didn't have available back then," I said. "Like, we could go into that house and spray the bedroom with Luminol. Doesn't matter if somebody came in later and cleaned the headboard and wall. As you know, these new forensic methods will pick up blood traces and cerebral spinal fluid in the walls and floors even after twenty-five-plus years. If Vulcuna got shot in the backyard like we think, then the bedroom won't fluoresce when we Luminol it, making his death a murder."

We all looked at one another. Finally McKnight broke the silence.

"This case has pissed me off for over a quarter century," he said. "It wasn't that me and Eddie were afraid to work it but once it was closed we had no way to proceed. If I can do anything to help you now, I'm in."

"We may need you to say some of this to our captain," I told him. "He's a straight shooter."

"You tell me when and I'll be there."

We shook hands all around and Hitch and I gathered up the evidence boxes. McKnight told us we didn't need a key to open the gate from the inside so we left him with his beer and carried the boxes up the ramp.

As we were loading them into the Acura, Hitch turned to face me. "Luminol. That's a good idea, homes."

"Then let's do it."

"How?" he said. "Stender Sheedy Sr. will fight a search warrant. If we make an illegal entry and find something that could reopen Vulcuna, we'll lose it all in court on the bad search."

"Stender Sheedy may not want us in there, but he's not the owner of the Skyline property," I said. "Neither is Thayer Dunbar. The owner of record is the Dorothy White Foundation, and if I recall, the legal proprietor and sole beneficiary is Brooks Dunbar. Let's get little Brooksie to agree to the warrant. I don't think he much cares what his father or mother think—at least not since they cut him off."

"He's a punk. I doubt he's gonna help us," Hitch said.

"I think he will. He just needs the right kind of motivation."

· CHAPTER ·
30

"I can almost promise you Brooks won't be at home after ten P.M.," Hitch said, looking at his watch. "From what I hear the kid clubs every night."

We were still standing beside our cars in the marina parking lot.

"So how do we find this little turd?" I said as I pulled the day-old arrest warrant for Brooks Dunbar out of my briefcase.

"I think I can track him down. Let's drop our cars downtown and take a slick-back. If I can find him, that black-and-white might be useful."

We left the marina and dropped our cars at the Police Administration Building. Light Santa Ana winds had started blowing, bending the tops of the palm trees with a warm desert breeze. We checked out a slick-back from the motor pool.

"Slick-back" is police slang for a black-and-white that is assigned to detectives and doesn't have a light bar on the roof, hence the name.

I drove the D-ride up the ramp and onto the city streets with Hitch in the passenger seat beside me.

"Let's start with the Ivy," Hitch said.

"He's at the Ivy?" I asked.

"Not as far as I know."

"Then why are we going there?"

"Watch and be amazed," he replied.

We headed toward Sunset and then to the Ivy on Robertson. It was after eleven P.M., but the restaurant was packed. About forty paparazzi were camped out across the street, their Nikon digital cameras at the ready.

We pulled up and got out of the car. As soon as Hitch was visible, a lot of the photographers started snapping his picture and calling his name.

"If we end up in *People* magazine over this, I'll kill you," I growled.

"Don't worry. I'm in the wrong age demo for *People*. They only want eighteen to twenty-four unless your name's Obama or you're a middle-aged actor who's beating the shit out of his girlfriend. These guys like me. They only take my picture so I won't feel left out."

Hitch told the valet we'd just be a minute and to leave our ride at the curb. The red coat reluctantly pulled the black-and-white up and parked it next to the valet stand where, immediately, it began to draw nervous looks from the patio tables, soiling the trendy ambience of the posh Westside restaurant.

Hitch walked across the street to the crowd of scruffy-looking photographers. I had no idea what he was up to, but followed.

Paparazzi are the tree squirrels of celebrity journalism. The guys were mostly wide bodies with plumber butts. The girls had stringy hair and bad complexions. They were nocturnal animals who surged around West L.A. like schooling fish, always hunting for the action with Vitaminwater and protein bars stuffed in their pockets.

"Hey guys, anybody see Brooks Dunbar lately?" Hitch called out.

"He was trying to get into Club Nine about an hour ago," one of the scruffy guys said. "But he owes that place a fortune, so they probably didn't let him past the rope."

"If you can scare him up for me, then the next time I'm with Jamie, I'll slow my man down so you can get some shots."

"Solid," several of them said as they flipped open cell phones and started calling other paparazzi around Hollywood.

"Got him," a tall, hefty girl wearing low-rider jeans said. "The Cottonwood on Melrose. He just got there but he's never in one place long, so you better hurry."

"Thanks, Julie. I owe ya." Catcalls and "See ya's" followed us back to our car.

"Not bad," I said. "Definitely a fresh way to do it."

I slid behind the wheel of the slick-back and we headed toward the Cottonwood Club on Melrose.

We got there just in time because as I pulled in, the Heir Abhorrent and his posse of hangers-on were already being escorted out of the club by a bouncer who was roughly the size of an old Wurlitzer jukebox. Brooks was screaming insults at this monster.

"You assholes overcharged my AmEx! I'm not paying you a fucking dollar until you make it right!"

He was trailed by his drugged entourage; two guys and four girls, all bone-thin losers. The bouncer shoved him to the curb and went back inside. Brooks then turned his ire on the circling pack of flashbulb-popping paparazzi.

"Eat my crotch, you shitsticks!" He flipped them off. He climbed to his feet as his friends all giggled. The photographers scuttled along behind this band of unruly brats who loved the fact that they were being chased by a pack of Hollywood photographers, while all the time pretending to be very pissed off about it.

"You fucking assholes need to get a real job!" Brooks, who had never had one, yelled.

Hitch and I cut them off. I grabbed Dunbar by the arm and shoved the arrest warrant in his face. Cameras flashed.

"You are under arrest for failure to appear as a material witness in a murder investigation."

We cuffed him and Mirandized him while the pack of teenagers and paparazzi looked on.

"Leave my mate be!" the Aussie girl I recognized from his Christmas party yelled.

We ignored her and shoved Brooks into the back of the car as the photographers circled, gunning off shots with the Cottonwood Club in the background. The tabloid headline over these photos would undoubtedly be something cute like "Heir Abhorrent Errs."

Our detective car had the desired effect.

"Am I being arrested?" Brooks said, suddenly aware of his predicament. "Whatta you doin'? I don't like this. I wanna leave." He was protesting loudly as we drove away.

Men's Central Jail is no damn fun at all. Especially if you're a pudgy white guy wearing a T-shirt that says EAT SHIT AND DIE MOTHER-FUCKER.

Despite his drug history, according to his yellow sheet Brooks Dunbar had never actually landed there before, having successfully used money and privilege to beat two possession beefs and one indecent exposure where he'd mooned sorority row at USC from the passenger seat of his dad's Ferrari.

Fifteen minutes later we were in the booking cage at the City Jail.

"For now he's being booked as a material witness on a seventy-two-hour hold," I told the sergeant in charge as I filled out the paperwork. "Put this guy in a dorm on the second floor."

The sergeant ran the night shift at MCJ and started processing my paperwork. I wanted Brooks in a group cell so he could experience the full ambience of our facility.

"You can't do this!" he shrieked, standing in the center of an outlined box painted on the floor while his picture was snapped. He looked terrible. His hair was mussed and his eyes bleary. I thought if it were ever published, this shot would live in perpetuity on the Internet.

"I can't stay here!" Brooks wailed.

I didn't blame him. The jail was a foreboding place with sliding metal doors, chipped yellow paint, and the faint smell of vomit mixed with desperation.

"I warned you, Brooks. You should've come to my office when you had the chance. Now we do it this way."

After he was processed Hitch and I left him with the booking sergeant and went to a restaurant across the street to get a cup of coffee. As we walked, I could feel the Santa Anas growing in strength. The trees on Bauchet Street were beginning to rustle in the desert wind. We went into the coffee shop and took a booth. After the waitress poured, we sat back and pondered our options.

"How long you want to keep him up there?" Hitch asked.

"He's not very tough. An hour ought to do it. We also need to get an ADA to chase us down a broad search warrant for both the house and yard at Skyline Drive. We need somebody who won't give us up if the pressure builds."

"I got just the one." Hitch smiled. "Frieda Wilson. She's been on the DA's staff for a year and she's got a huge case on the Hitchmeister."

An arrogant remark, but somehow Sumner Hitchens had the charm to get away with it. He dialed a number, then turned away and had a quiet conversation on his phone with someone, which included some whispered nuances before he finally disconnected.

"Frieda has a judge who will write it blind if she promises not to release the warrant without signed authorization from the primary property owner, which would be our man, Brooks. She said she'd be here in an hour."

"That works."

After three quarters of an hour had passed I said, "Let's see if Brooks feels any better about cooperating with our investigation now."

We went back over to the PAB and checked in with the booking sergeant, who told us he'd put Brooks into 2-15, an Eme gang car on the second floor.

I wanted him in a group cell but I wasn't sure he should be put into a cell with a bunch of Mexican Mafia. We followed the sergeant quickly into the elevator and rode up. As soon as I stepped out into the cell block, I could hear Brooks whining or whimpering. When we rounded the corner on our way to 2-15, we heard a slap followed by a squeal.

"Leave me alone. Please!" Brooks pleaded. "I can pay you money. My dad's a billionaire." Something you probably don't want to confide to a cell full of extortionists.

We stepped in front of the barred door and saw Brooks against the wall, surrounded by three Hispanic bangers, each with a large "18" tattooed on the back of his neck, indicating they were from the Mexican Mafia's hardened 18th Street gang.

"Hey *ese*, ease up. Don't go committing no assault on my arrestee," Hitch said sharply.

The gangbangers turned away from Brooks as the sergeant from the booking cage pulled out his keys and let the terrified Heir Abhorrent out.

Once he was in the corridor I saw he had a puffed lip from getting smacked around. Tears were wet on his cheeks.

Hitch and I led him into one of the I-rooms off the jail corridor and closed the door behind us. I took out my cuffs, and for effect, locked him to the ring on the table.

"What are you doing? What're you doing?" he squealed hysterically, pulling back. But once chained up, he wasn't going anywhere.

"How come you didn't come to my office?" I began. "You need to give me a good reason."

"Be . . . be . . . because," he stammered.

Hitch leaned forward. "Because is not a reason. We're looking for an action word here, Brooks. 'Because' is a conjunction."

"I had things to do."

"So, for no stated reason, you hampered and delayed our triple homicide investigation, keeping us from doing our job?" I said. "Don't you want us to solve this? You aren't somehow involved, are you?"

"No! Of course not. How could I be involved? I have an alibi. I was at my Christmas party. You already know that. And of course I want you to do your job." Brooks sniffled. "I'm very pro-police."

"Doesn't seem that way," Hitch said.

"I am, I really am!" he pleaded.

"How are you getting along with Stender Sheedy Senior?" I asked, abruptly changing the subject.

Now real anger flared. "I hate that fucker. He works for my father. Asshole made me fly all the way back from Amsterdam once 'cause he needed my signature on some stupid document that needed to be notarized."

"How 'bout Junior?"

"Sten is okay. He's a tight-ass, but he gets me stuff."

"Those two haven't exactly been helping me and my partner either," I said.

"Nope," Hitch agreed. "Makes us want to take it out on somebody.

Since you're handy I'm thinking we should park you in this jail 'til like, say, Easter. How's that sound?"

"No! No, please! Please don't!" he wailed. "Whatever the problem is, I can fix it, but you've got to let me outta here tonight. Those guys in that cell scare the shit outta me."

"Maybe you should stop wearing T-shirts that insult people," Hitch suggested.

"I'm not so sure we can just fix this," I said. "This isn't the Bel Air Country Club. You're not in here for throwing up in the pool. This is a triple homicide. Took place on your property. Until you convince us otherwise, we gotta assume you're part of it."

"I'm not! I promise you. What do you need? I'll do anything. Please!"

He was leaning forward. Tears again began to well in his eyes.

"I don't know." I looked over at Hitch. "What do you want to do?"

"I don't know," he said in deep theatrical thought. "I'm torn."

"Me too."

"Please! Just tell me what you want. I'll do anything. Just tell me. Whatever it is, I'll make sure it's done," Brooks whimpered.

"Okay," I said, rubbing my chin. "So here's the problem. In order for us to clear you, we need to make sure none of your DNA is on that crime scene."

"I wasn't there," he said. "How could my DNA be there if I wasn't?"

"You say you weren't there but you haven't been too honest with us up 'til now," I reminded him. "Like we know you met with Yolanda Dublin up on Skyline Drive to get her money, but you said you never go there. That was a lie. We lose trust when people lie. When trust is lost it's almost impossible to earn it back again."

"I just said that to you so my dad wouldn't find out I was renting that backyard to people. And I didn't exactly go *up* there. Sten showed her the property. I met her on Skyline Drive a day later and she paid me. We were out front standing in the street. I never even went up the drive."

Hitch thought about it, then pretended to have an idea. "Hey, if that's true, what if we go back there with a spit kit and check the house and the backyard for Brooks's DNA. If all he did was stand in the street and get her money, then his DNA won't be on the crime scene and we can cut him loose."

"'Cept we don't have a search warrant," I replied, furrowing my brow. Of course, all of this was patently ridiculous, but it was working because Brooks had a panicked look on his face.

"We'd need the owner's permission to go in there looking for the DNA," I continued. "Sheedy won't give it, so that's just gonna end up being a huge unproductive hassle."

"I have complete ownership of that property, not Sheedy," Brooks said, lunging at the idea. "I sign papers all the time on that place. For taxes and all kinds of shit. I can give the permission."

"I don't know," Hitch said, looking at me. "It's pretty late in the case now for that. Maybe we should just keep him here and sort it out later."

"No! Please. No! I'll sign it. I will." He was almost shrieking at us.

"We gotta think about it," I said. "Don't go anywhere."

We walked out of the room, leaving him chained to the table. Hitch notified the jail guard that our wit was to be detained in the I-room, and not put back in 2-15. We wanted to scare him, but we didn't want him killed.

Then we went to the lobby of the jail to wait for Frieda Wilson from the ADA's office.

She arrived twenty minutes later with our warrant and turned out to be another fox with great legs, wearing a very short skirt. The warrant she brought us was extensive. This one included both the house and the yard. There was a place for Brooks Dunbar to sign, granting us permission to search the premises.

"You're the best," Hitch told Frieda, who smiled longingly at him before she left.

The two of us went back upstairs to the jail. Brooks was crying softly when we walked back into the I-room.

Hopefully, this had been an eye-opening, life-changing experience for him.

"You left me. I was so scared you weren't coming back," he cried.

Hitch and I sat down facing him. "Here's the deal," I said. "You sign this and maybe . . . *maybe* we let you go home tonight."

"I'll sign. I'll sign."

"Since this is a sensitive case with a lot of media overtones, you better damn well keep this to yourself," I added. "You tell anyone and we slam you back in here."

"I promise," he said. "I won't tell anyone. Where do I sign?"

"Right here." I handed him my ballpoint. "Two copies. You keep the bottom one."

He signed without even reading.

▪ CHAPTER ▪
31

By the time we stepped outside the Men's Central Jail with Brooks it was after one A.M. The temperature was hovering in the low seventies and the Santa Ana wind condition had fully developed. Santa Anas clear the L.A. basin of pollutants, but they also drive up the pollen count and Claritin sales throughout the city.

As it turned out, Brooks had allergies, so as soon as we got outside he started sneezing. "You just gonna leave me here?" he whined, wiping his nose with his forearm after a big wet one. "Aren't you even gonna take me home?"

"We don't run a taxi service," Hitch said.

"Then how'm I s'posed to get there?" Another sneeze.

Hitch pointed at Brooks's four-hundred-dollar Gucci sneakers, which, miraculously, he'd not lost to his murderous cellmates. "The left one goes in front of the right one," Sumner said patiently. "If you keep repeating the process, you'll be doing something we call walking. Should get you home."

"Here's your copy of our permission to search Skyline Drive," I said, handing him the paper. "Do not talk about this to anyone."

He nodded, then sneezed again.

"You're just gonna leave me here?"

"That's the plan," I answered.

We got into the slick-back and left him standing there, wobbly and confused as a day-old changeling.

Hitch and I headed back to the crime scene. On the way, we stopped at the CSI equipment warehouse at the new forsensic lab at Cal State L.A. where we checked out a fire extinguisher–sized canister of Luminol spray with a nozzle.

As I signed for the stuff, I couldn't help but think about the paper trail I was leaving for Dahlia Wilkes. I pushed that troubling thought aside and in minutes we were again in the slick-back, heading to the Hollywood Hills.

When we arrived at the mansion, it was almost two A.M. We parked our black-and-white in the bushes off the road, then grabbed our equipment and briefcases and snuck up the driveway, through the main gate, and around to the far side of the house, where we wouldn't be visible from the Prentiss's second-floor windows.

The twenty-foot cypress trees in the yard swayed in the brisk Santa Anas over our heads, shaking their leaves like giant pom-poms. We paused at the back door and looked down at the big, commercial-sized Yale padlock.

"Shoulda brought some bolt cutters," Hitch said, studying the padlock. "We'll have to break a window."

"I'm not breaking a window," I answered. "If we don't find any-thing, I want to back out of here without leaving a trail. I'm still hop-ing this doesn't draw too much negative official interest."

"Including your wife's," Hitch said.

I hate keeping stuff from Alexa. Even when I was skating the edges of the rule book, I always eventually told her what I was doing be-cause she's the smartest cop I know and one of my best crime-solving resources. But there was no way Hitch could appreciate that, and since we were taking some career chances, I decided for the time be-ing to continue to honor my promise.

"Okay, okay. I won't tell her without at least talking it over with you first."

"Some vow of silence," he muttered. "How you planning to get inside if we don't break a window?"

I reached into my pocket and removed my little leather lock pick case. It's no bigger than a small manicure kit. I'd learned to pick locks from one of my training partners almost twenty years ago. It's actually not too difficult once you get the hang of it.

I unwrapped the leather case and pulled out the main pick. It was longer and thicker than the other ones and had a small right angle at the very end. Then I removed half a dozen shorter, thinner picks, each with a variety of different shaped bends at the end.

The idea was to slip the main pick into the guide slot, then jiggle it until it found the main tumbler. The smaller ones then slid in un-der it, fitting into the secondary tumblers, until you had enough trac-tion to turn the lock. There are easier, more high-tech ways to open locks, such as master tap keys or electric magnets. This was admit-tedly a little old school, but I liked the fact it took some skill and that I had mastered it.

"Shine your Mini Mag on this," I said, and Hitch aimed the small LED at the lock while I worked.

It took me about two and a half minutes before I had the padlock open.

"When we do the movie, I think the Hitchens character should work the lock pick and the Scully character should hold the light," he said. "Those picks are way cool. It's exactly the kind of thing Jamie digs in a film."

I was still fighting the idea there was going to be a film, so I just let that go and pushed the door open. We stepped inside and closed it quietly behind us.

The house was dark and creepy. We stood in the back pantry and listened to the mansion creak and groan in the growing wind.

I saw a documentary once about a bunch of little birds in the Amazon who have this unique relationship with the river crocodiles who live and hunt along the banks of that mammoth river. Part of the film told how sometimes, when a croc had meat stuck in the back of his mouth, he would open it for one of the little birds to hop inside. The bird would then stand on the huge reptile's tongue and feed himself by cleaning the croc's sharp, deadly teeth. The narrator called it an extraordinary act of synergy and trust. I remember thinking there had to be a better way for those little birds to feed themselves. To me, it just seemed stupid.

As I stood in the back pantry of that creaking, windblown mansion, I felt just like one of those little birds.

One snap and a crunch from oblivion.

▪ CHAPTER ▪
32

We left the large canister of Luminol inside the back door because it was too heavy to lug around, and took a slow walk through the downstairs, leaving our telltale footprints in the dust. I entered the solarium, and walked over to the curved windows to look out at the pool house, where the triple murder had occurred just days earlier. But tonight I was here to look at a completely different crime, one that had happened nearly thirty years ago.

I turned and saw a series of framed photographs on the far wall that looked like an exhibit of some kind. Hitch and I walked over and examined them. A wide framed placard above the shots said the mansion had been designated as a California landmark house in 1980. Since certification, no renovations other than standard maintenance had occurred to the historical structure. Prior to that freeze, previous

owners had photographed the different stages of the home's development and those shots were displayed on the wall.

It had always been a magnificent house, but when first built, it was
considerably smaller. There was a pool, but no pool house. In a photo
dated 1928, a big ugly-looking concrete building with a metal door
and a pitched roof was shown at the side of the house near where the
trash area now was.

"What the hell is that?" Hitch said, studying the shot.

"Some kind of poured-concrete one-car garage," I said. "Kinda
ugly. Musta been torn down during one of the renovations before this
became a landmark house."

There were other pre-1980 renovations displayed in the photographs. The solarium was a '60s addition, as was the pool house.
A second floor had been added on the east wing in '76.

Something heavy fell over and crashed upstairs.

We both froze.

"What's that?" Hitch whispered.

My heart was pounding. I could hear nothing but the Santa Anas
rattling the windows and blowing the branches of a large elm into the
roof on the east side of the house.

"It's nothing but the wind," I said, not exactly believing it.

Then we heard scratching.

"Rats," I said softly, under my breath.

"Rat must be on steroids," Hitch whispered. "Whatever's doing
that is big."

We now heard something moving upstairs, followed by some kind
of clawing, dragging sound.

"Thomas Vulcuna's ghost coming to get us?" I said, half in jest.

"Don't joke about shit like that," he hissed.

Hitch definitely seemed to be worried about a poltergeist factor.
Then I remembered him saying, "I don't get along with dead people,

they don't get along with me." Was it possible my new homicide partner believed in ghosts?

We listened in silence for almost a minute. When it didn't recur, I figured it was rodents. "See? Nothing," I said.

We moved cautiously into the living room, where I looked at the old, dusty Christmas tree and the twenty or so unopened presents.

"Let's see where the two Vulcuna women got killed," I said. "According to Norris and McKnight's murder book, the bodies were found over by the fireplace."

I went into the back porch area, grabbed the metal spray canister, returned to the living room, and pumped up the pressure. Then I aimed the nozzle at the fireplace area, wetting down the floor in front of the hearth.

It immediately lit up like a truck stop diner.

"Look at that," Hitch said softly.

Even though it had been a quarter century since the murders had occurred, we could see the outlines of both bodies in the Luminol's fluorescent glow. One had died over by the hearth, the other was farther out in the room, perpendicular to the fireplace. The women had bled profusely. Blood had collected around them, but not under them, leaving form impressions outlining where they fell.

"They were definitely killed in here," Hitch whispered softly, then added, "by the way, if we get Jamie to do this movie I think he should spray the Luminol."

"Yeah, you're right. Scully would be huddled over in the corner, shitting his pants."

Another clawing sound came from upstairs.

"There it is again!" Hitch whispered in fright, looking up at the ceiling.

I had to admit, it didn't quite sound like a rat. It sounded much bigger.

"I'm gonna unpack," Hitch said, pulling out his sidearm.

"This house is empty," I assured him. But because fear is even more contagious than a yawn, I pulled the Springfield from my belt holster.

"You wanta go up and check it out?" Hitch asked. "I'll cover you from down here."

"Don't you think Jamie would want the Hitchens character to man up and do the ghost check?" I whispered back.

"No," he said adamantly.

"Come on, numbnuts. Let's clear this fucking house."

We climbed the staircase. I took the lead with Hitch close behind me like a Marx brother in a forties comedy. Each stair seemed to creak louder than the last. Halfway to the landing we heard a frenzy of motion.

A lamp broke.

Glass shattered.

My heart leapt up into my throat. When I turned, Hitch was already back downstairs, standing by the front door, gun up in a shooting stance.

"If it's a ghost, that gun won't help you." I motioned for him to follow me up. "Come on, or you're not my partner anymore."

Reluctantly he rejoined me.

We finally got to the landing on the second floor. The walls were covered in some kind of old red flocked wallpaper. The floors were wood and creaked as we moved slowly and deliberately toward the master suite, where in 1981 Tom Vulcuna was supposed to have taken his life after killing his family.

As we approached the room, I had both my gun and my Mini Maglite out, pointing them at the threshold.

Then I saw a pair of yellow eyes shining brightly over by the window.

I swung the light and caught a huge raccoon in its beam.

It was the size of a fat beagle.

It screamed at us, then turned, raced along next to the floorboards, and jumped up on an old dresser, knocking a porcelain bowl over in the process before disappearing into the open heating duct.

The bowl, which was still teetering, suddenly fell and broke on the floor.

My heart was pounding even harder. Hitch's breath hissed out through his mouth.

It took us both almost a full two minutes to calm down.

"I think we should leave this out of the movie," I suggested.

"Solid," he replied.

· CHAPTER ·
33

After the raccoon vacated I went back downstairs and retrieved the canister of Luminol. Then we sprayed the bedroom.

Nothing fluoresced.

The bed linens and mattress had been removed and the box spring didn't glow. But the important fact was the headboard with the bullet hole also showed no sign of blood or CFS splatter. Neither did the wall behind it.

"Vulcuna wasn't killed in this room," I said and Hitch nodded.

I saw a color picture in a silver frame on the dresser so I walked over and picked it up.

The photo was of the Vulcuna family, done in studio by a professional photographer who had used a draped multicolor sheet as his background. They were a nice-looking family. Thomas was a handsome, middle-aged man with salt-and-pepper hair and a prominent chin. He was looking into the lens, his eyes projecting pride in his wife and daughter. Elizabeth was a fragile forty-five-year-old beauty with a long neck and wistful smile. The real looker, however, was their young daughter, Victoria. She had long dark hair and almost perfect features.

Somehow, seeing them made this cold case investigation more relevant. I now had a mental image of the family for whom I was attempting to seek justice. I carefully set the picture back down.

"I'm about ready to get out of here," Hitch whispered. "Let's go think this out in a crowded bar someplace."

"I want to open a few of those presents downstairs first."

"Why?"

"'Cause I had a shitty Christmas and maybe I'll like something," I said sarcastically.

"I want to go now," Hitch persisted.

"And I want to see what these people were giving each other for Christmas. Norris and McKnight got pulled from this case before they could fully investigate it. That's something you know they would've done."

Hitch followed me downstairs and I started with the presents marked to Victoria from her dad. The notes inside the cards were sweet. It was obvious that Thomas Vulcuna had cherished his eighteen-year-old daughter.

One read:

Dear beautiful Victoria,
   As you grow, you make your dad prouder with each day.
   Nothing in my life equals the joy you have brought me.

I hope you still like this necklace. You admired it in New York, so I snuck back and bought it for you.
    Merry Christmas, darling,
    Poppie

I handed the card to Hitch, who took it and read it carefully. After he was through, he said, "This guy didn't beat his daughter to death with a damn hammer."

I didn't think so either.

There were lots of presents to his wife, Elizabeth. One box contained a flimsy negligee and a note that said:

Open after Christmas—right after.
    —Tommy

More notes and cards to Vulcuna's wife and daughter followed. Each one was loving, all of them written in his neat, careful hand.

I looked up from my unwrapping project and saw that Hitch had gone wandering. I found him in the library looking at the Vulcunas' book collection.

"What are you doing?"

"You can tell a lot about people by looking at the books they read."

He began reciting titles. "Jacqueline Susann—*Valley of the Dolls*, Stephen King—*The Stand*, Jackie Collins—*Lovers and Gamblers*. The Vulcunas were populists."

"And that's unusual?"

"Where's the Shakespeare, the Chaucer, the Beowulf? This guy chooses *The Divine Comedy* to leave as a suicide note, yet there's not one piece of classic literature in here."

"Good get, homes."

Then he said, "I don't want you to think I'm scared, and in the movie, Hitch would stay all night if need be, but I really think we're done here. Okay?"

"I want to check one more thing," I said. "Let's Luminal the area out back where we found the 7.65 slug. That's probably where Thomas Vulcuna was actually killed."

"We aren't going to find anything with Luminol out there," Hitch said. "It happened over twenty-five years ago. If he was killed by the side of the house, the rain and weather has long ago washed all the blood evidence away."

"What about the trash shed? It's wood. Wood is porous."

"Okay," he sighed reluctantly.

We backed out of the house, relocked the padlock, and headed around the side to the trash area.

The wooden shed had an overhanging roof covering two new Dumpsters. I went inside and sprayed the area. The low glow of blood suddenly fluoresced everywhere. It was much fainter on the walls of the trash shed than it was in the living room, because, as Hitch said, over the years, weather had diluted the blood. But it had seeped into the wood out here in '81 and had managed to remain for the intervening quarter century.

"This is where Vulcuna got it," Hitch stated.

As we were leaving, I walked around the side of the trash area and caught a glint of something metal in the beam of my flashlight coming from behind the holly bushes that were planted there. I pushed the thorny growth aside, carefully threading my arm through the brambles. About two feet in, I touched cold metal.

"There's something back here," I called softly to Hitch. "Get the leaf strainer pole. It's lying by the side of the pool house."

A minute later Hitch came back with the long-handled pool net. I turned it around and poked the pole's handle into the holly bush.

Something very large and metallic was hiding back there. I probed several other spots and hit the same metal object.

"What the hell?" Hitch said.

"Let's cut these bushes back," I suggested.

We went in search of the gardener's shed, which was on the north side of the house in the back. The door was locked, but I had it open in a minute with my trusty set of picks.

Inside we found some long-handled hedge clippers and gloves. We returned to the trash area and began cutting away the holly bush. It took us almost half an hour.

When we finally had it cut back, we were looking at an anodized metal door that had been painted silver. It was on the front of a poured-concrete building the size of a one-car garage.

I realized that this was the structure we'd seen in the old photos hanging in the solarium. There was a raised metal plate on the locked door and I leaned forward to read it in the dim light. It said:

DEPARTMENT OF WATER AND POWER
1928

▪ CHAPTER ▪
34

"What is it?" Hitch said, crowding in to look over my shoulder.

"DWP seal."

"The electrical panel? Shouldn't it be against the side of the house? Why would they put it way out here?"

"They wouldn't."

I was beginning to remember where I'd seen one of these poured-concrete garages before. It was at an old turn-of-the-century house I'd visited at a party up in the Malibu Mountains a few years back.

"You know what I think this is?" I said.

"What?"

"This garage is covering an old water well. I've seen one of these before."

"A well. Why would they need a well?" Hitch asked.

"This house was built in 1908 and back then they didn't have an extensive water system in L.A. That was before the Owens Valley project. These old houses were built way before the water mains were installed up here. The owners would pay DWP to drill down to the water table and install these private wells. After the water mains were put into service, the private wells were decommissioned."

"So what's the garage for?"

"The guy who owned the house where I saw one of these told me you can't fill in a water well because it connects to an underground aquifer and whatever you pour down the well to fill it in just gets washed away."

"So they capped it, right?"

"Right, but the problem with that is vandals kept pulling the caps off. My friend told me in the mid or late twenties one or two kids fell down these old wells and died. DWP got sued, so they built these concrete garages and locked them shut to protect the wellcaps from vandals."

"Okay, so it's nothing, then," he reasoned. "It got planted out because it was ugly."

"Yeah," I said. "Probably."

But as I was turning to go, I started thinking that holly was a strange choice for that job. There were better and cheaper ground covers. Then I remembered that holly was often used by people who lived in areas where city-use ordinances prohibited high fences. If home owners wanted to secure their property, but couldn't because the city limited fence height to four feet, they often planted holly bushes, which reached ten or twelve feet high. Holly also has plentiful inch-long spike-like thorns. It was an effective barrier and a deterrent to prowlers.

I started to wonder if it was just a coincidence that the well house had been planted out with holly, or had someone, like Stender

Sheedy and Thayer Dunbar, not wanted this structure messed with like they didn't want anyone messing with the house?

"Let's open this thing up," I said.

"Why?

"Let's just do it."

I looked at the door clasp. It was held shut by a heavy chain with no lock. The chain had been welded to itself.

"Hang on," I said. "I'll be right back."

I ran to our D-ride parked down the street in the bushes, opened the trunk, and pulled out the jack handle. Then I ran back up the hill. By the time I got there Hitch had pulled the welded chain out as far as it would go.

"Okay, stand back."

I slipped the jack handle through the small loop he had created with the chain and tried to use its two-foot-long leverage to apply enough force to snap a link. It didn't yield.

"Grab on to this," I said. "Give me a hand."

We both hung on to the jack handle and put all our weight into it. After about two minutes of bouncing, one of the links finally broke and Hitch and I landed in the thornbush we'd just cut down from the front of the metal door.

"This better be worth it," Hitch growled, picking a painful-looking thorn from his palm.

We got up and pulled off the chain. Then we both yanked on the metal door. The hinges were rusted and the door was heavy, making it extremely tough to move. We managed to force it open wide enough to slip through. Musty air poured out of the crack and greeted us as we turned on our flashlights, both took a deep breath, and slipped inside.

The first thing I saw in the gloom was a large, boxy shape. I shined my light on it. It was a massive square object of some kind with a rotting tarp slung over it. The thing was sitting in the center of the rectangular space.

Hitch and I pulled off the canvas. Once it was removed, it revealed a thirty-year-old box-back armored truck. The faded red letters on the side read:

BRINKS
MONEY & VALUABLES, SAFETY & DISPATCH

"Damn. Look at this," Hitch said softly.

We moved around the truck. The tires were all flat from years of sitting here. Hitch climbed up on the running board and shined his light inside the cab.

"Auugh!" he screamed, and jumped back, almost falling down.

I moved up and shined my light where he had just been looking.

Staring back at me were two empty eye sockets and a bone white skull. A full skeleton was slumped over the wheel, its missing eyes turned to look out the window. All of the flesh had rotted away. A Brinks uniform hung on the bones like a scarecrow's clothing. In the passenger seat was another skeleton. This one was slumped against the passenger door, its uniform also in shreds. Bugs and bacteria had managed to get inside and do their work. Over the years, both guards had been eaten to the bone.

Hitch and I stumbled from the concrete structure and stood outside trying to deal with what we'd just discovered.

For almost two minutes, neither of us spoke. Once Hitch regained his composure, he looked over at me, pale but intense in the moonlight. His exact expression was hard to assess. There was excitement there, even avarice, but mostly he just seemed very happy.

"I told you once we got it worked out, the first act would be killer. In case you missed it, this is the rest of the big dark secret that was lying under Act One. It just exploded to the surface, changing every-thing."

"Huh?" I said, sounding like a Dunbar party guest.

"This is what we've been praying for, dummy. It's our major com-plication in Act Two."

Ten minutes later Hitch and I were sitting in the front seat of our slick-back, arguing about what to do next.

"We gotta take this to Jeb," I said.

"Forgetting the Permission to Search we got from Brooks, which I'm not even sure is completely valid, 'cause he was stoned; if our bosses find out we came up here to work on a whole second homicide without telling anyone what we were doing, we're capital-F fucked. The department will give us the grand tour, with that all-important career-ending last stop at Internal Affairs."

"But how can we sit on this?" I asked. "We got dead bodies stacking up like cordwood. These two have probably been in that truck since Thomas Vulcuna's death in eighty-one. They're probably part of the motive for his murder."

"I know. I know. Shit. Cool as this is movie-wise, if we divulge it to our bosses, we're gonna get sacrificed. We should've never come up here. Let's just think this out for a minute. Maybe there's another way to go."

"Look, Hitch. Even if we wanted to, we couldn't button up and walk away. Besides, since we've cut down that berry bush, somebody's gonna find that garage and truck tomorrow anyway. We gotta deal with this."

"I know."

"If you don't want to go to Jeb, then I say we start with Alexa."

"No."

"She's a good street cop. She thinks like a cop, not a suit. She'll understand why we went after this. Especially once Dahlia told us to take the 7.65 slug off our evidence sheet."

"Are you *nuts*? She's the head of the Detective Bureau."

"She's also my wife and a primary responder on the Sladky murder. We're gonna eventually have to tell Jeb too, so let's just get it over with and call them both. I don't see any way around it."

"A lot of people don't believe this, but I really love this job," he said. "I don't want to end my career on the LAPD with a blindfold and a cigarette."

"We'll get through it. Stick with me, here. I've been in tighter spots."

I took out my cell and dialed Alexa. It was after three A.M. but she was still in her office at the PAB.

"Why aren't you in bed?" she asked.

"I'm up at the house on Skyline Drive with Hitch. You need to collect Jeb and get up here now."

"What's up?"

"Plenty. Just get up here. I'd rather show you than tell you."

We spent a tough hour waiting for Alexa and Jeb, while we worked out our plan of attack and a few of our arguments. Captain Calloway arrived first.

"This better be either great or really, really good," Jeb said as he pulled in. He'd thrown on an old LAPD sweatshirt, jeans, and flip-flops.

"I'll let you assign the degree of greatness," I told him.

Alexa drove up a couple of minutes later and Hitch and I led them up the hill to the concrete well house. We had left the door ajar.

"Get ready for a shock," I advised as we accompanied them inside. Hitch and I turned on our flashlights, illuminating the Brinks truck for them.

"Drivers are still inside. Dead," I said. "Take a deep breath, 'cause it ain't pretty."

Both of them looked through the truck's windows at the skeletons. Alexa said nothing, but as Jeb looked, I could see he was breathing through his mouth and swallowing air. I cut him some slack though because he was born in Haiti where they still practice voodoo. When they finished, everyone backed out and we all stood outside.

"That truck is old," I said. "Late seventies or early eighties."

"I'll bet it's the armored car that disappeared off Wilshire Boulevard in eighty-three," Jeb said. "It was carrying something like fifteen or sixteen million in gold bullion from the Jewelry Mart. Case is still open, but very cold."

"It's still open?" I said for no other reason than to slow this down a little. I was getting overrun by events.

"Everybody thought the guards pulled the heist and escaped to Tahiti or someplace, to live the good life," Jeb explained. "Apparently not. I'll run the plate to confirm it, but I'm sure this is it."

"How did you find that garage?" Alexa asked. "I didn't see it before."

"You want to tell 'em?" I asked my partner.

"You can do it," Hitch replied.

"We found this because we were working an old double murder/ suicide from 1981. The Vulcuna family used to own this house in the eighties. The father was supposed to have killed his wife and daughter, then shot himself," I began. "Instead of working on closing loose ends for ADA Wilkes on Sladky, we were working that old double murder/suicide instead. We don't think Thomas Vulcuna was the doer. We think he was murdered too, shot back here. That's where the 7.65 slug came from. I'm really sorry about this, but cutting to the chase, I guess we were disobeying Jeb's direct orders."

"That may be an overly harsh assessment," Hitch jumped in, trying to massage it. Then the bullshit started flowing. "Put in a friendlier light, we were operating as good police officers, following the lead of our commander, Captain Calloway, who said that the 7.65 bullet we found over here should definitely stay in the Sladky case. But it needed to be explained and in an attempt to do that, we discovered it wasn't part of Sladky at all. So, in a dedicated and extremely professional way, we—"

"Please shut up," Jeb said softly.

Hitch fell silent. We all stood quietly trying to assess the situation.

"There's no way we can keep this from Dahlia," Alexa finally said. "This is going to affect her prosecution."

"We're fucked," Hitch whispered in my ear.

36

Jeb said he would make arrangements for a police tow truck to take the armored car back to the new Forensic Science Center on the Cal State campus while Alexa was trying to scare up a home number for Dahlia Wilkes. Before either could dial, Hitch and I moved in on them with an alternate idea.

"We need to talk to you guys for a minute," I started.

"You can't take this truck to the police garage at Cal State," Hitch said.

"Why not?" Jeb wondered.

"Once it's there a whole lot of people will know about it and this thing is gonna leak, Skipper."

"So then it leaks," Jeb said. "We're not the KGB, we don't conduct investigations in secret."

"Well, maybe this one time we should consider it," I suggested.

"And just how do we keep this quiet?" Alexa was tapping her foot as she asked this. I could tell from having known and loved her for years, it was not positive body language.

"Listen to all of it first," I said. "There's a lot you still don't know. Once you have the whole deal, then decide."

"There's more?" Alexa asked.

"Yeah," I answered. "A lot."

Hitch and I filled them in on the rest of the '81 Vulcuna case, taking them through everything we'd learned. Alexa had not been in L.A. back in '81 but Jeb remembered some of the Vulcunas' tragic story. We ran it down for them and told them about getting Brooks to sign off on a warrant so we could do the Luminol test in the master bedroom. They were both surprised to hear that it had been negative. We told them about the pressure from city government to close the case down, and how McKnight and Norris had only worked the Vulcuna massacre for nine hours before being pulled off and reassigned.

Jeb asked, "So what are you trying to tell us?"

"Thomas Vulcuna didn't kill his wife and daughter, then commit suicide," I answered. "We got that wrong in eighty-one. He was killed back here in that trash shed with the 7.65 bullet we found. The perp killed Vulcuna's wife and daughter in the living room, then shot Tom out here, reloaded the Luger, carried his body upstairs, placed him on the bed, and fired a second shot into the headboard to make it look right. That's why the headboard and wall wouldn't fluoresce. But this garbage shed did."

Hitch picked up the narrative. "The passage from *The Divine Comedy* was marked and left open on the bedside table as a suicide note," he said. "The Luger jammed on that second shot, but there was only one missing from the clip because the gun was reloaded by the killer then shot into the headboard."

Jeb and Alexa stood looking at each other, not sure how to proceed.

"Whoever put that Brinks truck in there probably also killed Vulcuna and his family," I said. "If this hits the papers and TV tomorrow, and the shooter is still around, he'll be gone before we can put a case together. The doer or doers will be in Mexico or France, where we can't extradite on a death penalty case, which this certainly is, because there are five murders so far, maybe six if the third Brinks guard is in the back of this truck."

"It's even bigger than that," Hitch said. "Brooks and the three Sladky killings are also somehow part of Vulcuna's triple and this Brinks heist. The two cases are tied together."

In my opinion he was overwriting the story there, but as I'd already learned, sometimes imagination is more important than knowledge.

"Brooks wasn't even alive when this Brinks truck was hijacked," Alexa reminded him.

"Not Brooks himself," Hitch continued. "His father, Thayer; or the guy who set up the foundation, that Century City lawyer, Stender Sheedy Sr. The reason they didn't sell this house for a quarter century is now pretty damn obvious. They didn't want a new owner re-landscaping and finding this well house and that armored truck inside with the dead guards."

"I still don't see how we keep this quiet," Jeb said.

"Hitch and I have been giving that some careful thought."

Jeb and Alexa seemed open to a better strategy, but didn't have one. At least they were listening. Our moment was at hand, so I jumped in.

"Okay, we know we can't keep this quiet indefinitely, but we may not need all that long. Let's say we can keep it under wraps for like seventy-two hours."

"There are at least fifty evidence tech workers at our new CSI science pod at Cal State," Jeb said. "There are a dozen more at the vehicle center. How's this stay quiet? It's bound to leak to the press. It always does."

"We limit the number of forensic techs to about six. We handpick people we know we can trust to stay quiet," I answered. "Then, instead of taking this truck to the new automotive garage at Cal State, we tow it to the old North Hollywood Medical Center on Riverside. That hospital is deserted and is being rented out for film and television shoots. Hitch woke up the location manager from *Mosquito* and that guy can rent it for us. The location fee is only fifteen hundred a day. It's got everything we need."

Hitch picked up the narrative. "We get one or two people from the ME staff who we can trust to keep a secret and get them to do their investigation of the remains in one of the old operating theaters there. Since it's just skeletons, they'll only be looking at bone and bullet issues. They'll need to do dental matches, but it's not anywhere near as complicated as a full soft tissue autopsy. It should work. Then we post a couple of patrolmen on this crime scene to protect the well house. Nobody gets in, especially the Dunbar family or their lawyers."

"And you think we can pull that off and keep this quiet?" Jeb said.

"I think it's a good idea," Alexa cut in. She was doing what I knew she would, thinking like a cop and not an administrator.

"What about ADA Wilkes?" Jeb asked.

"I think we need to keep her screened off," Hitch advised. "This old Brinks robbery touches her case and some of the same people may be involved. She won't see past the prosecutorial problems it causes. Murder defense is mostly about confusing the jury. She's gonna freak and start causing us major trouble when she finds out what we're up to."

"Doesn't matter," Alexa said. "We have to tell her anyway." Jeb nodded his head in agreement. "I'll stay here and help you with her, but if we fail to notify the DA's office on something this big, we're gonna be eating the fallout for years."

So Alexa made the call. She woke Dahlia up and told her to get to Skyline Drive immediately. She'd find out why once she got here. While we waited for her to arrive, Alexa looked at the search warrant Brooks had signed.

"You're learning," she said.

"Learn or burn," I replied.

A few minutes later, Sumner took me aside.

"That seventy-two-hour thing was brilliant, dawg."

"Thanks."

"It puts a tight clock on Act Three, and not for nothing, but we definitely needed a clock in this movie. You're showing some real producing promise. I'm telling you, when it's great, it's great. You just can't make shit like this up. This puppy is writing itself."

The problem was, he was completely serious.

▪ CHAPTER ▪
37

Dahlia Wilkes pulled up in a new red Lexus and parked down by the gate. It was five in the morning. The nights are long in December so it was still dark. As always, she was immaculately dressed. She set a fat designer briefcase on the fender of her car and regarded the four of us skeptically. Her hair ruffled in the brisk Santa Ana wind.

"So what's going on?"

"Something came up," Alexa said.

"It better not screw up my Sladky prosecution."

"It certainly touches on it," Alexa said. "It might affect it."

Dahlia turned on Hitch and me. "What have you two been doing?"

When neither of us answered, she started to walk up the drive to see for herself. Jeb blocked her way.

"This is a crime scene. It's restricted."

"Not from me. I'm the prosecutor on Sladky, or did you numb-skulls forget that already?"

"Except it's not Sladky," he said. "It's Vulcuna."

She stopped, then pinned us with a withering courtroom stare. "What do you mean, it's not Sladky? Why else would you call me? And who or what is a Vulcuna?"

"It's a cold case that just went active and it touches Sladky," Alexa said. "But unless you promise to give us seventy-two hours of confidentiality to work this situation, we can't let you on the crime scene."

"You're outta your mind."

"It's an unusual circumstance," Jeb said.

"By confidentiality, what exactly are we talking about?"

"Only you get to know what we've found here. We're extending this courtesy because you might have suggestions to protect your Sladky prosecution."

Dahlia's irritation had now turned to puzzled interest. "Of course, I have to tell Chase no matter what."

"Chase Beal doesn't need to know about this just yet," Alexa said.

"The District Attorney for the County of Los Angeles is to be kept in the dark? What are you smokin', girl?"

"This case has some political overtones. The DA is a politician. Without going any further, let's just leave it at that," my wife said.

Dahlia was definitely hooked. She wanted to know what we'd found, but she wanted to do it without putting her own ass on the line.

"What's to keep me from calling him right now, telling him what you people are suggesting? Our office will hit this property like a Panzer Division. Then we'll all know."

"If you intend to get the same excellent service from the LAPD on your cases in the future, I would advise against that strategy," Alexa warned.

"If I do this, I might as well tender my resignation to the section supervisor."

"I don't completely understand how things work in your office," Alexa challenged, "but we have solid reasoning behind this tactic. After Chase thinks it over, even he will acknowledge the wisdom of doing it this way."

"And I can't get filled in until I agree to this dumb-ass deal, in the blind."

"That's more or less it," Alexa said.

"Well, I've got to hand you guys one thing. You've definitely got my interest up."

She opened her calendar and looked at it. "Seventy-two hours is five A.M., Friday."

"That's right," Alexa agreed.

"Okay. I'll do you one better. Chase is in Sacramento this week meeting with some PACs to raise money for his mayoral campaign. He won't be back in town until Friday. As soon as he's back, I brief him. I should be able to get away with that."

"Deal," Alexa said.

"However, if he changes his plans and comes home early, he gets briefed then."

"That hardly works," Jeb objected.

"So nobody's completely happy," she said. "That's the way it should be in county government."

Alexa realized it was the best deal she could strike, so she agreed, and said, "Come on. We'll show you."

We all walked up the drive and headed toward the well house.

"Where the hell did that come from?" Dahlia said when she saw it.

We told her and then accompanied her inside. She looked at the truck and the two skeletons in the front seat. Five minutes later we were all outside again, standing in the predawn darkness, listening to the Santa Ana winds rattle through the forty-foot cypress trees.

"Where'd that Brinks truck come from?" Dahlia wanted to know.

Jeb had called in the plates and now confirmed that it was the armored car that went missing from Wilshire Boulevard in 1983 with fifteen million in gold bullion. He filled Dahlia in on the cold case.

"The third guard is probably in back," he concluded.

Dahlia sighed after he finished. She could see the trap we were in if this got out. "I'll keep it quiet until Chase gets back," she said, but wasn't happy about it.

We called two crime-scene photographers to the scene and six CSIs. Alexa and Jeb handpicked everyone. We worked fast. There wasn't any useful trace evidence inside the well house because over the years heavy rainwater had seeped in and anything that might have been there was long gone.

A police flatbed truck arrived at six and backed up the narrow drive.

The assistant coroner, Ray Tsu, pulled in at six thirty. The quiet Asian ME was called Fey Ray by almost everyone because he was rail thin and never spoke above a whisper. He'd worked half a dozen of my cases in the past.

He looked through the window at the two skeletons in the front seat. Because it was impossible to get inside the truck without torches, he made the decision to leave them in the armored car for transport back to the ambulance bay in the empty hospital in North Hollywood and remove the remains there.

As the sun came up, the tow drivers inflated the tires and winched the armored car out of the well house onto the flatbed. They tied a new tarp over the top to hide it from the neighbors, then drove the flatbed down the drive onto the street below.

Twenty-five minutes later we were pulling into the covered ambulance bay in the back of the old North Hollywood Medical Center.

The building was a big stucco four-story fifties-style rectangle with mismatching additions that architecturally resembled a bunch of shoeboxes. White with peeling green trim, it looked pretty run-down.

By ten A.M., our handpicked CSI team along with two forensic tech welders were hard at work in the ambulance bay opening the truck. The armored car was made of bulletproof steel so the techs had to use oxyfuel torches to cut through it. The door lock was finally freed.

Jeb had already assigned the armored car heist and its resulting murders to Hitch and me. As the new primaries on this three-decade-old cold case, we stepped up onto the truck's back bumper to open the rear door.

Because I now suspected that my new partner was afraid of ghosts, and because we were expecting to uncover a third skeleton inside, I did the honors.

I gloved up and pulled the door wide.

The truck was empty.

No third guard in the back, an interesting development.

"So the third guard probably did the deed," Hitch reasoned. "He jumped his buddies and made off with the fifteen mil in gold bullion."

He was visibly relieved a third skeleton wasn't lying around in the truck like some gruesome special effect from *Pirates of the Caribbean.*

"We need to get the identities of all three Brinks guards from the old case file and compare dental charts so we can identify the missing one," Jeb said. "That should tell us which one of these guys was the potential doer."

He turned to Ray Tsu. "You can remove the two guys from the front compartment now."

We were just getting set to let the CSIs come in to do a trace evidence sweep when I noticed four closed strongboxes pushed up next to the bench at the front of the compartment.

"I wonder why they didn't take those," I said. "Be easier to carry."

"Because you'd need a forklift to move fifteen million in gold bullion. The killer probably took it out in individual bricks," Hitch replied. "What would that much gold weigh anyway?" He reached down with a gloved hand and opened the top of the nearest box.

That's when we got the first big surprise.

Resting inside the strongbox were at least twenty-five gold bricks. They glittered brilliantly in the fluorescent light.

"Get the fuck outta here," Hitch whispered.

We opened the second box and, like the first, it was also filled to the top with bullion. So were the last two.

"Let's back out of here and think this over," I said.

We jumped down and told Jeb, Alexa, and Dahlia what we had just found. After they had all looked at the gold, everyone stood behind the truck talking at once.

The question was, why steal an armored car, kill at least two of the guards, and then leave fifteen million in bullion behind, parked with two skeletons in a concrete well house for over twenty-five years?

"Unless this gold is bogus," I offered. "Maybe somebody switched it out with painted lead or something."

"I'll get a metallurgist out here right away and find out," Alexa said. "The Jewelry Mart should have somebody who can assay this. I'll get someone who's bonded and sworn to secrecy."

While she was working on that, the rest of us tried to come to grips with this new find. It changed all my theories.

"What is going on here?" Dahlia said. It was the second time in two days I'd seen her off balance. "Was this a gold bullion heist or not?"

"We'll know more once these bars are tested," Jeb told her.

Ten minutes later I saw Hitch getting some coffee from a portable urn one of the CSIs had brought in. He carried an extra cup over to me behind the armored car. We stood, blowing steam across the cup rims, considering the new developments.

"I think you're wrong," I finally told him, pointing at the gold. "That's our Act Two complication."

He smiled widely at me. "You're absolutely right, dawg, and since we have Act One in place and this kick-ass complication in Act Two, now it's all about . . ."

ACT THREE

. . . .

■ CHAPTER ■
39

An hour later, Alexa had returned to her office and Dahlia to her trial in progress at the downtown courthouse. There were now fifteen men and women from the ME's office and CSI assembled inside the deserted hospital building. Some wore CSI jumpsuits and carried satchels full of equipment, others were from the lab or the ME's office and wore white coats. None of them had been told why they were here. They stood listening as Captain Calloway filled them in on the old armored car case.

Hitch and I stood behind Jeb and listened. He finished with the briefing and then launched into a rant on security precautions.

"It's extremely important that you protect the confidentiality of this investigation," he said to the roomful of earnest-looking geeks. "You cannot tell anyone about this. Not your wife, not your brother—nobody.

Because, while you may think you can impress upon them the severity of the situation, my experience has been once you tell anything to anyone outside the immediate scope of the investigation, it always leaks."

The tech team looked solemn, but who knew how seriously any of them were actually taking this warning.

Ray Tsu, as a supervising coroner, had agreed to personally wrangle the ME staff for us. He stood off to one side, looking like a wispy anime character: thin build, limp black hair pulled behind both ears, a hollow chest that was a concavity of bones. He may have looked frail, but he was well respected and one of the top MEs in the department.

"The perpetrators of this crime may still be around," Jeb warned. "We have to take every precaution to keep what we're doing here absolutely quiet so they don't cut and run."

He paused for effect and looked at each face of his handpicked team. "Okay," he finally said. "You guys know what to do. Get at it."

Everyone broke ranks and the work began. The truck was already open. After a quick round of crime-scene photographs, the MEs went in and carefully removed the skeletons from the front seat, placing them on plastic sheets before moving them onto gurneys and wheeling them off.

The power inside the old, deserted hospital was still connected for the movie companies who shot there, enabling the coroner's crew to transport the bodies by elevator to the OR theaters on four.

After everything got going, there wasn't much for Hitch and me to do. I was out by the loading dock making notes when my new partner drifted outside to talk on his cell. I overheard a little of his conversation.

"You gotta slow it down, Jerry. This is better than even *I* thought, but I'm under a police department cone of silence. I can't tell you or anybody else what's going on. But when it breaks, you're gonna kiss me. Keep our auction warm, but don't bring it to a head quite yet. This is definitely going to be bigger than *Mosquito*."

He listened, then said, "Back attcha," and hung up. He noticed me sitting nearby and shot a wide grin in my direction. "Working on your second mil, dawg."

"Hitch, we need to stop trying to make money off all these dead people and just work the case."

"It's been my experience that the dead are extremely forgiving." This philosophy supplied by a man who seemed unreasonably terrified of them.

"Jeb is pulling the old Brinks case record. Like Vulcuna, it was in the hard-copy room at the warehouse. A runner is bringing the stuff over right now."

"You don't even care what UTA just told me?" He had a little grin tugging at the corners of his mouth. "Not even a teensy-weensy bit interested?"

"Uh . . . well, I'm trying real hard not to think too much about all that money."

"It will make you happy," he teased.

"Not now. Can we just stay focused on the case, please?"

Twenty minutes later Jeb had a makeshift office set up in the ambulance dispatcher's old space. He had decided to watch over this part of the investigation personally, which was great by me. We were taking a big chance not telling Chase Beal what we were up to, and it's always good strategy to have a boss between you and any angry politician who's running for office.

The old hospital was basically without furniture. Hitch explained that on each production the set decoration department took care of that. Somebody had found a discarded desk and had moved it down to the ambulance bay along with an old scavenged sprung-back swivel chair. By the time the case file boxes arrived from the records warehouse, our captain was ready to go.

We started thumbing through two surprisingly thin case binders from '83 on the missing Brinks truck. The cops who had worked this heist were a couple of Metro Division bank squad dicks named Robert Carter and Jeremy Briggs. Hitch made a call downtown and found out both had retired in the late eighties and had subsequently gone EOW, which stood for End of Watch. Department-speak for dead.

"The Brinks truck was transporting this gold bullion to the airport, where it was scheduled to go to Switzerland," Jeb said, reading a page from Detective Carter's case binder. "An L.A. outfit called Latimer Commodities Exchange was in charge of the transport. We need to find out if Latimer is still in business. According to Carter's notes, they brokered gold, silver, and platinum contracts."

He licked his fingertips, taking more pages of case notes out of the binder. After reading, he handed each off to us one at a time. "Says here that the standard gold bar used for bank-to-bank trade is something called a London Good Delivery Bar."

Hitch and I had nowhere to sit, so we stood in front of the desk reading the pages after Jeb was finished.

"There were three guards assigned to this truck," Jeb said. "Driver was Alan Parks, age thirty-four. Married, two kids."

Jeb looked up at Hitch, who was in the midst of transferring this info into his snazzy red leather journal.

"Get another crime book, will ya, Hitchens? That fancy writer's journal is really starting to piss me off."

"Sorry, Skipper. I'll lose it as soon as I can." Hitch looked up from his writing. "We should probably see if Mrs. Parks and those two kids are still around."

"Wife was named Patty," Jeb said, as he found that on another page. "Carter and Briggs really shorthanded these write-ups. Didn't even put down the names of the children. Both were boys, ages six and eight, is all it says here. That makes them in their thirties today."

"Okay," Hitch said, and jotted that down as well. "We'll find out where Mrs. Parks and her two sons are. If they're available, we'll go talk to them."

"Damien Deseau, African-American, age twenty-nine, was the Brinks truck swamper," I said, reading a page in the late Detective Carter's binder. "That's probably the guy we just pulled out of the passenger seat. Unmarried. The GIB was Sergio Maroni, also un-married, age thirty." GIB was patrol division slang for Guy in Back.

"We need to get these two skeletons sorted out," Jeb said. "Find out who's who. Fey Ray will do the bone scans and dental matches. He's got a forensic orthodontist on the way over here, but we gotta figure it's gonna take a while to find their X-rays 'cause we gotta run down their original dentists from over twenty-five years ago if they're even still around."

The forensics team found two old thermoses in the front seat of the truck. There was dried coffee residue in the bottoms. Both con-tainers were quickly sent to the CSI techs, who were busily assembling a makeshift lab in the old ER and getting what equipment they needed sent over from the new Forensic Center at Cal State.

An evidence tech found the first bullet. It was buried in the passenger-side door panel of the Brinks truck's front seat. A .38 caliber standard-size round.

"We need to find out what kind of sidearm each of those Brinks guys carried," I told Hitch, who wrote down that note.

We were in a holding pattern until the crime techs got through with the truck and the assayer arrived, so we went outside again for some fresh air, sat on the loading dock, and worked on to-do lists. Ten minutes later a blue Lincoln Town Car pulled up and honked the horn. I walked over to the car.

"I'm from the Jewelry Mart," the driver called to me as I approached.

I directed the Lincoln to pull into the drive and park. When the driver got out, I could see he was a middle-aged dark-haired Hispanic man with a sagging beltline and a patch of male pattern baldness on the crown of his head about the size of a coffee saucer. He pulled a large rolling suitcase from the trunk, then turned to greet us.

"Hi," he said. "I'm José Del Cristo."

"Assayer?" I asked.

"You don't need to call me names," he quipped.

Great, I thought. *All we needs is another goofy character.*

Jeb didn't want the assayer to know that we had two dead guards and a Brinks truck from an '83 bullion heist stashed in the deserted ambulance bay. He instructed us to escort José Del Cristo up to the fourth floor and tell him as little as possible.

Jeb had set up a work area for the assayer in the old hospital administrator's office.

The three of us waited on the ground floor for the elevator. When it arrived we stepped inside.

"I was told you guys wanted me to do a gold assay and that it's very hush-hush, but nobody will tell me what it's about," Del Cristo said as he dragged his rolling suitcase onto the elevator.

"That's right and that's how it's gonna stay," I replied.

"'Zat why you're hanging out in this old deserted hospital?" he pressed.

"No comment."

I pushed the fourth-floor button on the elevator panel and we rode up in silence.

The doors opened and we stepped out into a long corridor with green walls and linoleum floors, with José pulling his rolling suitcase behind him. Jeb was at the end of the corridor waiting for us. I introduced him to José and we entered the office.

Jeb had chosen this room because it was spacious with a built-in desk and two badly functioning chairs. He had randomly selected a gold bar out of one of the strongboxes and had personally carried it up here. The brick was approximately the size of a paperback novel and was now sitting in the center of the large wooden desk, glittering in the flickering ceiling light.

José walked over and peered down at it. "London Good Delivery Bar," he said. "First test is the easiest. Just gotta lift it."

He picked up the bar. I could tell by the way he handled it that the brick was extremely heavy.

"So far so good. 'Bout the right weight," he said, setting it back down.

As he unpacked his equipment, he started a running monologue. Aside from being a character, José was also a nonstop talker.

"London Good Delivery Bars weigh exactly four hundred troy ounces, which, if anybody's interested, is about twenty-seven pounds."

"When I picked it up to bring it here, I wasn't prepared for how heavy it was," Jeb commented.

"Very few metals are as dense as gold," José rambled on. "For instance, gold is twice as dense as lead and two and a half times as dense as steel. That's why it's hard to counterfeit a gold bar. Even if there's a lead core, it's still way too light. One metal that's heavy enough to substitute is platinum, but it's actually more expensive than gold, so what's the point?

"Tungsten has enough density but it's impossible to work with because tungsten has a melting point one thousand degrees higher than most commercial furnaces or kilns can reach. Also it's an extremely hard metal. Gold is very soft. You can actually scar it with a fingernail like this." To prove his point he did just that.

He took a scale about the size of a shoe box out of the suitcase, then a bunch of vials full of different-colored liquid and a black sanding stone.

"Another metal that would work from a weight standpoint is depleted uranium," he went on. "It's heavy enough, easy to melt down, and at its heart not too expensive, but there are other drawbacks. Unless you're a government with a nuclear program, it's real hard to come by, and of course it's radioactive so if you make a mistake and touch it you're dead in a few days, which most counterfeiters tell me is a major drawback."

José lifted the gold bar onto the shoe box–sized scale that had PN 2100 PRECISION BALANCE stamped on the side.

"Four hundred troy ounces to the hair," he reported as he read the printout. "Means your bar here is most likely legit because it's soft like gold and it's exactly the right weight. But you can't be absolutely, positively sure without more tests."

"What's a troy ounce?" I asked.

"A troy ounce is 31.1 grams. A regular ounce, like the one they use at your grocery store or on your bathroom scale, is called an avoirdupois ounce and it only weighs 28.3 grams."

He took the bar off the scale and set it on a pad he'd just placed on the desktop.

"How do you want this?" he asked. "I can do a quick insurance appraisal or I can make you a big expensive enchilada with all the trimmings."

"I want to know exactly what we've got," Jeb told him.

"How about I do a standard viscosity X-ray fluorescence scan evaluation?"

"Can you do that here?"

"No."

"I don't want to let go of this bar. It's evidence. Can you tell us anything without taking it out of here?"

José leaned down and studied the brick carefully, then turned it over. "Yeah, I can tell you a few things. For instance, the forges that make London Good Delivery Bars are all bonded. See this little trademark here?"

We all leaned in and peered at a small stamp on the back of the bar. It showed tiny crossed swords inside a circle.

"That's an old refinery called Oswald Steel. They used to be located in Michigan but they went out of business in the mideighties. It was one of the big forges that produced these gold bricks back in the day. That gives us a few interesting facts. For instance, we now know the bar is at least pre-eighty-five. Also, they had fewer testing techniques for gold in the eighties. There were no X-ray or viscosity tests. Back then it was a lot easier to counterfeit one of these guys."

"How do we find out if it's real gold and not something else without taking it out of here?" Jeb asked.

"I can file off some of the bar, use my acids to make a solution, and give you a quick content assay right now. That will tell us how many karats it is and how pure the karats are."

"Is that enough of a test to be certain?" Jeb asked.

"Along with the exact weight, that's generally good enough for most insurance companies that write the transport policies on this stuff. However, when I do it, if this is real gold, you're gonna lose a little, about a hundred dollars' worth."

"That's okay," Jeb said.

"If you were buying it for an investment, you might want to do a more complete evaluation like a mass spectrometer test, but those can get pricey," José went on. "If it was coins and not a bar, you might do a standard heat conductivity test. Gold conducts heat at a specific rate which can be timed with a stopwatch. Works great with something as thin as a coin but it's not too practical with one of these big heavy London bars."

"Let's start by just doing the quick insurance assay," Jeb said.

We watched while José picked up the little sanding stone from the table and began filing some gold off the edge of the bar. It made a small pile of yellow powder on the work cloth he'd placed beneath the brick. He kept talking the whole time.

"That should be enough. . . . These vials contain different kinds of acid which I use in a mixture to break down the metal to measure it."

He picked up the filings with a small pen-sized battery-powered electromagnet and emptied them into a vial, mixing the gold filings with the acids from the smaller vials.

He set the mixed vial on the desk while he took a machine about the size of a small microwave out of his suitcase and plugged it into the wall socket.

"This reads the viscosity of the gold-acid mixture," he said as he put the mixed vial with the gold into the machine. "If we get the right viscosity we can assign purity. If your brick is a real LGD Bar and not a counterfeit, it should be at least ninety-nine point five percent pure. Could be more but it has to be at least ninety-nine point five to qualify as an official London Good Delivery Bar."

He flipped the switch on the machine and a minute later, read a printout. "Checks out. Twenty-four karat. Ninety-nine point seven."

"That can't be." I looked at Hitch, who also seemed puzzled. We'd all expected it to be fake. Why else would it have been left behind in that truck for all those years?

"You don't want this brick to be real?" José seemed surprised.

"Wait a minute," I told him. I pulled Jeb and Hitch into the hallway.

"We have to find out for sure," I said once we were out of Del Cristo's earshot.

"I thought we just did," Jeb said.

"He said there were more complete tests he could do. Let's have him take that one brick so he can do the X-ray scan. It should be safe to let him have it. He works for the Jewelry Mart. Alexa says he's bonded."

"What about our chain of evidence?" Jeb said. "Once I let go of it I can't swear it's the same bar if we ever get this case to court."

"It's just one brick. If you lose that one at trial, so what? You still got four strongboxes full to guarantee your chain of evidence."

But on principle, Jeb was torn. No cop likes breaking the chain of evidence on anything relating to a case, no matter the reason. Finally, he led us back into the office and faced the assayer.

"José?"

"Present and accounted for," the little man joked.

"How much do you think that gold bar is worth?"

"I can tell you to the penny. Gold today is about a thousand dollars a troy ounce. One thousand one hundred and six if you're a stickler for complete accuracy. I could do it exactly with a calculator, but throwing an ax at it, this one brick is worth about four hundred forty thousand dollars, give or take a Chevy Nova."

What a stitch, this guy.

"Excuse us again," Jeb said, and pulled me back into the corridor while Hitch stationed himself in the doorway, where he could keep José at a distance, but still hear what we were saying.

"We counted a hundred gold bricks in that truck," Jeb said. "At four hundred forty K a brick. That's forty-four million. According to Carter's case notes, the load was insured by Axeis Cargo Insurance. ACI only had it valued at fifteen million. So what's with that? How can there be more gold now than when the truck was hijacked?"

It was a damn good question.

Then Hitch whispered in my ear, "Don't ya love this, dawg? We're standing here doing absolutely nothing and Act Three is getting better by the moment."

· CHAPTER ·
41

I walked back into the office. José had a slight grin on his face.

"If you guys keep running out, I'm going to get an inferiority complex," he said.

"What was gold selling for in 1983?" I asked.

"A lot less. I'd have to look it up, but it was around three seventy-five a troy ounce."

I looked at Jeb. "Then that's the difference. It's worth a lot more per ounce today than it was in eighty-three."

José asked, "What's really going on here, guys?"

"Can we make arrangements for you to do a full assay at your place?" Jeb said without answering. He had made up his mind that I was right. It was better to risk the one brick as evidence and be absolutely certain of what was in that armored truck.

"Sure," José said. "But you gotta take care of the transport. I don't want to be responsible for that. You have my address on that card."

"What kind of test will you do?" Jeb asked.

"Probably the standard X-ray fluorescence scan. That's the one I'd pick 'cause I've got the right equipment in my lab. I'm pretty sure you're wasting your time, because I'm almost positive this bar is the real thing."

"Do it anyway," Jeb said. "We'll have it delivered to your office this afternoon."

José nodded and started to pack up his gear. While he was doing that I lifted the brick. It was amazingly heavy. When you're wearing a gold ring or watch, you're not aware of how dense it really is because it's so small. But melted down into one of these London Good Delivery Bars, the dead weight was impressive.

After José left and Jeb went back downstairs with the brick, I began cranking out yawns. It was only eleven A.M., but we'd gone another full night without sleep.

"Hitch, I'm not thinking straight. I think I need to get a few hours' rest. I don't want to take the time to drive all the way home, so I'm gonna rent a motel room nearby."

My yawns were becoming contagious and Hitch started yawning as well.

"I could use a little sleep myself," he said. "But I'm not gonna let my new producing partner crash in some no-tell motel. I got a guest bedroom at my place."

It sounded good.

We left the team of CSIs swarming over the Brinks truck, told Jeb what we were up to, then got in our separate cars and headed to Hitch's house up in the Mount Olympus development.

It was eleven thirty when we pulled up and parked in the circular drive under his porte cochere.

"Crystal starts early at the restaurant, making her pastries," Hitch said as we got out of our cars. "So she's not here."

We went inside and he showed me to the guest bedroom. It was large and inviting with a European ambience. The decor was Country French. Forest green walls with white trim. The furniture was mostly Italian and French reproductions. The upholstery was an expensive-looking French toile. There was a window that looked out over Hollywood.

Hitch set the clock radio alarm for me. We agreed to get up at five P.M. and he left.

I studied the view. We had to be over a thousand feet up. Low fluffy white clouds hung at eye level against the mountains like movie special effects. I stretched out on the extremely soft king-sized bed and closed my eyes. For a minute I thought I had died and was in heaven. I was already above the clouds and now I began to hear sweet voices singing harmonic madrigals a capella.

I realized after a moment that the music was coming from the clock radio that Hitch had inadvertently turned on when he set the alarm. It was set to a Christian station, the volume low. I was at peace on my supersoft cloud-nine mattress while a children's choir soothed my senses. Not exactly heaven, but close.

I considered turning the radio off, but the music was so soothing I didn't make the effort. Instead I stretched out and listened to the angelic voices. I fell asleep thinking, *So this is what real wealth feels like.*

Shane Scully had finally achieved his new exalted place, high above the toiling masses, at rest on Mount Olympus.

• CHAPTER •

42

I awoke to the smell of something delicious cooking in the kitchen. I lay still for a minute savoring the aroma. Then I looked over at the clock radio. It was five of five in the evening, just minutes before the alarm was set to ring.

The Christian choir was no longer singing and a preacher was in the middle of a sermon about enriching life. I listened for a minute as he told his radio parishioners that the secret to finding love was simply to be open to it. Nice concept, but not one you see very much of in police work.

I rolled over and snapped off the radio. I had slept in my clothes, so I padded into the bathroom to wash my face.

Hitch's guest bath was larger than the one Alexa and I shared in

Venice. The fixtures were little gold-plate dolphins that spit water from two ornate faucets into a hand-painted French porcelain basin.

I was beginning to see dolphins in a whole new light. They helped us wash. They helped us hold up our tabletops. It was probably time for me to step up and get some dolphins of my own.

While I was on this train of thought, I began to review the whole movie deal as well.

Was it really such a crime to sell this case to a studio? I mean, who did it really hurt? I'd heard that over twenty L.A. cops were members of the Writers Guild. Was I just being an asshole here? If Hitch and I didn't sell the case, wouldn't some other guy with flat feet and a column in the *LA Times* just scoop it up and make the sale instead?

I could feel my resolve weakening. It reminded me of those sand castles I used to build when Pop Dix took us to the beach on Saturdays way back when I was six. I'd spend half the morning building one only to stand there in horror as the tide came in and washed it away.

Back then I would curse myself because I hadn't taken the extra effort to build my castle farther from the water. As each wave got closer and stronger, I would watch with growing self-disgust as the foundation crumbled, leaving me to wonder why I didn't carry my plastic water buckets farther up the beach.

That's the way I felt now. How far up the beach should I go to protect the things that were truly important to me?

I took off my shirt and washed my face. There was a can of spray deodorant in the cabinet so I borrowed some and spritzed under my arms. Then I redressed, knotting my tie in a Windsor knot. I plastered on a jaunty, no-worries grin and looked at myself in the mirror.

Hidey-ho, ready to go.

I descended from my temporary sleeping quarters on Mount Olympus and joined Hitch in the kitchen. He was cooking.

"Good, you're up," he said as I entered. "I was just about to come get you."

Hitch had placed cubes of bread with the crust cut off in a greased nine-by-thirteen-inch pan with some sauteed sausage slices layered on top. He was sprinkling grated cheddar over the sausage.

"What is that?" I said. "It smells great."

"What you smell is the sausage I just browned. What you're about to taste is a culinary miracle known as the Hitchmeister's amazing eggs Portugal. Good at any time of day including dinner."

He went to the refrigerator and took out a concoction in a plastic blender. "Our eggs, milk, and mustard," he explained. "My secret sauce is a couple of jiggers of vermouth." He poured it on top of the bread, cheese, and sausage then popped the pan into the oven.

"We've got to wait an hour for it to cook, but I thought we could use the time to go over the case."

"Sounds good."

"I just got off the phone with NHMC. CSI did a test on the residue in those two thermoses we found in the truck. Both had strong traces of ketamine, so the two dead guards were drugged first. Coroner said both skeletons had bullet chips in their bones, making the probable cause of death gunshot."

"So the GIB drugged his two buddies then once they were asleep he executed them."

"That's what it looks like," he said.

"What about Del Cristo?"

"He just called over there and wants to talk to us. I was waiting until you got up to call him back because I know how much you, as senior partner, like to push the big red buttons."

"You da man," I said, and we slapped palms.

He handed me a cup of Brazilian coffee and we walked into the den to call José Del Cristo. As soon as he was on the line Hitch put him on speaker.

"What'd you find?" I asked.

"I ran an X-ray fluoroscopic and your gold bar checked out. I could do a few more tests if you want but in my opinion, the brick is good. Twenty-four-karat perfect."

I looked at Hitch to see if he wanted to add anything. When he shook his head, I said, "Okay, José. Thanks again. Don't do any more. We'll send somebody over to pick up the bar."

"I'm just getting set to leave now. I'll put it in our safe. You can pick it up first thing in the morning. I get in at eight and we close at five."

After he hung up I looked at Hitch.

"Makes no sense," he said.

"It makes perfect sense. The only problem is we just aren't looking at it in the right way yet."

We sat on the bar stools thinking. After a while I could smell the great aroma of eggs Portugal wafting in from the kitchen.

"Okay, look," I finally said. "The gold is real and we know that nobody in their right mind is gonna park that much loot in a sealed garage and just leave it. If it was hot, maybe, but then it would only be for a year or two to cool it off before moving it. But nobody's gonna leave it there for over a quarter century. That defies reason."

"Exactly." Hitch nodded.

"Unless whoever stole the money and hid it in that well house got killed himself. Maybe he was tortured by someone trying to find it, and when he didn't talk, they went too far and he ended up dead. Or less dramatically, it could be as simple as he got hit by a bus or killed in a freeway accident. If it happened that way, then it could sit there unopened for a quarter century with nobody finding it."

"I'm liking this. It ties Dunbar to Vulcuna."

"Not necessarily, because if the Dunbar family knew about it, wouldn't they pull the gold out of there and use it?"

"Then who planted out the well house with those holly bushes?" he asked.

"Maybe that was an independent event. Maybe it's just what you said. The well house was ugly, so they hid it."

"That means our great gold bullion heist with all these dead bodies ends back in eighty-three with our master villain going tits up in Act One." He was scowling.

"Kinda fucks up the movie, doesn't it?"

"What about Stender Sheedy and Thayer Dunbar and their crazy need to keep that house empty and unsold?"

"Rich people are often eccentric," I countered. "Too much money bends the mind. I offer young Brooks as Exhibit A. As you get richer it's something you might also need to keep your eye on going forward."

He looked at me or through me. Not sure which.

Then he said, "So your big idea is the GIB kills all three Vulcunas for some still completely unknown reason, then two years later he steals the truck, whacks the other two guards, and hides the truck with the gold inside at Vulcunas' well house, again for unknown reasons. Then the GIB goes out and gets picked up by a person or persons unknown who torture him to death without him talking or, better still, he gets hit by a bus, and the gold is lost, parked for decades in a well house owned by the estate of a pudgy twit whose father is a fucking multibillionaire. Now *I'm* gagging." He chewed a cuticle. It was a nervous twitch I'd not seen before. "We're running out of moves," he said.

"We still have two obvious ones," I countered. "Go out and brace Stender Sheedy is one. Lean hard on that asshole and see if he cracks. The other is we check with Axeis Cargo Insurance. If they examined the gold, see if we can get ACI's old assay tests. Then we find out who collected that insurance dough."

"Let's do Sheedy first," Hitch said. "I'd like to grind on that ass-hole a little just for fun."

"We have less than seventy-two hours before Chase Beal gets microphone fever and starts messing us up. We already lost five getting the truck open and the gold assayed. We just slept away another five. I think in the interest of time, we should split up."

He looked at his watch. "Business hours are over."

"That's why we got badges. So we can stop by a suspect's house unannounced and hassle him."

"No wonder you're so popular at Internal Affairs," he said.

I made a call to the research center. They gave me the name and address for the current CEO of Axeis Cargo Insurance, a man named Russell Meeks. They also told me where Stender Sheedy Sr. lived.

While I did that Hitch went into the kitchen and pulled the eggs Portugal out of the oven. He got a spatula and cut me a large section, placing it carefully on a china plate. He reached into the fridge and took out some cold mixed fruit squares in a honey sauce for a side dish, then made up a second plate for himself.

We took our food out onto the deck with two German lagers to eat dinner and watch the sun go down.

Hitch handed me a silver fork wrapped inside a green linen napkin and said, "Let me know what you think."

He waited for me to go first, eyeing me carefully as I took my first bite and swallowed.

"Aughhhh," I said. "Dry! You could caulk a boat with this."

"Huh." He seemed perplexed as he forked in a bite of his own.

"Go fuck yourself," he said. "It's great. Melts in your mouth."

"Yeah." I grinned. "It's pretty damn spectacular."

We finished our first helping and both had seconds. Twenty minutes later we were loading up and getting ready to go.

"I'll take Sheedy," I said. "You take this Russell Meeks character who runs Axeis Cargo Insurance."

"He lives all the way out in Thousand Oaks," Hitch complained. "Your guy is right down the hill in Bel Air."

"That's the problem with being junior man," I explained. "Junior man always gets the shit jobs. You're lucky we haven't been getting any flat tires."

We left his house in separate cars, riding down from Mount Olympus like mythic warriors.

We had no idea what awaited us. But to paraphrase my new partner, Act Three was certainly getting better."

· CHAPTER ·
43

Stender Sheedy's house on Oakcrest was nestled up against the Bel Air hillside. It was one of those classic Georgian Colonials that dot these old Westside neighborhoods like flowering magnolias in a verdant southern landscape. There was at least an acre of rye lawn. Stone lion statues that looked appropriately fierce and majestic guarded the drive. It wasn't as nice a spread as Thayer Dunbar's, but it was pretty good for a man who had made his career by flushing the other guy's toilets.

I pulled the MDX up and parked on the street. It was still early, only a little past eight o'clock in the evening. There was a Mercedes S600 sedan parked in the drive with personalized plates that read BAR'STER. The lights on the ground floor were all festively lit.

I got out, walked by some expensive cars parked at the curb, and continued up the drive past Leo and Cleo. Neither of the stone beasts snarled at me, a hopeful sign.

I rang the bell and the door was answered by a slender middle-aged Chinese woman in a crisply ironed maid's uniform. According to my recent observations, the Chinese seemed to have cornered the Westside domestic services market.

"Yes?" she said hesitantly.

"I'm here to see Mr. Sheedy," I replied.

"He no come right now. Dey eat dinner."

"It's official business."

I showed her my badge and it was like I had just pulled a rattlesnake out of my pocket.

She took a quick step back and said, "Oh . . . oh."

"May I come in?"

She took another step back so I just followed.

"Wa Sun," she called out.

A Chinese man appeared in the entry hall. He was a little older than she, and when he spoke, there was no trace of an accent.

"This man with po-leece."

"How can I help you?" Wa Sun inquired.

"I need to see Stender Sheedy Sr."

"He's not available."

"I'm not looking for a place setting at dinner, but I'm also not going to stand around out here and wait."

I showed my badge. It had little effect on him.

"What's this regarding?" he said.

"At least five dead people, but it may actually be more because I'm keeping the count open."

"I suggest you make an appointment to see Mr. Sheedy at his office during business hours."

He turned and spoke harshly in Chinese to the woman who had

let me into the house. I didn't have to understand Mandarin to know he was bitching her out for giving up the family threshold without shedding blood.

Enough of this, I thought. As he continued to berate her, I walked past them toward the dining room, which I assumed was down the hallway to my left. Wa Sun hurried after, calling out for me to stop.

I ignored him.

On my way I passed some magnificent rooms with expensive furnishings. The Sheedys leaned toward upscale European antiques with a sprinkling of early American maple. No dolphins in sight, but they usually reside in ornate marble or nautical settings. The oil paintings that lined the walls were rich and probably very expensive. The carpets thick and inviting.

I entered the dining room a few steps ahead of Wa Sun and found Stender Sheedy in mid-story, entertaining his wife and six dinner guests.

". . . the odds were extremely long in the racing form, but since I had all six of that colt's morning workouts—" He stopped mid-sentence and looked up at me, a startled expression on his face.

"I'm sorry, sir. He pushed past me," Wa Sun said by way of explanation.

Everybody at the table was dressed expensively. It appeared I'd blundered into a high-toned dinner party. Sheedy was facing me at the far end of the room. There were three other couples having dinner, plus his wife, all of them seated in high-back Queen Anne chairs around a long mahogany table.

Mrs. Sheedy was at the near end, with her back to the doorway where I was standing. She craned her cosmetically peeled porcelain face around to study me. Silver hair, nice tight nip-and-tuck job, great blue eyes.

The other people varied in age. The youngest couple was midthirties and the husband was instantly hateable. One of those "ain't I cute" kiss-ass political ladder climbers that every business seems to have a few of. You can almost spot them by the way they comb their hair. There were two other older middle-aged couples seated around the table.

"You must leave," Wa Sun persisted, putting his hand on my arm.

"Back off or you're gonna be put under arrest," I said. He dropped his hand.

"Just what on earth is this?" Stender said, blundering to his feet as if about to protect his dinner guests with heroic feats of mortal combat.

"Good to see you again, Mr. Sheedy. Do you remember me?"

"Haven't a clue," he snarled. "Get out."

"At the Skyline Drive house. I'm the homicide detective you let in there a few days ago."

"Oh, good Lord. When will you people ever learn?"

Probably a pretty good question, but he wasn't going to get the answer from me.

"You will leave my house immediately," he blustered. "This is outrageous. I'm having a dinner engagement."

I crossed to him. "It's a police matter. However, there's no need for us to go to the mattresses. I only need a little of your time. Now happens to be extremely convenient for me, but if you disagree, I can start making phone calls."

"Absolutely preposterous! Get out!" he thundered, bobbing his head and waving his arm at me.

He was so used to pushing people around, he'd completely forgotten what it felt like forty years ago when he was still stuck in the mail room.

"Stender, who *is* this person?" Mrs. Sheedy asked.

He didn't answer. He looked at his wife and then at me. This intrusion and my refusal to leave embarrassed him in front of his guests, causing his temper to boil over. Then as I watched, he reined it all in.

He lowered his voice and said, "Come with me."

▪ CHAPTER ▪
44

I followed him out of the dining room into the den, or maybe the Sheedys called it the great room. Either way, it was huge and overlooked a rectangular-shaped swimming pool.

The room was done in a macho hunter-killer theme. Elk and deer heads, nail-studded bar stools, brown leather furniture, forest green walls, and a Kilgary plaid area carpet. Old flintlock hunting rifles from the seventeen hundreds hung like crossed sabers over a magnificent walk-in fireplace.

"How dare you invade my house while I'm entertaining?" he began. "I've been told that case on Skyline Drive is over. They've caught the man. This is outlandish!"

"Mr. Sheedy, despite all that, I still have some questions."

"You obviously have no idea who you're dealing with."

"I know who you are. That doesn't get you out of this." Then I decided to just hit him with it hard. A blitz interview technique can often unnerve a stubborn witness and, in the ensuing confusion, cause them to make mistakes.

"Do you represent now, or have you ever represented, the Latimer Commodities Exchange?" I said without warning.

He just stood there; his jaw began clenching. He obviously wasn't going to answer.

"You might as well tell me and not make me go to a lot of trouble, because I *will* find out. It's going to be in somebody's records somewhere. Court or corporate documents."

An awkward moment followed while he silently ran through his options. Then he said, "I don't believe I have any obligation to reveal my business practices to you without first knowing the scope and context of the inquiry."

"Let's move on then. I'll get it myself. Do you handle any clients that trade in precious metals?"

"No."

"I'm curious as to when you started your business relationship with Thayer Dunbar."

"You are going to have to tell me, without prevarication, to what end or in what context this inquiry resonates."

Damn, he talked fancy.

"I'm trying to solve a murder case."

"It's solved."

"Not the one I'm working."

That stopped him. "And just which one is that?" he asked.

"Did you have any dealings with Thomas Vulcuna before his death in 1981, or with Eagle's Nest Productions before you acquired it through the Dorothy White Foundation?"

"You know, I've had just about all of this nonsense I care to deal with."

He turned to his desk and picked up his cell phone from its charging dock. Then he started scrolling through the call log until he found a number on speed dial. He hit the Send button and put the phone to his ear.

"You can't avoid answering my questions by calling someone for help," I said.

"Wanta bet?"

He turned slightly away from me and spoke into the phone. "Chase, it's Stender."

Uh-oh, I thought.

"I have one of your police officers here. He rudely interrupted a private dinner party at my residence and is asking damn fool questions about God knows what. I do not appreciate this kind of harassment and if you and I are going to continue in our little quest, I demand that you muzzle this man and make sure he never be allowed to return to my home."

He listened and then said, "No, I don't know his name. A police person of some kind."

He turned and handed me the phone. "For you," he said coldly.

"Hello?"

"This is Chase Beal. Who am I speaking to?"

"Detective Scully, Homicide Special, sir."

"What are you doing bothering Mr. Sheedy, Detective?"

"I'm trying to deal with a case I'm working on, sir."

"It's over. Ms. Wilkes has thoroughly briefed me on the Sladky shooting. We won't be requiring any further assistance from you on that, so leave Mr. Sheedy's house immediately."

"It's not Sladky I'm working on."

"Not Sladky?"

"No. It's an old case that was just reopened."

"And what case is that?"

His voice was ice-cold. I wanted to keep our armored car heist a secret for a little longer, but I needed something to pop Sheedy open. I decided to give them half of it.

"The case is the Vulcuna family murder-suicide from 1981," I told him. "We had Thomas Vulcuna down as the murderer of his wife and daughter who then shot himself. It was closed in eighty-one. Now we think it's a triple murder with the killer still at large."

As soon as I said this, Stender Sheedy abruptly straightened up. It was as if somebody had jerked him upright by an invisible cord attached to the top of his head.

"What is that case?" Beal asked. "I'm afraid I don't know it or what it could possibly have to do with the Sheedys."

"The Vulcunas owned the house on Skyline Drive that Brooks Dunbar now owns. The same address where Sladky committed the triple murder. Mr. Sheedy was the attorney who acquired that property for the Dunbars in 1982. That's why I'm over here."

There was a long silence on the other end of the line. Sheedy was now beginning to twitch as if he had suddenly developed a nervous disorder.

"You get your ass out of there right now," Chase Beal ordered. "Be in my office at eight A.M. on Monday morning prepared to defend this behavior. If I get another call from Stender about this, I'll fall on you like a mountain of shit."

"Yes, sir."

I handed the phone back to Sheedy. He listened for a moment, then whispered his thanks and disconnected. He was pale when I arrived but now he was bone white.

"What kind of quest are you on with Chase Beal?" I asked. "You helping him with his campaign for mayor?"

"You will leave my house immediately," he said.

I had accomplished what I came here to do, so I said something

I've always wanted to say, but which is never said in real life, only in films.

"In that case I'll see myself out," I intoned elegantly, then spun on my heel and left.

It was a movie moment.

I wished Hitch had been there to see it.

· CHAPTER ·
45

I left the Sheedys' Georgian house, passing the three expensive cars belonging to his dinner guests, which I'd failed to take adequate note of before.

I slid behind the wheel of my MDX and pulled up the street, then hung a U-turn and parked half a block away where I had a view of his front door. I had a hunch something was about to happen.

I didn't have to wait too long.

Ten minutes later Stender Sheedy Sr. ran out on his very important dinner guests, almost falling down the front steps in his haste to get to his car.

He climbed into the Mercedes and backed out, clipping one of the stone lions on the way. He bounced over the curb cut in his driveway, threw the car in gear, and raced up the street.

If I'd set fire to a cat's tail, I wouldn't get this much reaction.

I pulled out after him, keeping the lights off for the first few blocks before switching them on.

Single-car tail jobs are hard because if the subject is paying even the slightest bit of attention, it doesn't take much effort to pick you off. But judging by the panicked way Sheedy was driving, I didn't think he was wasting much time on his rearview mirror.

After he turned up Coldwater Canyon, I was pretty sure I knew where he was going—the deserted house on Skyline Drive.

Was he worried about that Brinks truck?

I followed him up into the hills, dropping farther back as his destination became clearer. When he turned onto Mulholland, I let him get far enough ahead so that I wouldn't be in his rearview at all.

I turned onto Skyline and pulled behind a van parked about a block down from the mansion. Then I got out of the Acura and walked to a place where I could see what he was doing.

He was in a moonlit argument with the two patrolmen stationed at the foot of the drive, guarding the property. They were denying him access and it wasn't hard to figure out what he was saying. His arms were flapping. He was bobbing his head as he shouted at them. It was the same sort of behavior he'd displayed less than an hour ago when he was shouting at me.

His dialogue had to be something like, "Have you any idea who you're dealing with?" Punctuated with words like "outlandish," "outrageous," and "preposterous." He seemed to be very frustrated with all us little people who for some reason were being uncharacteristically disrespectful tonight.

He got back into his car and burned rubber to display his anger to the cops. He flashed right by me going downhill without so much as a glance in my direction. He was having a bad night.

I jumped back into the MDX and followed. In the next few minutes I almost lost him because I'd assumed he would turn left on Mulholland and head back toward Bel Air. Because of that assumption I turned in the wrong direction, but fortunately caught a glimpse of the distinctive taillights on his Mercedes in my rearview mirror. He was going the other way on Mulholland, toward Laurel Canyon Boulevard. I backed up, swung around, and followed him. He took a left on Laurel, heading down the hill into the Valley.

He was on a mission, running yellow lights, occasionally leaving me stuck at intersections behind a line of traffic. Just past Moorpark Avenue I thought I was going to lose him so I took a big chance and put on my hidden flashers in the grille, growled the siren, and broke through a red light. Despite my light show, I somehow remained undetected.

I followed him onto the 101 North heading toward Ventura. I kept several car lengths back. Once on the freeway, he was a little easier to follow.

I had put Hitch's number on my cell phone's speed dial so I jammed the Bluetooth into my ear and hit Send. No answer. I left a voice message for him to call back ASAP.

I kept driving, trying Hitch every ten minutes or so. He was either out of cell range or had turned his phone off while he was interviewing Meeks. The fifth time I called, I was deep into the West Valley.

This time Hitch answered on the first ring. "Whatup, dawg?"

I told him briefly about my meeting with Stender Sheedy and that I was tailing Sheedy, Devine & Lipscomb's senior partner on the 101, heading toward Santa Barbara.

"I'm liking this," Hitch said. "This is all great Third Act stuff."

"I'm trying to stay on this guy, but he's going fast and once he gets back on city streets my single-car tail is gonna be tough. I could use some help. I just passed Thousand Oaks. You still anywhere out here?"

"Yeah. What's your next exit?"

I saw it coming up on my right. "Royal Oaks."

"Okay, I'm not that far. Let me know when he turns off."

Sheedy exited on Lynn Road, turned left, and headed toward the ocean, which lay on the other side of a chain of low hills about ten miles to the southwest. I stayed on the phone with Hitch, giving him my changing location as I kept driving.

Finally, I followed the Mercedes into a green valley that was home to some big, lush horse-breeding ranches with expensive-sounding names like Arabian Acres and Kensington Farms. The properties stretched out magnificently on both sides of the road. Huge ranch houses and miles of lush grass were bordered by white slat fences.

Sheedy kept going straight until he turned onto a road marked W. Potrero. Half a mile farther on the Mercedes slowed and pulled up to a large arched gate with a white security shack.

I saw it just in time to shut off my headlights as I approached, rolling to a stop off the road about a quarter mile back. Hopefully I had remained out of sight of the guard shack that protected the drive. Sheedy spoke with the uniformed security cop for a moment before he was passed through.

The Santa Anas had by now cleared L.A.'s night sky of its normal brew of hazy pollutants, and a bright three-quarter moon was putting a soft silver glow on everything. I took a pair of binoculars from the glove compartment and panned the huge, meticulously maintained ranch before me.

Arabian horses stood in the fenced fields, some with their beautiful shiny necks arched gracefully down to graze. A large racetrack outlined by white-painted rails could be seen in the distance. On the top of the hill the sloping roof of a magnificent old Spanish-style ranch house was silhouetted in the moonlight.

Then I panned over to the white arch spanning the light brown two-lane granite driveway. There was something spelled out on the arch in gold letters. I worked the binoculars until the words came into sharper focus and I could read the sign.

RANCHO SAN DIEGO

▪ CHAPTER ▪
46

Ten minutes later Hitch's Porsche flew by the spot where I was parked, his headlights off as I'd instructed. I flashed mine and the Carrera squealed to a stop fifteen yards beyond. He backed up and parked behind me. A minute later he climbed into my passenger seat.

"What's this?" Hitch looked at the ranch protected by the guard shack and arched gate that spanned the lane at the end of the road about three-tenths of a mile up ahead.

I handed him the binoculars. First he panned the farm with the grazing thoroughbreds, then the house on the hill before he focused on the archway over the gate.

"Rancho San Diego," he read aloud.

"I wonder if the guy who owns this place has any Italian poetry in his library," I said.

"You're right. 'San Diego' was written in pencil on the inside cover of *The Divine Comedy.*"

I filled Hitch in on the rest of what had happened at Sheedy's house and how I'd tailed him to Skyline Drive and then here. After I finished, he was silent, a pensive look on his face, chewing it.

"He's worried we found that truck," Hitch said. "That means he was probably in on the gold heist."

"Maybe."

"My money says Sheedy Sr. was the tall, pale, black-haired guy in the Chief of D's office when McKnight and Norris were yanked off the Vulcuna case in eighty-one."

I nodded. "I've been meaning to get a photo six-pack together and have McKnight take a look. See if he can pick Sheedy out. We better get that done now. I'll have somebody downtown to go on the company Web site and download a current picture."

We both pondered it for a moment. Then I turned to face him. "You get anything worthwhile from Russell Meeks?"

"A few things."

Hitch opened his red journal to a page but didn't look down at it. "Meeks is real young for a CEO, only about forty, so he obviously wasn't at Axeis Cargo Insurance in eighty-three. He had to make a phone call to find out about that Brinks truck. He got some guy who lived near the office to go down there and log on the computer. Unlike the department, they actually put their old paper files on disks. He accessed the old insurance report on that stolen Brinks shipment. Apparently, the Latimer Commodities Exchange wasn't the owner of the bullion."

"Then who owned it?"

"Latimer was transporting it on contract for an outfit called . . ." He consulted his notes. "Farvagny-le-Grand Jewelry Consortium. Back in eighty-three they were a big manufacturer of expensive jewelry located in Switzerland. Apparently, Farvagny-le-Grand traded in large amounts of gold and platinum as well as gemstones. That bullion was heading to the L.A. airport for a transfer flight to their jewelry manufacturing plant outside of Geneva."

"Fifteen million in bullion?" I said. "That's a hell of a lot of watches and rings."

"Sounded like a lot to Russ Meeks, too. But apparently, this outfit supplied retailers throughout the world with product. Had offices in South Africa, London, Singapore, and Cartagena."

"Cartagena?" I said, looking over at him sharply.

"Looks like some cocaine cowboys just galloped into our movie." Hitch was smiling. "A drug angle could be very cool. Figures too, 'cause it was snowing pretty good in this town back in the eighties."

"Who at that jewelry manufacturer paid the premium on the insurance and then collected the payment after the truck was lost—did you get that?"

"I get everything, dawg. I'm the Roto-Rooter of crime." He thumbed through his notes. "The guy on the insurance form was Manfred West-erling." He spelled it out then added, "*Jawohl, mein herr.* Westerling was Farvagny-le-Grand's wholesale manager here in L.A."

"Okay. Gives us somebody to look for and question."

"German national," Hitch added. "Hopefully he didn't get transferred back to Switzerland."

Ten minutes later Sheedy's Mercedes came back down the private road and passed the guard shack. He was driving much slower. Hitch and I ducked down as he went past.

When we sat up, Hitch said, "Aren't we gonna follow?"

"No. He's already talked to whoever he needed to. He's driving like a normal person now. My guess is he's going home to pout."

We continued to sit there, both of us running through our options.

"I want you to do me a favor before we leave," I said.

"Name it."

"Get in your car but keep the headlights off. Then back up about a hundred yards and drive towards the gate at around sixty miles an hour. Once you get past me, turn your lights back on, then go by that guard shack as if you didn't know Potrero ends at that arch. I want the guard to leave his post and chase you up onto the property."

"Why?"

"I've been sitting here, looking at that fancy mailbox down by the gate. I think I know a quick way to find out who owns this place."

"Forgetting for the moment the illegal search aspect of reading their mail, the gate guard probably collects it every day and delivers it up to the main house, so the box will be empty."

"If this guard is like most of the other plastic badges I've met, he's hijacking a few magazines to read on cold nights. Then he sends them up with the following day's mail. It's not an illegal search if I steal something that's already been stolen."

Hitch smiled. "That's very fine hair you're splitting, dude, but I like it. You've always got some devious shit happening. That's gonna be very good for your character, movie-wise."

Sumner grinned as he got out of the MDX and into his Porsche. A minute later he had backed up and was speeding past me. I watched as he snapped his headlights on, then flew past the guard shack and up the drive.

The uniformed guard came running out, shouting as Hitch's Carrera disappeared up the long lane leading to the ranch house on the top of the hill. The guard got into an electric cart that was parked nearby and gave chase.

I put the MDX in gear, and as soon as he was out of sight, I drove up to the guard shack, stopped, left the motor idling, got out and went inside.

The shack was empty, but as I suspected, there were six or seven magazines with address stickers lying on the counter. I took one, got back into my car, hit reverse and backed out of there. Then I turned and reparked in about the same spot I'd been in before.

A minute later Hitch's Porsche came back down the lane followed by the electric cart. He was being escorted off the property. Once he was through the arch he continued down W. Potrero.

Then he switched off his headlights, hung a U-turn, and reparked behind me. A moment later he was again seated in my front seat.

"How'd you do?" he said.

I handed him the sports magazine I'd just lifted.

"Who the hell is Diego San Diego?" he said, reading the label.

"That's what we're going to find out first thing tomorrow."

▪ CHAPTER ▪
47

I arrived home twenty minutes behind Alexa. It was almost half past midnight. We agreed to finish a few more work items and meet in fifteen minutes for a nightcap on our patio before bed.

I sat in the big chair in our den and began to make notes in my casebook about what I'd learned that day. I made a chronological list, starting with what José Del Cristo had told us about London Good Delivery Bars and gold bullion, followed by my meeting at Sheedy's house, the trip into the West Valley, and finally Rancho San Diego.

Next I went on the Internet and Googled Diego San Diego. He was not too widely written about. You had to make a concerted effort at anonymity to be that wealthy, own a multimillion-dollar Arabian horse ranch, breed thoroughbreds, and at the same time stay nearly invisible to the press. However, the few stories I did find proved thought-provoking. As I read the meager selection, I accumulated some interesting facts.

Originally from one of the hill towns above Cartagena, Colombia, Diego San Diego came to the United States as a teenager in the early forties. Cartagena is the capital of Colombia. It is a known haven for drug dealers and money launderers and is one of Farvagny-le-Grand's main marketing centers. I was beginning to wonder if the Farvagny-le-Grand jewelry company was actually some kind of elaborate Colombian drug laundry.

San Diego's business interests sounded semi-legit, unless you'd spent the last two days investigating the Vulcuna case. He'd been a polo player, which was only interesting because it hinted at too much disposable income, a little like those South American drug lords who build zoos in their backyards. Diego had also been a show-business financier all through the nineties, and a commodities broker since 1978.

As I read all of this, it seemed to hit all the right hot buttons. My Colombian mystery man was quickly rising in this twenty-five-year-old pool of yellow shit.

In an article about a cancer fund-raiser in 1998, I found an out-of-focus picture of him obviously taken without his permission. His left hand was thrown out toward the lens, partially blocking the shot. The article noted that he was notoriously publicity shy and abhorred being photographed. Interestingly enough, it was a personality quirk shared by Al Capone, Carlos the Terrorist, and a dozen other killers and world-class criminals.

I searched around and found another photo taken in 2004. The quality of that one wasn't very good either. He was moving in the shot, causing it to blur at the edges. His back was slightly turned to the camera, so he was caught in a three-quarter profile.

From what I could see, Diego San Diego appeared to be a very tanned, fit man in his mideighties. He had a full head of steel gray hair. His teeth looked big and strong, reminding me again of the Amazon River crocs and those foolish birds that wandered into the jaws of death to feed.

The story under the photo stated that Arabian horse breeder Diego San Diego had been a large benefactor of the City of Hope Oncology Center since the death of his wife, Maria Elaina Blanca San Diego, from breast cancer ten years earlier.

Diego was continuing to gain energy as the primary focus of my investigation. But I was so tired I couldn't plot a decent course of action. My head felt like a ball of cotton.

I shut off the computer, grabbed a bottle of Corona beer from the fridge, and went out to the backyard. Alexa was just finishing her e-mails so I sat in one of the metal chairs to enjoy the view while I waited for her.

My thoughts quickly turned away from the beautiful moonlit water and fresh ocean breeze to more venal, monetary concerns. For instance, where was my twinkling jeweled carpet of city lights? How come I had no large bubbling Jacuzzi at my elbow and no plate-glass windows that looked down on the clouds?

Hitch parked his expensive sports car under a porte cochere while my leased Acura was pulled up next to my neighbor's trash cans.

I was trying not to let any of those pesky flies land on me when my wife came out holding a cold beer and sat down. She also looked extremely tired. It had been a long day for us both.

"My detective commanders all got their estimated budgets in late," she said. "It gets worse every year."

"Well, they have divisions to run," I replied, wondering as I said it if Jamie Foxx would really agree to star in *Prostitutes' Ball*, doubling our potential domestic gross.

She sighed. "It's getting way tougher to make a decent financial plan with all these city budget cuts."

"Right," I agreed as I sipped from my bottle. *Corona is good beer,* I thought, *but just for the hell of it, maybe I should pick up a few six-packs of that imported German lager that Hitch drinks.*

"How's the armored car case coming?" Alexa asked.

"We have a person of interest. Two, if you count Stender Sheedy Sr."

She looked at me and raised an eyebrow, so I brought her up to date. I also filled her in on the few things I'd just learned about Diego San Diego.

"Sheedy is the nexus," she said, cutting to the bottom line, like she always did. "He touches both cases. He was making noise in the eighties and he's still barking."

"Yeah."

Alexa sat for a moment thinking about the case. Then she turned and looked directly at me.

"You know, for two smart guys, there's one thing here you and Hitch aren't dealing with, but you should because it makes absolutely no sense."

"The abandoned gold."

"Exactly. You've got this guy, Diego San Diego, who you think may be a big-time Colombian money launderer, making him a time-sensitive cash broker, yet he leaves fifteen million in gold bullion parked in that well house for over twenty-five years?"

"I know, but José said . . ."

"I don't care what José said. José seems a little flaky to me anyway. Something this out of whack has to be wrong."

"You think it's counterfeit?"

"It's gotta be counterfeit," she said, and set her beer down. "Look, it's not my case, it's yours. But I *was* one of the primary responders on the triple that got this whole thing started. My opinion is, get a second assay opinion."

I took another sip of Corona and thought about it. She was right.

"Hang on a minute," Alexa said. Then she got up, went into her office, and returned a moment later with a slip of paper. There was a name and number written on it.

"Who's Materon Smith?" I asked.

"She's the contact person I talked to at the Jewelry Mart. She gave us José Del Cristo. I took him because he was immediately available. That doesn't mean he's necessarily the best. There are others who do gold assays down there. She said I could call her anytime, day or night."

I was still holding the slip of paper when Alexa pulled her cell out of its holster and handed it to me. I dialed and got Mrs. Smith. She sounded like she'd been asleep, but after I told her who I was, she said it was okay, she was used to taking midnight calls from their brokerage contacts in Europe.

"I think we need another assay done for the purpose of legal verification," I told her somewhat vaguely.

"I have three more firms I can call for you."

She read off the names. One was the Latimer Commodities Exchange in downtown L.A. She told me they just went into that business a few years ago. I put Materon Smith on hold and looked over at Alexa.

"Latimer just started doing assays."

"Go for it," Alexa said. "Might tell us something."

"Can you set me up an appointment with Latimer first thing in the morning?" I said into the phone.

"They open at seven. How's seven fifteen? I can meet you there."

"Perfect." I hung up, then handed the cell back to Alexa. "Seven fifteen tomorrow morning," I told her.

"Good. You should probably call Jeb and have an armed patrol officer get one of the gold bricks out of the evidence room and meet you there."

I made the call, waking Jeb up too. But he wasn't ticked off either because this case was now weighing down on all of us.

After I hung up, Alexa looked at me and said, "I'd like to come up with something else, but my mind is putty."

"Mine too."

"Race you to the bedroom."

I didn't know what she had in mind, but I got up and headed that way. I was going about as fast as a man who'd only had five hours of sleep in seventy-two could go.

Naturally, she beat me.

We made love in our big queen-sized bed. It calmed my nerves and raised my spirits, lightening my mood. When we finished we lay in each other's arms. She didn't speak and a few minutes later I realized the reason. She was already asleep.

I looked up at the ceiling, then pushed my thoughts about the case into a cupboard in the back of my head and slammed the door shut to wait for morning.

As I often did before sleep, I lapsed into a confusing personal inventory of my assets and liabilities. It was something I'd been doing since I was in the Huntington House group home as a child. Back then, I would sit on the toilet in the big, shared bathroom in Sharon Cross Hall with the door locked and my meager collection of stolen treasures on my lap.

I would look at my money, most of it lifted from the purses of social workers at the group home. I would count it, then stuff it in my pocket. Each time I examined the broken gold watch that I'd filched off some guy's towel at the beach I'd wonder if I got it fixed what it might be worth. A few rings and trinkets completed the stash. It was a collection of questionable worth, because I had paid for most of it with my own loss of self-esteem.

Lately these bedtime inventories tended to be more psychological than material, but now, all these years later, I again found myself fantasizing about wealth. It felt like lost ground. Was I still building my castles too close to the water?

As I lay in my bed listening to Alexa's rhythmic breathing I suddenly realized that I was having a midlife crisis. I was nearing the end of my police career and had very little set aside. As a child, my life had only been about me. I was the most important part of every equation. As I got older, I felt smaller and smaller inside my surroundings. This whole movie deal seemed to have kicked these hidden insecurities into overdrive. Now I tried to put things into a better perspective.

Sure, it would be nice to be wealthy, to drive a Carrera and have a huge house with a city view. But I knew if I wanted to have true happiness, I needed to rein all that bullshit in. It just wasn't me. At least not anymore. I had built this castle in exactly the right place.

It wasn't on Mount Olympus. It was in Venice Beach, California. That was *my* reality. And you know what? That reality was pretty damn good.

There were no angels singing, but I got to hold one in my arms.

As I fell asleep I was thinking not many guys got to do that.

▪ CHAPTER ▪
48

Alexa was out of the house early. I left a few minutes behind her so I could make it to Latimer Commodities Exchange by seven fifteen. I also wanted to start the spade and shovel work on Diego San Diego's background.

I was on the freeway by six forty-five, heading into town, when I finally got through to Barry Matthews, my contact on the white-collar squad who handled business and financial crime. He swung on better vines inside of L.A.'s complex financial jungle. I thought if anyone could pierce Diego's aversion to the press and get me some dirt, Barry was the one.

Once he was on the line I said, "I need a deep background check, state and federal, on Diego San Diego." I told him what little information I'd found—horse breeder, polo player, commodities broker, film financier. "Also, anything you can give me on his financial and banking affairs."

"Point me in a direction. What, exactly, are you looking for?"

"I think there's a decent chance he used to be a Colombian money launderer in the eighties. That hunch is supported by the fact he dealt in easy-to-move, high-value international commerce, like gemstones and gold bullion.

"He might have a connection to a Swiss jewelry company called Farvagny-le-Grand in Geneva. I'd also like you to see if he connects to Thomas Vulcuna, who owned a production company named Eagle's Nest and was supposed to have killed his wife and daughter then shot himself. We cleared it in eighty-one."

"Supposed to have?" Barry said, alert to every nuance.

"I think we got it wrong. San Diego might have had silent dealings with Eagle's Nest. Go back before 1981 and be sure to check with DEA."

"Anybody else?" I could hear him turn a page. For a computer geek, he had some old-school habits.

"Yeah. He has a connection to Stender Sheedy Sr., the managing partner of Sheedy, Devine, and Lipscomb, a white-shoe law firm in Century City. I'd like to know what those two have been doing. Also, there might be a Thayer Dunbar connection as well."

"The oil billionaire?"

"Yeah, and listen, Barry. This is kinda hush-hush. I'd really appreciate it if you didn't farm any of it out."

"What's your timetable?"

"ASAP."

"ASAP," he repeated. "What ever happened to WYCGI?"

"Never heard of it. What the hell is WYCGI?"

"Whenever you can get it."

"We'll do that one next time." Then I thanked him and hung up.

The Latimer Commodities Exchange was located on the top floor in an old brick building off Sixth Street in the Jewelry District. Jeb Calloway had signed out another gold brick from the evidence locker and brought the twenty-seven-pound London Good Delivery Bar over himself, along with a police escort to help guard it.

They arrived in a black-and-white and pulled in next to where I was waiting. The uniform carried a heavy canvas satchel with the bar inside, following Jeb and me into the elevator. We rode to the twelfth floor.

Materon Smith met us in the lobby and escorted us down the hall. She was a heavyset African-American woman in her midforties with a friendly face. Her hair was pulled back in a ponytail.

"I got Valentine Rosinski to come in early," she said. "He's one of the best assayers in L.A."

The lab was large, and filled with an impressive array of equipment. We were greeted at the door by Rosinski, a man with a laurel wreath of gray hair fringing his head. He was wearing a white lab coat and sixty extra pounds.

Jeb put the gold bar on the table and Rosinski studied it carefully. "Is right size for London Good Delivery Bar," he said in a semi-thick Russian accent.

He lifted it, nodded, then set it down on its face and, like José Del Cristo, read the Oswald Steel identification trademark on the back. Then, exactly as José had, he told us the bar was made pre-1985 and put a nail mark in the gold to test its softness. He weighed it, getting the same four-hundred-troy-ounce reading.

"What tests have been done?"

I looked at my case notes. "An acid test for purity which said the gold was twenty-four karats, and ninety-nine point seven percent pure. Then it was taken to an assay office downtown for an X-ray fluorescence scan, which it also passed."

Rosinski continued to study the bar. "London Good Delivery Bars would be hard to make counterfeit, yah? Very expensive to do this. Top-quality fake today would cost maybe fifty thousand U.S. dollars to produce, because today, you would need to use much real gold to pass our new tests. In 1983, not so much. Back then, they have no neutron activation analysis, no speed-of-sound tests. Weight is always a problem unless you use tungsten."

I said, "I understand that tungsten is very hard to work with because it melts at extremely high temperatures."

He smiled. "When you are stealing gold, a little hard work is not such a bad thing, no?"

"I guess not."

"Since you already do X-ray fluorescence scan, I suggest a neutron activation analysis. It's more thorough, is nondestructive, and will tell what we need to know."

"And the X-ray won't?" Jeb asked.

"If your bar has a one-sixteenth-inch layer of gold on top of a tungsten base, the X-ray will not pass through. This makes it read pure. This neutron analysis is better."

"How long 'til we know?" I asked.

"I can't start until tomorrow because I have other work," Val Rosinski said. "But tomorrow, maybe an hour or two after we open, we know."

We left the gold bar in the same spot where it began its journey over twenty-five years ago, right here, at the Latimer Commodities Exchange.

It was only a little past eight when I got back into my car. As soon as I did, my Bluetooth beeped. I answered and instantly had Hitch's voice in my ear. He sounded excited.

"Listen, dawg. I just got a strong bite."

"On San Diego?"

"On Jamie Foxx. He wants a meet this morning. A guy from his production company just called me. I'm not sure exactly what Jamie wants to discuss, 'cause his assistant didn't have any details, just that Jamie wants to see me. The agency isn't open yet so I can't call Jerry and get a heads-up. One of my UTA guys musta given him a sniff of this yesterday."

I didn't say anything. I was getting mad.

"Shane?"

"Listen, Hitch, this is supposed to be on the DL, remember? Now you're telling me UTA is out there blabbing it around? Did you leak this to them?"

"No. I haven't told them a word about the gold. But agents are scavengers, man. They root in other people's trash. That's how they go for the gold. Excuse the double metaphor. . . . You can't stop them 'cause it's in their DNA. Of course I told UTA about the old Vulcuna murder-suicide, but you already knew I did that. If they called Jamie, that's probably all they told him about." I didn't answer that either. "Shane, are you there?"

"Yeah."

"This could be huge, man. We gotta drop everything and go see Jamie right now."

"What about that other thing?"

"What other thing?"

"Our case, dipshit. The twenty-five-year-old gold heist with five corpses. You *do* remember that, don't you?"

"Of course."

"It's picking up speed. We don't have time this morning to be messing with your movie-star friend."

"Listen, dawg—"

"I'm a lot of things, but not a dawg," I interrupted. "I'm sometimes a jerk, even an asshole, but I'm not a fucking dawg."

"If that's your call, fine. But here's the 411. Jamie is headed off to London on a European promotional tour for his new flick that's just coming out. Then he's in Prague for six months on the new Michael Mann film. He's leaving at noon from Van Nuys Airport on his G-5."

"So what?"

"Right now, this morning, he happens to be in Malibu looking at some property he wants to buy. He happens to want to talk to us about *Prostitutes' Ball*. If we get our asses up there, he'll hear me out, but it's kinda time sensitive. We blow this meet, unless we wanta spend a fortune to go to Prague, we lose our chance at getting any face-time with him for half a year."

I remained silent. Or maybe I just groaned slightly.

"Okay, okay. So I'll say no. I just had to check with you, dawg—I mean, Shane. Because, like it or not, I've become sort of fond of you. I'm trying to keep my partner from throwing away a bloody fortune so you and Alexa won't get stuck eating dog food after you've pulled the pin and shot through your measly police pension."

I suddenly realized I was so distracted by this conversation I was driving erratically and straddling two lanes. Cars behind me on Sixth Street started honking. I corrected and felt myself caving in to this new lust for money.

The canal house was nice, but beachfront would be better. Instead of taking our retirement sitting on lawn chairs in some public campground, wouldn't Alexa and I be happier on a sleek sixty-foot sailboat with silk spinnakers, cruising the California coast?

"I'll call him and tell him no." He paused. "So that's the decision. That's what you want, right?"

"Uhhh, well . . ." I was vapor locking.

"Good. I hear indecision in your voice. You're finally coming to your senses. Listen, I got directions here. It's off Trancas Canyon, but it's a little confusing. Meet me at Moonshadows restaurant on the Coast Highway out by Malibu in half an hour. Can you make that?"

"I don't know," I said. "I'm not sure we should be doing this."

"It's a lousy two hours out of your life, get a grip, Scully."

"Okay, okay. I'll see you there."

I turned around, headed the other way, and got on the Santa Monica Freeway to the Coast Highway. All the way, I kept wondering who I was turning into. Was I now just a Donald Trump wannabe with a badge?

Hitch was waiting in the restaurant parking lot with the top down, looking like a GQ photo spread in his tan suit, pink shirt, and matching tie. I pulled in and he shouted.

"Park over there. We'll take my ride."

I parked and got in the Porsche. We buzzed out onto PCH heading farther up the coast toward Trancas Canyon. As we drove, I told him I'd set up a second gold assay test at the Latimer Commodities Exchange. He didn't seem too interested. He was deep in movie producer mode.

"Okay, look, when we get there let me do the talking," he said.

"Jamie doesn't like a hard sell, but he's got a shrewd eye for a hit. He also knows what works for him. This is right in his sweet spot, so he's gonna know it without us overdoing the whole story pitch. Sometimes less is more."

"We can't tell him the whole story. Remember, the gold bullion thing is still off-limits."

"Shit, he's gonna be in Prague. Who's he gonna tell in East Europe? We can trust him."

"It's off-limits. We can only pitch Vulcuna, not the Brinks truck." I was hanging on to this slender distinction as if it was some sort of important moral distinction. "You tell him about the gold bullion, I'll put you under arrest right in front of him," I said hotly.

"Okay, okay. Don't go all Dirty Harry on me." Hitch downshifted as he made the turn away from the ocean onto Trancas Canyon Drive.

"So how's this?" he said. "We use the fact that we can't tell him anything to tease him. Y'know, like, 'We can't tell you everything, J, because it is so fucking hot, we've been sworn to secrecy by the LAPD, FBI, and the entire Department of Homeland Security. But it's huge and involves over thirty million in liquid assets. And once it goes public it's gonna be on the cover of *Time* and *People* magazine.' How's that?"

"Nothing about money," I said, my neck bowing.

"A liquid asset isn't money. It could be stocks or even real estate priced to sell. Come on. If we get Jamie to do this, we just doubled our back end in one hour."

"No," I said. I had my teeth clenched as I spit that one word through them.

I felt ridiculous having this argument. After all, selling out was selling out. The only thing we were arguing about was degree. I was so far out of character, I was afraid I would meet myself coming the other way down Trancas Canyon Road.

At the top of the hill, the landscape was rolling grass and majestic rocks. The view was spectacular up here. The ocean stretched out two thousand feet below us, blue as sapphire and just as ageless.

"Jamie's assistant said Canyon Ridge Drive." Hitch was looking at his scribbled directions. "He's buying twenty acres up here as an investment. Fuck if I can find it." Then he put the car in gear and pulled farther up the road to read a sign.

"Ah, there it is."

He downshifted again and turned onto a small unpaved feeder road. After we were about two hundred yards in, we were forced to stop because a large pile of boulders blocked the way.

"Fucking rock slide," Hitch said. "Even God has turned against me."

"Hitch."

He didn't answer.

"Hitch."

"What is it?" he snapped. "We're running out of time. We gotta get around this rock slide."

"I don't think it's a rock slide. There are no loose rocks or boulders up there." I pointed up at the grassy hillside above us.

"If it's not a rock slide, what is it?"

"A barricade."

As soon as I said this, the first rifle shot rang out.

The windshield on the Carrera shattered right by Hitch's head, but the tempered glass saved his life because it ricocheted the bullet.

That shot was followed by two more. I felt the wind from the second one as it whizzed by my cheek and hit the headrest behind Hitch. It was almost a full second before I heard the retort. From that one-second sound delay, I knew whoever was shooting at us was a long way off using a scoped rifle.

Hitch ducked low, threw the car in reverse, and roared out of there, churning up dust and gravel.

The fourth and fifth shots slammed the front of the sports car, blowing furrows into the hood. Fortunately, on a Porsche, the engine is over the rear wheels so nothing vital was hit and we kept going.

"Hold on!" Hitch screamed. Then he put the Porsche into a smoking one-eighty bootlegger's turn and we were back on Trancas Canyon, burning rubber from all four tires. Two more shots followed, but they were wild and missed.

We were finally out of range. Hitch pulled over at the first turnout while I snatched up the radio.

"This is Delta-28. LAPD officers need help on Trancas Canyon Road in Malibu. Cross street—Ocean View. Shots fired. We're in the county. Notify the sheriff's substation in Malibu."

"Roger that. LAPD D-28 needs help on Trancas Canyon Road and Ocean View. Shots fired. Contacting LASD. Stand by."

"We can't run away. We gotta go back up there and catch that shooter," I said.

Just then a red and white Bell Jet Ranger rose up from the hilltop behind us. The helicopter hovered for a moment before it headed north, speeding away.

"Too late," Hitch said. "There goes our Michael Bay factor. The two assholes in a chopper." He heaved a frustrated sigh. "Look what they did to my beautiful car!"

"Forget the car. You can fix it. We need to move fast. The shit just jumped off. They're gonna go back to that ranch in the Valley and tell Diego San Diego they missed us. He's gonna run. We got less than an hour to pull this together."

▪ CHAPTER ▪
50

After the chopper left, we didn't stick around for the L.A. Sheriff's Department to arrive. I called in a Code Four as Hitch sped along Trancas Canyon toward the ocean.

We'd decided against going back up to find the shooter's nest and look for brass in favor of making a move on Diego's ranch.

"I hate what they did to this car. Can't see shit through this busted windshield," Hitch groused, squinting through shattered glass.

"Forget the car. I can't believe all this materialistic bullshit."

"It's not just the car that's got me so bummed. It's also the fact they got to Jamie," he said. "How could he have given me up? The guy was my tight."

"They didn't get to Jamie. Jamie doesn't even know about this unless you blabbed it to him, too."

Hitch looked over at me as he snap-shifted into third and simultaneously took a hairpin turn too fast. His eyes were off the road.

"Watch where you're fucking going!" I yelled.

He looked back, swerved, stayed on the road. "You're right. Of course Jamie's not involved. He couldn't be. Guy loves me. But then how did they know to call us and lure us up there?"

"I don't know. How much did you really tell your dumb-ass agents?"

"Nothing! Do I have to take a damn polygraph?"

I didn't answer, but when he looked over I was probably scowling.

"If we're gonna be partners, you've gotta develop a little trust," he said, sounding pissed.

I snapped my fingers. "Your plates. That security guard at Rancho San Diego. I bet he got your license plate when he followed you down the hill."

"That's gotta be it. Powerful guy like San Diego must have some police connections. He could have run it. My association with Jamie is all over the Internet. Once they knew who I was, one of San Diego's guys could have called me, pretending to be Jamie's assistant."

"Listen, Hitch. We're way behind here. We're chasing this. We need to get out in front."

"Gee, whatever gave you that idea? The five fucking bullets in my car?"

My mind was racing. "We've gotta get back to the PAB fast. We got no time, but we've gotta set up a takedown."

"I'm going as fast as I can," he said, roaring around some slow-moving traffic.

"We've got to hit that horse farm and bust San Diego this morning. That means judges, warrants, even SWAT."

"Exactly!"

We were now on the Coast Highway roaring past Moonshadows. Hitch started to downshift. "Forget my car. Leave it," I said, shouting over the slipstreaming wind.

I pulled out my cell phone and dialed the office. "This is Scully. Gimme Jeb," I told the probationer on our call desk.

A minute later I had the captain on the line. "Jeb, the Vulcuna case went hot. Hitch and I were just fired on, ambushed up in Trancas Canyon." Then I told him about Diego San Diego and explained what I needed.

"I think this guy is some kind of retired Colombian scumbag," I said. "You need to get Dahlia to start writing warrants."

"What kind of warrants?"

"Anything she can get a judge to sign. Search, arrest, evidence gathering. We need to lock that ranch of his down before he splits."

"That's kinda vague for a warrant," Jeb said. "You need to give me some probable cause."

I looked at Hitch. "He says we need PC."

"Tell him what those assholes did to my car."

"They dumped six or eight rounds down on us from a hillside with a scoped rifle," I told Jeb. "That's attempted murder of two police officers. We've got some of the slugs with us in Hitch's car. That's gotta be good enough to get us paper. This has to happen now. These guys are shooters so you better notify SWAT. We'll need to use their warrant delivery team."

"I'm on it. Get in here," Jeb instructed. He'd been my boss for several years and I knew he trusted my instincts. I could hear nervous energy in his voice as I hung up.

We raced onto the freeway, made it to the interchange in a miraculous ten minutes.

Then I called Barry Matthews in Financial Crimes. "We're out of time," I told him. "I'm about twenty blocks away. What have you got for me?"

"I'll meet you in your office in ten," he said.

"You got something?"

"Yeah," he said. "Get ready to be very happy."

▪ CHAPTER ▪
51

We got to the Police Administration Building in record time. The last few miles of the trip the Porsche had begun making loud growling sounds that didn't sound too healthy. Hitch pulled his bullet-riddled Carrera into an empty parking spot.

"Those assholes are gonna feel the Hitchmeister's full and complete wrath over what they did to my ride," he said, slamming the driver's-side door in frustration. When he did that, most of the windshield glass fell into the front seat.

We hurried upstairs. Jeb, Dahlia, and Alexa were already there. Because she had been a primary responder on the original case, and because she really missed this stuff, Alexa was taking some time away from the department budget wars to help us sort it out.

Two or three other Homicide Special cops were already talking to a warrant delivery team, lining up tactical support.

"I think we're gonna want more than one SWAT," Hitch suggested. "These guys have already piled up five corpses. This morning they tried to make it seven. They're a bunch of trigger-happy assholes with long guns and helicopters. How much PC do we need before we can make a move?" The Hitchmeister on a rant.

"Slow down and talk me through it," Dahlia said.

She set a digital tape recorder on Jeb's desk between us. We gave them everything we had, including all of our suspicions. When we finished, Dahlia weighed in.

"You can't pin any of that on San Diego. You got nothing that sticks to him except the fact that Stender Sheedy ran out there after you braced him in his den, which is not a crime. No judge is going to write this."

"I didn't say we had it completely nailed down," I defended. "But these people have somehow tripped to our investigation. Sheedy went directly out to Skyline Drive after I started talking about gold contracts. My bet is he wanted to check that well house to be sure we hadn't found the truck. When he couldn't get on the property, he went straight to San Diego. That tells me they're all involved in that eighty-three bullion heist and the deaths of at least two guards."

"Circumstantial, nonbinding, probative, and inadmissible," Dahlia said, firing these legal concepts at us like clip-fed bullets.

"Maybe, but how 'bout this?" I said, switching tactics. "An hour ago we were both shot at. The slugs are in Hitchens's car. We search that ranch. If we find the long gun out there that fired those bullets and ballistics can make a match, that's physical evidence tying the gun licensee to an attempted double cop killing."

"It's upside down, Scully, and you know it," Dahlia said in frustration. "You need the gun and the ballistics match first, *then* you get the search warrant. I'm trying to help here, but it's all speculative. You need to give me more."

Of course she was right.

Just then, Barry Matthews from the Financial Crimes desk rode in on a white horse and saved us. There weren't enough chairs so everyone stood as he launched into his report.

"In eighty-one the DEA thought Diego San Diego was a silent partner in Eagle's Nest Studios," he began. "But it was never proven. There were also rumors he was funding that studio's bank overdrafts."

"Why would he do that?" Hitch asked.

"The DEA thought Diego San Diego was a silent partner in the company and was setting Eagle's Nest up as a potential money laundry for the Columbian drug cartels. Apparently, this was going on without Thomas Vulcuna's knowledge. Vulcuna found out in December of eighty-one. They had at least one public argument over it. It almost came to blows at the studio Christmas party."

"The night he supposedly killed his wife and daughter, then shot himself," I said, looking at Dahlia. She had a neutral wait-and-see look on her face.

"A lot of the DEA stuff I got dealing with Diego's past relationship with Vulcuna was redacted," Barry continued. "So I don't know exactly what was going on there, but somebody in our federal system wanted to keep San Diego out of that murder-suicide case and blacked out about ten paragraphs of their own report. Back then, the DEA was running a big probe on the Colombian drug cartels. From all that blacked-out language, it looks like the feds had flipped Diego San Diego and he had started giving up names on his drug buddies."

"So the feds protected him," I said.

Barry nodded. "They didn't want him compromised as a witness before they could get their major drug case to court. He wouldn't make much of a wit if in advance of those cases, he got accused of Vulcuna's triple murder."

I said, "That's why McKnight and Norris were yanked off the Vulcuna case and it got closed down so abruptly."

Hitch now took one of the few chairs, opened his journal to a fresh page, and started writing furiously.

"How does a production company operate as a drug laundry?" Alexa asked.

"You invest dirty drug cash in the production company and take ownership in the shows it produces," Barry explained. "Then after two network runs, when Eagle's Nest finally sells the shows into syndication, the owners take their money out in distribution and syndication profits. Everybody pays their income taxes and walks away rich and happy."

"And how does the Dorothy White Foundation fit?" I wondered.

Barry started grinning. "That's the really neat part. You'll never guess who Dorothy White really is." He paused for effect.

We all just waited him out and the moment was lost, so he shrugged and pushed ahead.

"Dorothy White is Diego San Diego's sister-in-law. Diego's wife was Maria Elaina San Diego, but her maiden name was Blanca. Blanca is white in Spanish."

"Duh," Hitch said.

"Yeah, duh. But you guys walked right past it. Dorothy and Maria Elaina were sisters," Barry continued. "Dorothy married Thayer Dunbar. Maria Elaina married Diego San Diego. Their grandfather changed his name to White from Blanca when he emigrated from Colombia in the fifties. It was a very common practice for immigrants to do that."

It's exactly what Chrissy Sweet had done when she married Karel Sladky. Another weird parallel between those two cases.

Hitch finished writing this and shouted, "He shoots, he scores!"

Everybody in the room turned to look at him. His red journal was still open in his lap. His left fist up pumping air. The smile on his face quickly faded under the roomful of glares.

"He's excited because that's the main subplot that's been lying beneath the surface since the inciting event that nobody saw until it finally jumped up in the third act and tied these two cases together," I said.

Now everybody was staring at me.

"Maybe we should explain it later," Hitch muttered.

"So, Brooks Dunbar is what? Diego San Diego's nephew through marriage?" Alexa asked.

Hitch nodded. He was still grinning.

In the next hour an arrest warrant came through for Diego San Diego and twenty John Does as material witnesses and potential suspects in the hijacking of the Brinks armored truck and the killing of its two guards. A search warrant was written for Diego's ranch located at the end of W. Potrero Road.

Jeb called a Realtor in the West Valley and found a nearby farm that was for sale near San Diego's spread. He made arrangements for us to use it as a staging area.

I was tapping my foot impatiently while I imagined the ranch house emptying out, with the old Colombian drug boss scurrying to his jet for an escape to the town of his birth somewhere in the hills above Cartagena.

We were on the road less than ten minutes after we had the warrants in hand. I was in the back of an armored rescue vehicle with Hitch, Jeb, and a SWAT warrant delivery team.

"We need more SWAT shooters, Skipper," Hitch said, leaning forward, an intense look on his face.

"We have one unit," Jeb told him.

"Two SWAT teams would be better," Hitch pressed. "Three if possible."

Jeb wasn't convinced, so Hitch went into verbal overdrive. "This shoot-out will soon become LAPD campfire lore. The heroics of your takedown will be talked about for years, Skipper. They write folk songs about shit like this. It could end up being called the Battle of Simi Valley or, less favorably, Calloway's Catastrophe." Then he lowered his voice. "You want to protect your guys, Skipper. It's better to have extra SWAT and not need it than to need extra SWAT and not have it."

Jeb was still reluctant, but a sense of caution finally prevailed. He made the call.

"I'd also get the SWAT chopper up over the target with a couple a Colt CAR-15 assault rifles," I suggested in the clutches of the moment.

We sped along on the 101 freeway. A caravan of five Suburbans full of armed cops in flak vests followed by a SWAT team in a black ARV, with two more on the way.

"We're over twenty-five years late serving this warrant," Hitch said. "But the LAPD is on a collision course with justice."

It sounded like the tagline for our movie.

52

The ranch Jeb had found was small and only a quarter of a mile from Rancho San Diego. It was a holdout property that had finally been sunk by California's high state taxes. The few farm buildings were in desperate need of repair. We pulled up the drive and parked next to an old barn with faded, peeling paint.

Hitch and I walked over to the SWAT van and borrowed a couple of Second Chance flak vests, strapping them on over our clothing. Then we each checked out Heckler & Koch MP-5 9 mm submachine guns from the weapons box. These full-autos were acknowledged by most cops to be the Rolls-Royce of assault guns.

LAPD SWAT squad teams were commanded by a sergeant and consisted of two five-man elements. There was a hard-entry team and an intelligence officer who was assigned the job of detailing everything about the target and the location.

The two-man sniper teams consisted of a shooter who carried a long-barreled AR-15 and his spotter, who was assigned the job of identifying potential targets with a scope.

We waited for our two additional SWAT teams, who had just called to say they were ten minutes out.

The first pictures appeared on the intel officer's closed-circuit monitor in the back of our black ARV, sent down to us by a camera in SWAT's hovering air unit. Everyone in the truck huddled around the screen and looked at the shots being beamed down by the chopper, currently flying at five thousand feet over Rancho San Diego. We could hear the faint THUMPA-THUMPA of the rotor blades.

The air unit was broadcasting a front-down view of the huge ranch house. Even on TV, it looked impressive. The two-story California Spanish with its magnificent courtyard sat facing a stable building and horseshoe-shaped paddock.

"Looks like nobody's left yet," Jeb commented, watching the monitor, which showed half a dozen Lincoln Town Cars and Suburbans parked in front of the house, being loaded with bags. Off to one side, next to the big horse barn, I could see the red and white Bell Jet Ranger that had been out at Trancas Canyon this morning.

"You need to keep that bird from leaving," I told Jeb, who relayed that instruction to our air unit.

Then the two arriving SWAT units rolled up the drive in their new black Armored Rescue Vehicles. The commanding officers of the three SWAT teams began making geographic drawings of the site.

About ten minutes later we reviewed the layout of Rancho San Diego. As we watched the monitor, we could see the red and white chopper was now being loaded with big suitcases.

"If you want to keep it contained, we need to do this now," the SWAT lieutenant advised. He was a tall, raw-boned guy with too much chin named Rick Sherman.

He called his guys together and huddled with his SWAT sergeants, working out the plan.

Jeb, Hitch, and I were given radios and told to stay on TAC frequency six. We were also instructed to follow the entry teams up the drive, but to stay well back until the site was secured.

"We don't want you guys getting hurt or in the way," Lieutenant Sherman said.

"In the movie, we can take a little creative license with that," Hitch assured me after Sherman left.

There were over thirty of us as we drove off the borrowed property and headed up Potrero. The first line of resistance was the guard shack, which sat under the driveway arch. When the plastic badge saw our armored black caravan, he stepped out and held his hands high over his head.

"I surrender," he said. "Don't shoot."

The security guard, in his late sixties, was ordered to toss his gun in the dirt and was quickly cuffed.

We left two men to secure the exit and our army of flakked SWAT officers drove up the lane in the deadly looking black ARVs toward the beautiful two-story Spanish farmhouse that sat at the top of the hill. Hundred-thousand-dollar grazing thoroughbreds turned their heads and watched placidly as we rumbled past.

The SWAT teams poured out of the vehicles just below the house and, with their MP-5s at port arms, quickly fanned out to secure all first-floor exits. Several stewards who were just coming out of the house carrying luggage stopped in surprise.

"LAPD! Hands in the air! Everybody on the dirt. Spread 'em!" Sherman shouted.

The men dropped Gucci bags, threw their hands in the air, then proned out on the ground and were handcuffed.

The SWAT teams ran up the short hill and went through the open front door into the main house. Hitch and I brought up the rear. In the entry hall, five more Colombians were carrying suitcases down from upstairs. All of them surrendered without incident.

"The shooting's gonna start any time now," Hitch panted in my ear, still out of breath from running up the hill.

We followed a SWAT team into the kitchen, where we found two more men and one woman packing food into a wicker basket.

"SWAT. Put 'em up. Assume the position!" a SWAT sergeant shouted.

They all hit the floor and spread their arms, then laced their fingers behind their necks. They were cuffed and pulled into the entry.

Hitch and I stood with them under an old Spanish wagon-wheel chandelier, pointing our MP-5s at these frightened employees who sat handcuffed as SWAT teams continued to sweep through the house.

We heard doors being thrown open upstairs and officers yelling, "SWAT! You're under arrest!"

Several minutes later one man and three women in household staff uniforms were herded down the staircase by SWAT members and secured next to our picnic basket packers.

So far, not a single shot had been fired.

"I think there's a large contingent of shooters in the backyard," one of the SWAT sergeants said over the radio TAC frequency.

"That's where they'll make their stand," Hitch told me earnestly.

"Right," I replied. We were both gripping our 9 mm machine guns with sweaty palms.

SWAT took the backyard in less than ten seconds.

Every single person back there threw their hands up and submitted immediately to arrest without incident.

We followed SWAT into the courtyard, where ten or so *celadores* were being arrested, cuffed, and pushed down on their haunches next to a garden wall. There was only one person left.

An elderly gray-haired gentleman was seated in a high-backed wicker chair beside a large Spanish fountain. He had a blanket over his knees and was holding a calico cat on his lap.

"Diego San Diego?" Lieutenant Sherman demanded.

"Yes," the old man replied in a weak, shaking voice. He was no longer the powerful, fit man I'd seen in the picture from four years ago. He looked sick. He had lost weight. His hair had thinned.

"You are being issued an arrest warrant as a material witness and potential suspect in the hijacking of a Brinks armored truck and the murder of two guards," Sherman said as he put the paper in the old man's hands. "Get up, we need to cuff you."

"I'm sorry, I can't stand," the almost ninety-year-old man said. "My doctor forbids all movement. I've got severe phlebitis in my legs."

"In that case, stay where you are and remain absolutely still," Sherman said.

"We're clear upstairs," one of the SWAT teams called out.

"Clear in the main house," another called.

"Courtyard is clear," someone behind us shouted.

Lieutenant Rick Sherman turned and looked at Jeb.

"We're secure here, Captain."

The cat on Diego San Diego's lap stood, arched its back, and yawned.

Then Hitch leaned in toward me and whispered, "This ending is gonna need a big fuckin' rewrite."

· CHAPTER ·
53

When I first came on the job I had a training partner who used to say that runny shit always floats. A gross but often accurate work metaphor in law enforcement.

The first thing that floated was the Kalashnikov Series 100 assault rifle that had fired on us up in Trancas Canyon.

It was still in the red and white helicopter tucked behind the back passenger seat. When we ran the AK-100, it came back registered to Diego San Diego. The stock had been wiped clean of prints, but Ballistics was able to match the slugs to the ones we dug out of Sumner's Porsche.

That afternoon, Stender Sheedy Sr. was called in to the district attorney's office. Chase Beal was strangely unavailable for this interview, so Dahlia Wilkes did the questioning for the county.

With his attorney at his side, Stender first denied knowing Diego San Diego at all.

My statement about having followed him up to Rancho San Diego was read to him. It quickly turned into a case of my word and Hitch's against the word of one of L.A.'s most powerful power brokers and prominent legal minds.

Sheedy insisted we were mistaken. That it was a preposterous claim. For the time being, it was a standoff. Next he was questioned extensively about his relationship with Thayer Dunbar. Dahlia wanted to know how Stender was connected to the suspected money launderer Diego San Diego.

"Preposterous," Sheedy said. "Outrageous."

Dahlia had found some billing records that revealed Sheedy once did some real estate work for the Colombian. Stender Sheedy Sr. finally admitted to knowing Diego San Diego, but tried to claim attorney-client privilege, saying he knew nothing about the Vulcuna triple murder.

That's when Jack McKnight drove in from Marina del Rey and identified Sheedy's picture out of a photo six-pack. He nailed him as the man who had stood silently in the Chief of D's office in 1981 to make sure McKnight and Norris closed the Vulcuna case.

Sheedy had no explanation as to why he would involve himself in that particular murder-suicide, but he was starting to panic. He could feel the case slithering out of a deep black hole in his past and, like a giant anaconda, it was starting to wrap itself around him.

Sheedy had been the legal counsel for Thayer Dunbar and his wife, Dorothy, since the seventies. As their attorney, he did have privilege, but it was pretty obvious to all of us that he was also the conduit funneling cash between Thayer and his criminal brother-in-law. Diego's money had paid for all those Houston oil-lease deals.

Thayer Dunbar was at the very least complicit in the Brinks truck hijacking because it now seemed he had allowed that armored car with its two dead drivers to be parked on his property at Skyline Drive over a quarter century ago.

Another good piece that floated was a weathered, nut-brown guy named Daniel Morales. He was in the group of people we'd pulled in during the raid on Rancho San Diego. When we ran his fingerprints, they matched up to an old Brinks Company's employee ten-card for Sergio Maroni.

So our missing armored truck guard had, at last, been found. He had changed his name and gotten a cushy job from his patrón, breeding thoroughbreds. He was now fifty-seven. A day later he was charged with double murder in the deaths of his two fellow guards and the hijacking of the armored truck. Maroni lawyered up and immediately started trying to cop a plea.

The twenty-five-year-old criminal Gordian knot that had been so baffling was finally coming unraveled.

None of this was good news for Stender Sheedy. He could see his chance to turn state's evidence slipping away and instructed his lawyer to start negotiating for a lesser charge with the DA.

Hitch and I stepped out of the way when this deal-making frenzy began, but the red leather journal was never far from my partner's hand.

The DA doesn't like to cut deals with actual murderers, so it was Stender Sheedy, not Sergio Maroni, who won the chance to turn state's evidence. Sheedy pled to five counts of conspiracy to commit murder, felony obstruction of justice, and a pile of lesser charges. He agreed to a twenty-year sentence, reducible to eight for good time served. Then he started giving up everybody. When the facts of his statement were evaluated, it ended up pretty much the way Hitch and I had figured.

Diego San Diego had invested millions of cartel drug money into

Eagle's Nest Studios in the eighties. The cartel had intended to cash out big when the shows went into syndication. But because Thomas Vulcuna wanted to make high-quality television more than he wanted to make money, he'd spent more than he had received from the networks in licensing fees. In the process, he had run his studio deep into debt with his primary lender, City Bank.

And that was when things got critical.

Diego San Diego couldn't let the bank seize a studio where he'd placed millions of dollars belonging to his violent Colombian drug bosses. He confronted Vulcuna and told him to stop losing money on production costs or the Colombians would come after him.

When Vulcuna found out his money partner had invested drug cash in Eagle's Nest shows, he first told his wife and daughter, then threatened to go to the DA.

Vulcuna and his family were killed on Christmas Eve to keep them all quiet.

More than a year later, San Diego hijacked his own insured shipment of gold to pay back the cartels. He parked the Brinks truck in the well house at Skyline Drive, which he controlled through his sister-in-law's foundation.

During the days that followed Sheedy's statement, Dahlia Wilkes was filing so many charges her designer suits began to wrinkle and she looked like she'd been sleeping in her office, which, it turned out, she was.

A couple of weeks later Alexa and I were invited up to Hitch's house for dinner. He and Crystal prepared a Country French meal of liver paté with onions as a starter. The main course was rabbit in plum sauce with vegetables al dente. Crystal made a chocolate mousse pastry for dessert. They didn't serve me another dish of bullshit prepared in the French style for which I was grateful.

After dinner Hitch supplied bathing suits and we relaxed in his bubbling Jacuzzi. The lights of Bel Air and Hollywood twinkled like jewels across the canyon below while progressive jazz played softly from the hundred-thousand-dollar sound system.

I tried not to notice any of this seductive luxury and kept telling myself I was more than happy in Venice.

After a while the girls got out of the bubbling brew and went inside the house. My new partner and I sat opposite each other, warm water frothing up under our chins, and grinned happily.

"More wine?" Hitch suggested, reaching for a bottle of cabernet.

"Thanks. Better stay sober, I'm driving."

"You guys can bunk in the guest room and go home in the morning," he offered.

"That room is bad for my *emotional* sobriety."

Hitch chuckled and said, "By the way, I've got a breakfast meeting with my agents at the Polo Lounge at nine in the morning. The auction on *Prostitutes' Ball* is kicking ass. Jamie Foxx just got in. He's our new high bidder."

"He is?"

"My guys are still working out the fine points. We're down to negotiating a definition of rolling break even on the back end."

"Whatever that means."

"It's the way you figure when the picture is in profits. There are releasing costs that roll forward, changing the break point. We have to agree on what those costs are. It's important because after we hit break even, that's when our back-end points kick in. Since you're a thirty-percent partner, I want you to come to the meeting, Shane. The Porsche got shot up, so I could also use a lift."

"You know, Hitch, this has turned into a big midlife crisis for me. I'm not dealing with it too well. I'm sort of thinking that you should take my two back-end points and keep the story money. Leave me out of it. I don't think it's good for my psyche to be around too much money. I'm starting to think like an asshole."

"Because the auction went so well, we're probably talking around two million up front with another million for every ten over fifty million in domestic gross. When it's all over, factoring in DVD and network TV sales, your end could come to seven or eight mil."

"In that case, how 'bout I pick you up here at eight sharp?" I said.

After our feast in the clouds, Alexa and I drove down from Mount Olympus and headed home to a more earthly existence.

"When you get him out of the office, Hitch is much different than I thought he'd be," Alexa commented as we passed through the ornate gates separating the gods on Mount Olympus from the rest of us.

"He takes some getting used to, but he's a damn good guy and he's sure a smart cop," I said.

When we got home, Alexa and I went out to the backyard off the canal and after a few minutes of fidgeting, I finally came clean and told her that I had agreed to meet Hitch's agents from UTA tomorrow morning.

I confessed sadly that I had let my principles get flushed to the almighty dollar. I finished by telling her that I was such a shallow asshole that I had actually been worried for the last hour about what to wear to the Polo Lounge tomorrow.

Alexa sat looking at the reflection of the moon that was wavering in the waters of the canal. She didn't say anything. I was afraid she might be making a dangerous reevaluation about the man she had chosen to marry.

"I feel sort of like I'm selling out," I said, trying to reclaim some high ground. "I mean, I've been really struggling with it. I sort of don't know who I'm supposed to be anymore. I know all about Joe Wambaugh and his books and movies. I know about Popeye Doyle in

New York, who sold *The French Connection* for millions, and about Joe Pistone and *Donnie Brasco*. I know there are more than twenty members of the LAPD who belong to the Hollywood Writers Guild. I know all of this, but still—"

I stopped and looked over at her. She was just sitting there, a strange contemplative look on her face.

"So, what do you think? You got an opinion about any of this?"

"Yes."

"What is it? I'd really like to know."

She set down her beer and kissed me on the lips.

"Stop being such a self-righteous asshole and let's go to bed," she said.

EPILOGUE

. . . .

▪ CHAPTER ▪
54

Hitch explained to me that the epilogue is the final few beats in the story. So here goes:

Karel Sladky was eventually convicted of the triple murder he'd committed up on Skyline Drive. Dahlia Wilkes put on a blistering case that earned him the death penalty.

She never smiled at us once during the trial. An Ice Goddess from gravel to gavel.

The London Good Delivery Bars turned out to be fake, just like Alexa had suspected. According to Val Rosinski, the original forgers of the bars had ground down some tungsten ore and mixed it with an epoxylike clay so they could mold it into the right shape and weight. Then they plated a sixteenth of an inch of pure gold on top, which was enough depth to keep José Del Cristo's standard fluorescent X-ray scan from reaching down and reading the viscosity of the tungsten.

Latimer estimated that each counterfeit gold bar only had a value of five hundred dollars, making it not worth the effort or potential criminal risk to recover.

Hitch and I sold *The Prostitutes' Ball* to Jamie Foxx's production company for a million eight plus change. After agents' commissions and legal fees, my thirty percent of that will come to slightly over four hundred thousand dollars. After taxes, a quarter of a mil.

I'd been fantasizing about a house on the sand, so Alexa and I looked at condos on Venice Beach. They seemed too expensive, so I'm using the money to fix a lot of delayed maintenance on the house and redo the garage addition for Chooch's room instead.

We're going to wait for the movie to come out and pray we get to break even quickly. Our pari passu payout kicks in at rolling break, and Hitch says that's when we'll start banking the really big profits.

Then comes the house on the sand. . . .

Maybe.

I subscribed to *Daily Variety* at Hitch's insistence, but I don't read it. Headlines like "Ten Percenters Shutter Pic Pact as Cruise Loses" scared me off. The issues pile up on the hall table and are thrown out at the end of the week, but I am getting better and better at movie speak. Hitch and I can now shorthand our frequent discussions about deal points.

Not for nothing, but we've decided to stay a team. Strange as it seems, Sumner Hitchens turned out to be a perfect partner for me. Fast, loose, funny, and smart. With Hitch, I'm never bored.

The night after we closed the deal on *Prostitutes' Ball* with Jamie's production company, Alexa and I celebrated with a drink and dinner at our favorite restaurant. Then we came home and got in bed.

Before I fell asleep, I turned on the TV to catch the late news. As I was lying there, flipping through channels, I came across Brooks Dunbar on *TMZ*.

He was being pulled out of a bar by two Hollywood Division cops. According to *TMZ*'s managing editor, Harvey Levin, he had assaulted a bartender and was being further charged with sexual misconduct. Harvey reported that Brooks had mooned a table full of German tourists.

"Lick my balls, you shitsticks!" he shouted at the paparazzi as the cops led him past. At least, I think that's what he said because half the sentence was bleeped.

"Not much going on there," Alexa said. She was lying in bed beside me, an arrest-to-conviction percentage analysis for the Detective Division on her lap, looking at the TV over half-glasses perched on her nose.

On New Year's weekend, just after the case wrapped, Alexa and I had taken our son, Chooch, out to dinner. At the Emerald Bowl game on Christmas day, he'd held a clipboard and never got on the field, but we were proud of him, and for me, more important than him playing was the effort he'd displayed in his years so far with the Trojans. He was a good teammate. He continued to strive, despite disappointments, and never gave up on his dream.

You can't do any better than that.

I couldn't help but note the difference between Chooch and Brooks Dunbar.

They were about the same age, but Chooch honored me and his mom with his life and his values. Brooks, on the other hand, pursued nothing. The Heir Abhorrent was about nothing and, as a result, cared for nothing. Brooks was already bored with his life and that boredom was destroying him.

One final irony: because of his need to finance a nose candy habit, Brooks had illegally rented that backyard on Skyline Drive to an Internet madame so he'd have money to buy eight balls.

It was an event that had led to a triple murder, which in the end brought down his parents and eighty-nine-year-old uncle for five murders and an armored car heist committed more than twenty-five years earlier.

As I watched Brooks being shoved into the back of one of our Hollywood Patrol Division units, my phone rang. It was Hitch.

"Hey dawg, turn on *TMZ*," he said. "You won't believe this."

"I'm watching."

"This just gets better. That little turd, Brooks, is the throughline that holds our whole plot together."

"He is?" I asked, puzzled. I'm still not as good at this as Hitch.

"Yeah, he is," my partner purred. "This club bust is the final event that concludes our story."

And so, months later, when the script was finally written, that's exactly how it ended.

FINAL CREDITS

■ ■ ■ ■ ■ ■ ■ ■

■ ■ ■ ■ ■ ■ ■ ■

There are always so many people to thank when I write one of these. My office assistants at Cannell Studios, Kathy Ezso and Jane Whitney, are my toiling Egyptians pulling word boulders uphill, trying to get them to resemble a pyramid. Thanks again for an amazing effort.

Jo Swerling Jr. is my early reader. Jo supplies the encouragement I need at exactly the right time.

My agents at Trident Media are always there for me. Robert Gottlieb is my downfield blocker. He's the best.

At the publishing house, there are so many. . . . In some movie credits they are listed alphabetically, in others, in order of appearance. Most authors do it in order of importance, but at St. Martin's Press, this is almost impossible for me, because they are all so important. So this time I'm going to do it in order of first telephone contact:

Charlie Spicer is my editor extraordinaire, my real friend, and a great cheerleader inside the publishing house. He makes this work fun.

Sally Richardson, our publisher, has guided us through the years. Sally has great vision and helps us be better.

Matt Baldacci is our secret weapon in marketing. He has never let me down or told it other than exactly the way it was.

Matthew Shear is VP and publisher. He has helped with overall planning, marketing, and advertising. He's a great supporter.

Yaniv Soha helps move everything along. He's the grease on the wheels of this enterprise.

Thanks to Tara Cibelli in Marketing and to Rachel Eckstrom in Publicity for their energy, enthusiasm, and creative ideas.

Thanks to Judy Hilsinger and Sandy Mendelson at Hilsinger-Mendelson. They are my book publicists and have helped me on fifteen novels. Also, thanks to Meghan McPartlan and Rogers & Cowan, my entertainment publicists.

At home is my emotional support. My wife, Marcia, who is my Alexa. My kids, Tawnia, Chelsea, and Cody, who shine bright and light everything in my path.

My cat, Buster, who keeps my feet warm at night.

So that's it. Cue the end music. Roll the production logos. Bring up the final card and we're at:

THE END

∎ ∎ ∎ ∎ ∎ ∎ ∎ ∎